Simon's Song

A TALE OF ADVENTURE AND FRIENDSHIP

SIMON'S SONG
Copyright © 2013 by Carolyn Williford
All rights reserved.

Cover Illustration: Original painting by Robert Fobear
White Buffalo Gallery
www.thewhitebuffalogallery.com

Cover Design by Julia Wright Design

ISBN-13: 978-1492789710
ISBN-10: 1492789712

Library of Congress Control Number: 2013919322
CreateSpace Independent Publishing Platform, North Charleston, SC

ALSO BY CAROLYN WILLIFORD

Devotions for Families That Can't Sit Still

More Devotions for Families That Can't Sit Still

An Appreciation Book for the Pastor's Wife

Questions from the God Who Needs No Answers

*Faith Tango: A Liberating Approach to Spiritual Growth in Marriage
(co-authored with husband Craig)*

*How to Treat a Staff Infection:
Resolving Problems in Your Church or Ministry Team
(co-authored with husband Craig)*

Jordan's Bend: A Novel

Bridge to a Distant Star: A Novel

With much love, this book is dedicated to
Sandy and Perry Downs.

Because of your enormous hearts and loving care for children,
you have enriched and blessed so many.

I count it pure joy to be considered your friend.

ACKNOWLEDGEMENTS

I'm in debt to so many who've made this dream of mine a reality:

- Lewis Carroll, for his masterful work, *Alice in Wonderland*

- If not for these encouragers, I would've given up years ago on Simon's story—Don and Ruth Pape, Bob Fobear (who believed in this project enough to do several beautiful paintings as illustrations; thank you, my gifted friend), Carol Smith Walter, Kay Kleinschmidt, June Sorensen, Joann Gay, Perry and Sandy Downs.

- My agent, Steve Laube, who's believed in my writing abilities and supported me through good and lean years.

- Julia Wright (Julia Wright Design)—an answer to prayer for editing, typesetting, cover designing, marketing, all-around expert in coaching me through this entire project.

- Craig (I love you so much, Sweetheart) and my whole family (special thanks to Mom and Dad, for all their prayers; Bob and Sharon; Jay and Rachael and all my wonderful grands: Tucker, Abby, Tyler and Nathan—it's your imaginations I hope to inspire). You all have loved and encouraged and put up with me when it was so undeserved!

- My Lord and Savior, Jesus Christ. *"I am the Lord's handmaid; may it be to me as you have said."* (Luke 1:38)

CHAPTER 1

"Oh, Kitty, how nice it would be if we could
only get through into Looking-glass House!
... Let's pretend there's a way of getting through
into it, somehow, Kitty.
Let's pretend the glass has got all soft like gauze,
so that we can get through."

—ALICE IN WONDERLAND BY LEWIS CARROLL

Simon burst out of the schoolyard doors among a mob of excited children, swept along with the boisterous, laughing group as they bounced against anyone or anything in their way. They moved en masse down the chipped cement steps, finally spilling out onto the grounds to board tired-looking, fume-spilling buses; find Mom waiting in the family car; or race to the bike racks. This was where Simon headed, but with none of the bubbling, happy exuberance his classmates demonstrated.

Unconsciously chewing his bottom lip, he glanced around for Abbey, his younger sister, knowing it would be next to impossible finding her in this out-of-control crowd but still hoping he would. Dad had been in an especially ugly mood this morning, already beginning his usual weekend binge by grabbing the dreaded cans out of the refrigerator. The next two days stretched ahead of him like an eternity, and Simon breathed the sigh of the often seen weary placard-holder (*"Will work for food"*) on the street corner.

Anxiously searching the grounds for others in Abbey's class, Simon found no one. When the thought suddenly struck him that Abbey's teacher may have let her class out early and Abbey could already be on her way home, he raced determinedly for his bike. *I don't dare let Abbey get home first*, Simon thought, ducking and dodging kids in his way. *If Dad sees her first, he might....* Near panic now, he jumped on his bike and quickly maneuvered it over the pathway by the playground. "I've got to get home before Abbey," he muttered to himself. "God, please don't let her get home before me."

Peddling at full speed now, Simon passed other children along the path, driving his already beat-up and badly dented dirt bike way beyond its obvious limitations. He'd just reached up to wipe a small trickle of sweat from his upper lip when he noticed the new pothole at the curbside where pathway and roadside meet, but it was already too late. Jerking up the front wheel anyway, Simon tried to avoid the inevitable. The slow response of the failing brakes was the final blow, however, and Simon realized—as if he could view the entire crash in a slow-motion replay—that he was doomed.

His front wheel turned sharply to the left while Simon went flying right, crashing into rough pavement and tearing away tender skin. At the last moment he managed to mostly protect his face from the forceful hit with an outstretched hand, but still his chin bounced off the curb and the poor hand surely felt the brunt of it. His jeans sported a fresh tear at the knee, revealing a nasty scrape underneath, and his shoulder immediately began to throb.

"Hey, dork! Wow, that was some fall." The boy, David, offered no assistance but merely stood over him, ogling his cuts and scrapes. "Knee's looking pretty good already. And you 'bout tore off your chin, from the looks of it."

Simon sat up, rubbing his shoulder and reaching up to gingerly touch his chin. There was blood on his finger, but he said nothing, hadn't even cried out when he'd fallen.

"Why'd you fall?" David asked, shaking his head and kicking at the tire of the pitiful bike.

Simon nodded towards the broken pavement. "Stupid pothole." A close observer would've caught a brief grimace as he stood, and then Simon righted his bike, trying to determine if it could still be ridden. Spinning the wheels, gingerly moving it back and forth, he decided it wasn't bent much more than it had been to begin with. "Gotta get home. See you later, David," Simon offered, and then instantly corrected himself. "Um, no. Actually, Monday."

"Don't you wanna play ball tomorrow? Everyone's gonna be there." David jerked his ball cap farther down on his head, peering at Simon from under the lowered brim through narrowed eyes. "*Come on!* Don't you dare cop out on us again. We need you to have enough guys to play!"

"It's just that, well, I got stuff to do on Saturdays. I better go now." Suddenly remembering his worries for Abbey—and forgetting any aches or pains—Simon pushed off.

David watched him go a moment and then hollered after him, "Didn't want you to come anyways. Forget you, Simon Thompson! Do ya hear me?" Fuming still at Simon's retreating back, he added, "We'll get a *girl* to take your stinkin' place!"

But Simon hadn't even heard the last remark; once again he was pedaling as fast as the damaged bicycle would go. Having seen no sign of Abbey, he knew she must be home by now. When he winced this time, it was not because of his pain.

Rounding the bend that led to his street, Simon made a sharp turn to the left, deciding to cut through grumpy old Mr. McCauley's yard. Most likely he'd be noticed and then Mr. McCauley would gripe to his dad, adding more fuel to his dad's drink-induced anger. *I'll worry about that later*, Simon thought to himself. *If Dad's mad at me, that's one thing. But if he goes after Abbey....*

Simon didn't hesitate for a second, but still scanned the large yard, searching for any sign of the cantankerous old man. Mr. McCauley *was* old—way over eighty. He was the grouchiest person Simon had ever known (unrelated to being drunk, that is), stingy, stubborn and loud, since he was hard of hearing. But one thing he wasn't: blind. Nor was his eyesight any less keen, despite the bottle-thick glasses he wore, for he could spot an invader on his property anywhere, at anytime, day or night, even when it was pitch dark, as Simon had experienced many times before.

"You hoodlum. Get that blamed bike off my property! And you with it!" Mr. McCauley'd spotted him all right, and now he came running as fast as his arthritic legs would allow, brandishing his cane like a weapon. Horn-rimmed glasses bounced on his leathered face, below amazingly bushy, wiry eyebrows and on a thin, mean looking pinched nose. Beady, piercing eyes—magnified and accentuated by those thick lenses—glared towards the trespasser with intense determination to reach the target.

Simon glanced over at him with worry, trying to gauge how fast his bike could go versus how long it would take Mr. McCauley to reach the spot where they'd intersect: the strip along the side of Mr. McCauley's property that led to his front yard and then finally, the street. Freedom was just ahead! His knee burned from pumping those stiff, resisting pedals and his shoulder ached from leaning over the handlebars, but Simon ignored the pain completely. Shut it out like it didn't even exist. *Abbey*, he thought to himself. *She's all that matters. Just Abbey.*

Simon closed in on the patch that led to escape, noting that this time luck was with him. "I'm going to beat the old man," he muttered, and just as he did, he felt a sharp blow to his back. When Simon glanced around to find the source of the hit, he saw Mr. McCauley's cane rolling across the grass just behind him.

"Gotcha. See what happens when you trespass, you hoodlum!" Mr. McCauley yelled, shaking a trembling, clenched fist. "Someday you and all the likes of you will really feel the sting of my cane. I'll catch you! And then I'll…"

Simon allowed himself one glance back at the old man, one fleeting grin of victory. But then all his attention turned to his own home, just two houses down.

It sat on a pleasant looking street, lined with an assortment of elms and maples, filled with the typical middle-class homes that had simple landscaping in the front and cement porches in the back. Backyards sported cedar picnic tables, charcoal grills, numerous evidences of children—swings (the metal kind), sandboxes and tricycles, bikes, balls of all kinds—and a garden dotting here and there. The homes, though older, were well kept ranches or split-levels with siding, pretty much resembling subdivisions from family television shows so popular in the early 1960's. Simon and Abbey's home blended in naturally with all the others.

Glancing through its windows with the green shutters and lace, Simon strained to see a glimpse of his dad, listened intently for the sound of his voice. Everything appeared calm, quiet. He laid his bike on the ground to the side of the driveway (the kickstand having broken long ago) and hurried around to the back door. He'd just closed the screen door softly behind him when the nightmare started again. He instantly felt sick to his stomach.

"What do you mean bringing home a paper with a *D* on it? Do you have any idea how this makes me look as a parent?" A stream of curses was followed by a sickening silence. "Well, do you?"

Instinctively, Simon moved towards the source of the conflict. He acted out of a subconscious reflex of love for Abbey as he approached the seething man; moving towards the furious voice was purely hopeless, completely senseless. There was nothing he could do to protect Abbey, but he'd try again. Just like he always did. That's what big brothers were supposed to do. Walking resolutely from the kitchen to the living room, Simon noted that his dad— hair uncombed, ugly stubble of beard, wearing his ratty bathrobe—slouched forward in the worn recliner. The television droned in the background, a western complete with a gunfight, good guys and bad. Abbey stood, trembling, by the steps that led upstairs to their rooms. She had one hand on the banister, gripping it so tightly that her small knuckles were white, and one hand behind her back. Simon moved to position himself in between his dad and Abbey.

"Who invited you to this party?" His words were slightly slurred, the consonants weak. "Just get outta the way, Simon. I'm talkin' to your sister."

"Abbey can't help it if she gets *D*s sometimes. She has a learning disability, Dad." Simon looked at his dad pleadingly, still feeling the waves of nausea washing over him. He knew it was inevitable, but he had to try. "She does the best she can, Dad. Honest."

The room was crowded with faded green-and-gold-plaid furniture; family pictures scattered here and there on the walls (one of his mom on her wedding day, innocently gazing out at the world with a naïve look of hope for her future); dusty, fake plants hanging in the corners from macramé roping. A table in front of the couch held the daily paper—the page open to the television listing—an ashtray full of cigarette butts, and several empty beer cans. The air was heavy with the smells Simon always associated with his dad: rank cigarette smoke; the stench of beer; stale, closed-in, suffocating hopelessness. From Simon's view, hopelessness had a smell, a very definite one.

"I said get outta the way, Simon!" Cursing again. "Why are you forever an' always in my way?" His rage filled the room now, and Simon knew it would find physical form.

The blows came then, just like they always did. He heard them, flinching each time the *"smack!"* hit skin or clothing. Holding out his hands to ward them off was useless, for there was no way to protect anyone from his father's fury. And yet still he stood there, hearing the awful sounds, watching the hated hands hit their mark time and time again. Finally, there was silence— except for Abbey's soft weeping.

"Why do you always make me do this?" he demanded of them now, his voice softer, but accusing still. "I don't want to. But you *make* me, you know. I wouldn't hafta do this if you didn't make me!" He turned and walked unsteadily towards the kitchen; Abbey and Simon could hear the sound of the refrigerator being opened, another can being removed.

"Come on, Abbey, let's get you upstairs to your room," Simon whispered urgently. "Before Dad comes back in here." She glanced up at him with a vacant look, but she obeyed, almost crawling up the steps. Simon winced with nearly every step too; his knees, shoulder, back, and chin were all throbbing. He'd ignored all of it to get to Abbey, to protect her. *Why do you let him do it?* he denounced himself. *Can't you ever do anything right? You* are *no good, just like Dad always says!*

Once they'd reached the top step, Simon picked her up, carrying her slight form gently to her room. Abbey was six, a first grader, but small for her age. Her spindly legs, frail arms and overall petiteness made her look one, maybe even two years younger than she was. But it was the despairing, vacant look about her eyes that alarmed Simon the most. Sometimes he worried she was in danger of withering away to nothing, and all that would be left was that hollow look, a way of staring out at the world as if she were so afraid she was hiding elsewhere. When she pulled into herself like that—and she was pulling away from them more all the time—Simon knew she was retreating within herself to escape the brutalities of their home. He laid her on the bed and Abbey reached up to put one trembling finger to his face. Putting aside her own trauma, she winced at the sight of Simon's chin. "What happened?"

"Fell off my bike." Simon shrugged off Abbey's concern. Accepting sympathy opened the possibility of too much vulnerability. "It's nothing." He glanced over at her desk, noting the scattering of colored markers, construction paper, tape, and scissors. "Finished your project yet? Need any more help?"

She shook her head. "Mommy said she'd help me finish it this weekend, if she didn't have to work Sunday." Abbey's eyes took on a frightened look again as she suddenly realized the implications. "Simon, Mommy has to work tomorrow. What if she has to go in Sunday too? We can't…you can't…"

Simon stuffed his hands into the pockets of his faded, torn jeans and sauntered casually to a window overlooking their front yard, the pleasant street, the neighborhood filling now with the soothing sounds of happy children. "Eh, ain't nothin' to worry about." He leaned his head wearily against the screen, envying the stark difference between those children and Abbey and himself. Two boys tossed a baseball back and forth; Simon's eyes followed the ball as it went *smack!* from one glove to the other, that glove back to the first. Somewhere a dog barked incessantly—probably wanting loose from his chain in order to run with kids—and he could hear the excited cries of several children playing tag. Three girls biked by, laughing, pointing to old Mr. McCauley pulling weeds. Carefree, happy children. "Wonder what's it like to be like them?" he whispered, a plaintive yearning filling his question.

"Like who?" Abbey climbed across her bed and came to stand by Simon. She looked out at the scene before them, scanning up and down the street. "You want to be like those boys?"

"Nah. Not like them. Just different from me." Simon absently scratched his head, flinching when he found yet another sore spot. "Want to…be someone else. Be somewhere else."

Abbey looked up at him with panic moving across her features and she reached up to grab at her brother's shirtsleeve with clutching fingers. "Please don't leave me, Simon. Please don't ever leave me." Tears instantly filled her eyes again, and Simon looked down at her with deep love and embarrassment at the same moment.

To disguise the awkwardness, he ruffled her hair, sending the mass of golden curls into even greater confusion. "Couldn't. I know you. You'd tag after me if I went to…well, even old McCauley's doorstep. You'd be right behind me, pestering, 'Can't I go?'" Simon mimicked her in a whiny voice, and Abbey grinned up at him now. "'Please, Simon. Old McCauley's got his nasty cane!'" he continued. "'I wanna beating too!'"

He stopped suddenly, the horror of reality striking up against the teasing. Both looked at each other for just a moment before glancing away, knowing too much was left unspoken. And too much had been spoken at the same time. They stared out at the street again before Simon announced, resignedly, "Better get to my homework." With one last longing look, he followed the boys with the baseball now trotting along the path to the park. And then he turned and walked out the door, pausing just a second to say, "Don't worry about Sunday, Abbey. I'll be here. Promise."

Simon's room was just across the hall, and though he pushed the door closed behind him for privacy, he always left it open at least a crack. It was necessary, he felt, absolutely necessary, to hear Abbey if she should cry out for him at any time. The need left him constantly on edge, tense, and emotionally weary.

Moving to the mirror above his dresser, Simon leaned close to inspect his wounds. "Geez," he said out loud, shaking his head at the mangled chin, bruised cheek and various cuts, scrapes, and black-and-blue marks all over his body. If not for these remnants of such a bad day, however, Simon would've been described as cute. At least, nearly all the fifth grade girls in his class seemed to think so.

Blessed with blond hair and eyes that were a startling bright blue, Simon also had thick lashes and deep dimples that sent girls into a frenzy. It seemed to Simon that one or more was always "in love" with him, and the chanting teases of "Jennifer loves Simon!" or "Kathy loves Simon!" were a normal part of his school day. But he ignored all that stuff completely. Which, in turn, seemed to heighten the girls' frenzy (to his dismay) and (even more to his disadvantage) alienate the boys. Somehow he felt too old for any of it.

Simon tilted his chin up towards the light, frowning at the wide scrape and dried, caked blood. But then he stopped the close scrutiny of cuts and bruises and instead gazed over the entire reflection of his boyish self. Tall for an eleven-year-old, but definitely still only a boy, Simon smirked at the baby fat that clung to his arms and waist. Bringing his arms up into a body builder's stance, he flexed the muscles in one arm and then the other. He grunted and gritted his teeth at the reflection, and then grinned.

"You *do* look pathetic," he finally pronounced to his reflection. Glancing from his dirty t-shirt with the faded image of a former basketball star (and since this afternoon's bike crash, a brand new hole right above the player's head) down to the grease-stained, ripped jeans, Simon shook his head in disgust. "How are you ever going to be able to protect Abbey?" he asked. "If you don't do something soon—something, anything!—you never will be any good, just like he says. *No good!*" And then whirling away from the incriminating mirror to flop onto his bed, he buried tear-filled eyes in his pillow.

But Simon didn't cry. Not ever. So just as quickly as his eyes had filled with tears, he stubbornly blinked them away. When he rolled over and stared up at the ceiling, the only feeling he knew was anger. Furious, heart-pounding rage directed towards his dad. Towards himself. And mostly, at God. A God his mother still relentlessly clung to through all the emotional pain, all the humiliation, all the disappointment. When he glanced towards the mirror again, he saw only an unhappy boy glaring back at him and…something odd. *What is that?* he wondered, scrambling out of bed and moving to inspect his mirror more closely. Leaning down to peer at the bottom corner, he squinted his eyes and tentatively reached out to touch the queer sight before him. For there, in one small section, the mirror appeared to have completely changed; suddenly, it looked like a window.

For a moment Simon stood up straight, closing his eyes and shaking his head. "Maybe I hit my head harder than I thought," he mused. And then he leaned over to peer into the same part of the mirror again, wondering to himself, *If this is a window, then what on earth could I be looking into?* The images before him were fuzzy, but there was definitely something—some *things*—in there. Because they *moved*.

Quickly turning and opening his door—after looking up and down the hallway and hearing no sounds from Abbey's room—Simon tiptoed into the bathroom, which was on the other side of the wall from his mirror. Crossing his arms over his chest, he stood in the doorway, examining the bathroom like he envisioned a detective would. Sink, toilet and tub were in place just like always; the rust-stained tub spigot dripped like normal too, its familiar *plink! plink!* echoing against the mildewed walls. He reached for the adjoining wall and ran his hands along the dingy striped wallpaper, searching for anything that would explain the strange sensation that there was a window just on the other side of that wall. Finding nothing unusual, Simon straightened, glanced into the bathroom mirror, and shook his head at himself yet again. "You're going crazy!" he whispered, and then tiptoed back into his room.

But as much as he tried to ignore that tiny section, it was as if it were pulling him towards it like a black hole in space. With no conscious will of his own, Simon edged towards the mirror. Only this time, when he touched one finger to the curious area and leaned in closer for a better look, he found himself losing his balance as he fell forward towards the mirror. And slipped right through.

CHAPTER 2

*"Who are you?" said the Caterpillar.
This was not an encouraging opening for
a conversation. Alice replied, rather shyly,
"I—I hardly know, Sir, just at present—at
least I know who I was when I got up this
morning, but I think I must have been
changed several times since then."*

A startlingly cold, wet nose pressed against his face, waking him slowly from a languid, dreamy sleep. Simon fought the awakening, for the sleep had been deep and peaceful, with no worries lurking, no responsibilities demanding his watchfulness. He opened his eyes with weary resignation...and stared into the enormous eyes of a big, black dog—a mere inch from his chin.

Simon instinctively froze, but pressing its (from Simon's close perspective, at least, what appeared to be) *gigantic*, freezing nose against Simon's face once more, the dog excitedly asked, "Wanna play? Dowgers love to play ball!" And then the dog picked up a ball—chewing it so voraciously that gobs of slobber literally oozed from its jowls—and plopped it onto his lap.

The boy stretched out cramped arms and rubbed his eyes, attempting to shrug off the lingering haziness. "Am I out of it or what?" Simon mused, stifling a yawn. "For a moment there I thought *you* were talking," he said to the dog. "And is this ever gross!" Simon exclaimed, gingerly picking up the offensive ball and pitching it away. "That ball's so disgustingly soaked that it got my jeans wet too. Yuck!"

"Beauregard always gets things oogey. If he wouldn't chew the blamed thing like that, it wouldn't happen. But that's Beauregard for you." The voice seemed to come from just above him, so Simon searched the overhanging branches of the tree that he was leaning against. "Hope you don't mind my asking, but what on earth happened to your face? I haven't seen so many bruises, cuts, and scrapes since Beauregard ran smack into the hickory tree when he was chasing that very ball. My, but was he a sorry mess."

"So where are you anyway?" Simon asked, craning his neck as he continued scanning every part of the tree for the source of the voice. "Was it you I heard before?"

"Yoo-hoo! I'm right up here. It's me. Atticus. And who, pray tell, are you? This is most strange. Humans don't talk, you know. At least, that's what I've been told. You are the first one I've met, however."

The voice came from a raccoon that was peering down at Simon from a tree limb just above. Or at least, that's where the voice *appeared* to have come from. Simon stared up at him with mouth gaping open. But then the obnoxious dog came back, retrieving the ball joyfully as if Simon had tossed it simply for the dog's pleasure rather than throwing away a disgusting thing. After chewing it several more times—and obviously making the thing that much more gooey each time he flattened it in his slobbery mouth—he dropped it at Simon's feet and hunched down in a playful, anxious stance before him, eyes alight with excitement and tail wagging furiously.

Simon blinked his eyes. Rubbed them once again—only more seriously this time. He frowned, shaking his head. "This is crazy. Just crazy." He glanced up at the raccoon—*Was that a smirk on his face? Nah, couldn't be*—and then at the dog before him. "*I've* gone crazy!"

"Dowgers love to play ball. Frow it!" the dog exclaimed.

"*Dowgers?* Why does he talk like that?" And then Simon grabbed his head, moaning, "Geez. This is totally ridiculous! Here I am wondering why a dog calls himself something silly like *dowger*. And I'm asking a raccoon to explain it!"

"What an insult, Beauregard. You should take that oogey ball and go home." The raccoon stretched a fingered paw along the tree branch, drumming it impatiently. He looked just like the raccoons Simon had seen at the zoo: masked face, giving him a rakish bandit sort of look; fingered paws resembling miniature hands; and a bushy, ringed tail which he draped casually along the branch. But at the same time he was totally different from those…well, those *animals.* Somehow the total effect of this raccoon—as he continued to inspect Simon from head to toe and now twirl a small twig in one paw—was debonair. He leaned farther out over the branch and twitched his whiskers. "Of course animals talk. Why wouldn't we? It's humans that don't. Nary a word."

The dog shook his head in response to the raccoon's speech, but he still kept his alert eyes on the ball at Simon's feet. The dog was coal black, a Labrador retriever. "Atticus's right. Peoples don't talk. Never did. Never will."

"Well, I do!" Simon nearly shouted, and the raccoon and dog both jumped. "And would one of you talking animals kindly tell me where on earth I am, please?"

"Please is nice. Dowgers fink manners is good."

Simon frowned. "So why does he talk like that? Saying *dog* like *dow-jer?* And why does he talk about himself like he's…well, someone else?" he asked the raccoon.

"My name is Atticus. You can call me that."

"Fine. Atticus, one last time: why does this stupid dog talk funny?"

"The dowger's not stupid," the dog explained as he plopped down and cocked his head to one side. "But the dowger is simple. That's a fact." Simon shook his head at him. Clearly the dog wasn't insulted. He *was* simple.

"He calls it Dowger Talk, and he's always talked like that." Atticus shrugged his furry shoulders, if a raccoon can do such a thing. "And his ball is always oogey. We just tolerate it." Atticus turned and skillfully worked his way across the branch and down the knotted, aging tree towards where Simon leaned against the ample trunk.

"Oogey?" Simon asked.

"Describes it rather well, doesn't it?"

Simon nodded his head. "Yeah, I suppose. That and several other words for *gross.* What's his name again?"

"The dowger's name is Beauregard. Frow the ball, okay?" Beauregard jumped up, wagging his tail feverishly again. Amazingly, Simon could not resist the dog's innocent excitement for such a simple pleasure.

A simple act for a simple dog, Simon thought to himself. *Well, this is one strange world I've tumbled into.* Putting aside his revulsion for the slobbery ball, Simon picked it up and threw it a good distance this time. He grinned as the dog bounded after it. "Does he ever get tired of chasing it?"

"Nope." Atticus smiled too as he watched the joyful dog. "Never."

"So where am I, Atticus?" Simon asked, as he gazed around him at lush grass, a gurgling brook, the bluest sky and gentle sloping hills dotted here and there with trees. "One minute I was looking into my mirror and then whoosh!—I'm in this strange place where animals talk. And, according to you, where people aren't supposed to. Maybe I should ask *what* is this place instead of *where.*"

"Well, this is…it's here!" Atticus put one tiny finger to his head and scratched. He had climbed up onto a good-sized rock next to the tree trunk, and now he studied Simon again, curious eyes moving from the top of his head to his badly scraped knee. "I suppose the real question is, where did you come from? Amazing blue eyes you have, quite amazing. Never seen anything like them before. And I can't help asking again about all those wounds. What happened to you? And would you like Beauregard to lick that nasty scrape?" He pointed to Simon's knee. "Dogs do that sort of thing, you know."

After glancing once more at Beauregard—and the disgusting, now nearly foaming ball—Simon grimaced. "Uh, no thanks. And my name's Simon, by the way, and I came from earth." Simon's mouth fell open a moment and his eyes were wide with sudden alarm, realizing what he himself had just implied. "Oh geez, don't tell me I'm on another planet or something weird like that."

"Oh no, no. This is earth, I'm sure it is," Atticus responded thoughtfully, although the look on his face implied otherwise, it seemed to Simon. Beauregard dropped the ball for Simon and he threw it again absentmindedly, evidently getting used to the squishy feel of the ball between his fingers. "We need Caleb here, that's all there is to it. And Mary, Mr. and Mrs. Barton Beaver and their baby, Kit. They would have much more insight than me. To help you. Simon-by-the-Way."

"What's that?"

"Simon-by-the-Way. You *said* that was your name." Atticus stared at him matter-of-factly as he laid one arm (or should it be called a leg?) across his plump belly, his other elbow (leg joint?) on that arm, and then finally, rested his head in the palm (pad?) of that tiny hand. "And you still haven't told me how you managed to incur such tremendous wounds. Was it a horrible fight? Did you win in the end?" Atticus squinted as he stared at Simon's chin.

"First of all, let's get my name straight. It's just Simon, okay? And I fell off my bike."

"Hrmph! I've never seen such injuries from a bike." He leaned towards Simon, sniffing. "What's a bike?"

"Thwilly! Iht'sa fwish th…" Beauregard began, but Atticus immediately cut him off with an impatient wave of his hand.

"Beauregard, I just won't have it anymore," Atticus scolded. "Talking with your mouth full of that ball. Ugh. Now put it down and converse with Just-Simon-Okay and me in a decent manner." Beauregard obediently dropped the ball and plopped down once again. Only this time he lay all the way down, resting his head on his front paws and staring up at Atticus with a sorrowful look. "There's no use trying to manipulate me with that wounded expression either, Beauregard. Martyrdom is not becoming to you. Now, what were you trying to tell us?"

"That a bike's a fish. What lives inna river."

Simon started to laugh, covered his mouth, and then couldn't keep a giggle from escaping after all. Beauregard looked up at him, thumping his tail against the ground, nudging Simon's elbow with his cold nose. "Beauregard made you laugh, eh? Petting's nice. Petting the dowger is very nice."

Simon smiled at him, finding the dog's soft eyes and gentle nuzzling irresistible. He stroked Beauregard's head and Beauregard closed his eyes with pleasure. *Amazing how he evidently delights in such simple things*, Simon thought again to himself. "Let's set some things straight," he announced, still petting Beauregard's head. "First of all, my name is just *Simon*. Understand? Next, a bike is not an animal, Beauregard. It's a thing you ride, with wheels." Both Atticus and Beauregard looked at him in total confusion, staring blankly. Beauregard tilted his head even more and lifted both ears slightly. Simon spoke. "You don't know, do you? Oh well, you're just going to have to trust me on this one. It's got a metal body with two wheels that you balance on, and it's fun to ride."

Atticus looked skeptical as his gaze roamed over Simon's bruises and cuts. "Doesn't look much fun to me."

"Well, it is. Unless you fall. And now who are these other people you were talking about? Can they help me get out of here, wherever I am?"

"Them's not people," Beauregard informed him. He turned his head so Simon could rub the other side.

"I should've known. What are they?"

"Caleb's a bird. A red-winged blackbird," Atticus said, capping his eyes with one hand and searching the sky now for some sign of him. "He should be along anytime now. Had to help Barton Beaver with a small problem at the dam."

"So Barton is a beaver?"

"Yup. He and his sweet wife and their roly-poly little Kit."

"Wasn't there someone else—er, another name—you mentioned?"

"Mary. Such a deer she is."

"A dear what? And can *they* help me get out of here?"

"Not a dearwhat. Just a deer, Just-Simon. And you've only arrived here moments ago! Why on earth would you want to leave so soon?"

"Atticus!" Simon snapped. "Honestly, if I'd known that communicating with animals was going to be this difficult…"

"What's so difficult, Just-Simon?" But something overhead caught his attention, and he pointed towards the sky, shouting excitedly, "Look there! Here comes Caleb now! And that must mean Mr. and Mrs. Beaver and Kit and Mary are not far behind. Oh, I've missed them. Haven't you also, Beauregard?"

Beauregard jumped up, too, starting to reach for his ball and stopping suddenly, remembering to speak first. "Oh yes. Kit whacks the dowger's ball good. The dowger likes Kit!" And then he grabbed it up, chomping the ball repeatedly as he ran in circles in his excitement.

Simon slowly stood up, finding that his many bruises had caused him to stiffen a good deal. *How long have I been here?* he wondered to himself. *Time seems so different in this place, as if it's stretched out. Or is it bunched up?* Cupping one hand over his eyes to shield them from the bright sun, Simon searched among the clouds scattered here and there for the bird. When he caught sight of the beautiful splotch of red against the black background, he watched in fascination as the blackbird glided towards them and gracefully landed on a branch just above.

"Oh, Caleb, welcome. Welcome!" Atticus gushed, nearly tripping in his excitement to scramble up the trunk and out onto the limb to sit beside the beautiful bird. He held both arms out before him and then dramatically pointed both hands towards Simon. "And Beauregard and I are de-*lighted* to introduce you to our new-found friend, Just-Simon."

Caleb blinked once, eying Simon before elegantly bowing his head in greeting. "My sincere pleasure to meet you, Just-Simon."

"Um, you, too, Caleb. But Atticus keeps messing up my name. It's *Simon*. Only Simon."

Atticus leaned over to whisper in Caleb's ear, but he whispered like someone who's hard of hearing would whisper: loud. Quite loud enough, actually, so that Simon and Beauregard both could hear him without any trouble at all. "The boy's very nice, Caleb, but he's terribly confused. Keeps telling me different names for himself. Suppose it could be because of those nasty bumps and bruises all over his head?"

"I can hear you, you know," Simon interjected, giving Atticus a disgusted look. "I'm not deaf."

Suddenly Beauregard raced around Simon's legs, knocking him off balance and nearly causing him to fall down. "Kit's come. And Mr. and Mrs. Beaver. Mary too! Let's have a party!"

A beautiful deer bounded towards the assembled group, her gait delicate and yet somehow strong and assured at the same time. Her huge, deep brown eyes with amazingly long, curled lashes turned quizzically towards Simon and seemed to draw him into liquid depths. Instantly, Simon was entranced with the graceful, enchanting creature that stood before him. "Who is he?" she asked simply, but the emotion in her voice was strong and deep.

Atticus sighed. "Well, let me see if I can remember the list. One minute he goes by Only-Simon. And then it's Just-Simon and next Just-Simon-Okay." He put one hand to the side of his face, absentmindedly pulling at one wiry whisker. "Lastly, Simon-by-the-Way." Atticus looked over at Simon. "Did I miss any?"

Now Simon sighed. "I never—"

"He's come. He's the one, don't you see?" the deer whispered, so softly that everyone leaned slightly towards her so as not to miss a word. Her voice reminded Simon of tinkling bells, the music and melodies of Christmas. "The one we've been awaiting for so long has come!"

"Oh my. You're right, Mary," Caleb said, a hushed awe in his voice now.

All of them moved to form a semicircle around Simon—Atticus (rubbing his hands together nervously); the lovely deer; Caleb (now perched on the deer's back); the family of beavers (who had come just before the deer's pronouncement and immediately huddled together, wide-eyed, before Simon); and even Beauregard, who paused his exuberant running and dropped the slobbery ball to sit, perfectly transfixed, at Simon's feet.

Simon eyed them all nervously, slowly turning to look at each pair of eyes staring at him, expecting…what? "What do you mean, that I'm the *one*? The one what?"

Caleb ruffled and lifted his wings, suddenly gifting them with a glorious demonstration of scarlet against black. Simon would soon learn that Caleb always did this before an announcement, before he said anything important. "All the Father's Creatures listen to this Word! The one will come to complete the image of the Way, the Truth and the Life! And when he has come, the Three will journey from Knowing in Part to Knowing Fully. Then they shall be Fully Known, and the Father of all Creatures will be glorified! Amen and Amen!"

With great reverence they all repeated, "Amen and Amen!" while seven pairs of eyes turned to stare at Simon, waiting expectantly.

Unconsciously, Simon took an awkward step backwards, away from them all, trying to escape their scrutiny and their obvious expectations that were nothing but nonsense to him. "Now look, all of you. I don't know who it is you've been waiting for, but it's clearly *not me*. This is all just crazy!" He threw his arms up into the air before slapping them to his sides in total frustration. "Maybe somehow I fell into another world, a parallel one like in the sci-fi book I read last week. Or maybe I'm just dreaming." His eyes suddenly lit up. "Yeah, that's it! I just read about this mirror-image world and now I've created my own world in my dreams!" He attempted to stare down Atticus. "You all don't even exist."

Dramatically—that was definitely beginning to appear to be Atticus's forte—placing one paw over his eyes and sighing loudly, Atticus moaned, "I'm crushed! Such a nasty, cruel thing to say, when Beauregard and Mary desperately need you to fulfill the prophecy. And of course the rest of us," he went on, motioning with his other paw to the beaver family, Caleb, and himself, "are here to help and serve and protect you in any way we can."

"The prophecy? Is that what Caleb was pronouncing?" Simon shook his head at them in total dismay. "I don't understand any of this!"

"You mean you've never heard the prophecy?" Kit asked, obviously amazed. Simon merely shook his head.

"Come, come all of you," Caleb encouraged them. "Simon-by-the-Way, please sit by the oak tree once again, dear friend, and we'll try to make it clear. All of you now, gather around and let us truly get to know our new friend." He gave Simon a reassuring look and somehow, the slightest smile from his rigid black beak.

Simon sat down in resignation, feeling mentally drained from his inability to comprehend what was happening to him. And more so, from that fact that mere animals seemed to grasp so much more than he did. The animals gathered around, settling into comfortable positions and giving Simon a sense of security and belonging as they did so. Atticus climbed back onto the rock that he'd sat on earlier and the deer lay next to the rock with Caleb perched on her back. The beaver family huddled together—with Kit protectively in the middle—by Simon's feet, and Beauregard turned in circles several times before plopping down and nonchalantly easing his head onto Simon's lap. When Beauregard nuzzled his arm to be petted again, Simon complied and thought to himself, *It sure would be easier if I could just wake up from this ridiculous dream.*

"But you are awake, Simon-by-the-Way," the deer whispered calmly.

He stared at her in amazement. "How did you know…? Can you hear what I'm thinking?"

"Not always. But sometimes words are…well, mere imitations of the truth that is so much more plain to see." The musical lilt to her voice was tender and soothing to Simon. He listened to her eagerly, and her words and tone soothed him like drinking a cool liquid on a sweltering day. "Surely you have experienced this before? The ability to know what another is thinking, feeling?"

Simon nodded. "With Abbey, my little sister. I know when she needs me. And that's one reason I just have to get back home. Abbey might need me—"

"If you can sense when she needs you," Caleb interjected, "does she truly need you right now?"

Closing his eyes a moment to concentrate, Simon shook his head no. "I guess not just now, but I don't know how quickly she might. And besides, I promised."

"Promises of protection must be kept," Mr. Beaver announced solemnly. He and Mrs. Beaver looked into each other's eyes a moment before gazing proudly at the baby between them.

"Absolutely," Mrs. Beaver agreed. Kit merely looked up at Simon and smiled broadly, nodding in agreement. All three were obviously designed for maneuvering in water, not waddling about on land—for their sleek fur smelled of the river and their tails stretched out awkwardly behind them. Kit, ever one with an eye for mischief, had planted himself atop his father's flat tail.

"The promise will be kept," Caleb assured them all, glancing around the entire little group before turning a steady, unwavering gaze towards Simon. "When Abbey needs you—or if anyone should need you from your world—you will hear that person calling."

"But how can I—?"

Mary gazed at him with eyes filled and overflowing with promise. "Remember the knowing without words. You will hear. And you will know."

It was impossible to look into Mary's eyes and not believe her. Simon nodded, accepting this truth. "But why am I here? What is the prophecy and what could it possibly have to do with me?"

"Total understanding only comes with completion of the journey," Caleb explained, "the journey you and Mary and Beauregard must take that has been foretold by the prophecy. The rest of us will come along to help."

"But why do you think *I'm* the one designated to go on this journey of yours?"

"Because you've come. And you're Simon-by-the-Way," Mary said matter-of-factly.

Simon closed his eyes and shook his head in exasperation. "First of all, I haven't the faintest idea how I got here. So my coming is just one big mistake. Or a joke, more likely! And secondly, Atticus never did get my name right."

"Did so. Heard you perfectly well. Raccoons are well known for their excellent hearing, among a veritable multitude of other gifts, talents, and abilities," Atticus stated, appearing insulted and crossing his arms over his stomach again.

"Better add *humility* to that list," Simon added. Atticus merely nodded, accepting the comment as a compliment. "But, hey. Where I come from my name is Simon. *Simon!* Not any of those other things Atticus said and certainly not Simon-by-the-Way!"

"But this is here!" Kit chirped, bouncing his baby fat fur as he left his parents to climb boldly—and a bit clumsily with a grunt or two—up onto Simon's unoccupied knee. "Names can be different for different places, can't they, Mama?" he asked, squinting his tiny eyes at Simon's face and studying him curiously.

"Yes, Kit, they can," Mrs. Beaver agreed. "When I go to my garden club every Monday afternoon I'm called Mrs. Beaver. But at home, in our lodge, I'm called Mama, am I not?" They all nodded in agreement.

"I don't think that's quite the same—" Simon began.

"But it is!" Kit insisted, placing his two front paws on Simon's chest and sniffing at his scraped chin. The whiskers tickled something awful and Simon chuckled.

"Okay, you win. I give up! Call me Simon-by-the-Way or whatever you want. Just stop tickling my chin, will you?" Simon pleaded, between giggles.

Kit sat back down on his lap, giving Simon an astonished look. "But you don't understand. We can't call you 'Whatever you want.' We must call you by your rightful name. The name from the prophecy."

"I don't—" and then Simon looked to Caleb for an explanation. "Caleb?"

"For so many years now, Simon-by-the-Way, our little group has been incomplete, waiting. Oh, we've experienced joy as we've lived and worked together as friends. Kit's birth being chief among them." At this, Mr. and Mrs. Beaver beamed proudly (Barton's furry chest expanded considerably) and Kit climbed down off Simon's lap to snuggle up between his parents once again. Soon he would be fast asleep and snoring slightly. "But we were always looking, waiting expectantly for that which the prophecy promised us. We knew the Father of all Creatures would send us the completion of the image of the Three. And so we waited."

"The Three?"

Caleb nodded solemnly. "Beauregard is the Truth. We judge that his being selected may have something to do with his simpleness. He's quite accepting of this, actually." The dog gazed adoringly up at Simon, thumping his tail. "And Mary is the Life."

Simon looked over at the beautiful deer and reached out to stroke her soft, sleek coat. Even though she wasn't currently speaking, he swore there was still a hint of music hovering in the air. "Why is Mary the Life?"

Caleb shook his head. "This we do not understand. The prophecy can be explained and understood only by completing it. By attempting to finish the journey."

"You said I'm the third one. Why are you so sure?"

"Because you are Simon-by-the-Way," Mary said softly, looking deeply into his eyes again. "We are the image of the Way, the Truth, and the Life. And together we will attempt to complete our journey." She bowed her head in a hushed silence, a quiet that became suddenly a being itself, as it took on a life of its own somehow. Suddenly all inanimate things—the trees, the sky, the clouds, the sunshine, the rock next to him and the very ground that Simon sat upon—responded to Mary's words as they moved against and rustled and whooshed into the stillness. Simon could have sworn that even these objects whispered reverently, "Amen and Amen," for the silence was recognized, welcomed and grasped expectantly by all of creation around them.

CHAPTER 3

"How am I to get in?" asked Alice again,
in a louder tone.
"Are you to get in at all?" said the Footman.
"That's the first question, you know."

It must have been the gentle rustling of the tree branches that stirred up an inspired breeze—one that caressed Simon's hair against his forehead, rippled the beavers' thick fur and Atticus's tail, lifted the feathers on Caleb's wings and stroked Mary's back. Soon, they all drifted off to sleep in that soothing wind, joining in with Kit for a chorus of soft snoring.

It must have been mystical too, a gift from the Father of all Creatures, for they all knew a sleep so deep and peaceful that it brought not only rest for any weariness they may have known, but also left much healing in its wake. When baby Kit—bright-eyed and eager for adventure in his youthful exuberance—crawled up onto Simon's chest to sniff his chin, he discovered only a slight redness where the nasty scrape had been.

Simon twitched his nose once, and reaching up to scratch the tickling sensation, he discovered the baby beaver. Kit grinned mischievously up at him. "Geez, every time I wake up here I've got an animal's nose in my face." Simon stretched out both arms, yawned, and sat up straighter, jostling Beauregard's head and awakening him also. Kit continued to perch exactly where he was, staring unblinkingly at Simon's face.

"What?" Simon asked, as he glanced over to Beauregard and noticed the same transfixed look on his face.

"Your cuts and bruises," Kit said, sniffing curiously at Simon's chin yet again, "they're lots better!"

Simon smiled but gently pushed Kit back down onto his chest. "Can't be, unless we've been asleep a lot longer than I thought." But when Simon reached up to feel his chin and cheeks, he discovered only a slight tenderness. And when he reached for his knee, he discovered it to be mostly healed also. "How on earth could—?"

"It's the first sign. The first miracle," Caleb said. "And now we know without doubt that we are to begin our journey. Do you not agree, Mary?"

Mary stood, stretching her legs and rubbing her neck against the tree. Kit bounced (it appeared to be the only way he moved from one place to another—by bouncing) over to his parents and all three immediately began grooming themselves and each other at the same time. "Oh yes, Caleb, definitely. The sleep was a gift of preparation for all of us for the rigorous journey ahead. And it was mystical and wonderful too. Did anyone see visions?"

"The dowger did," Beauregard announced, standing and arching his back. "The dowger was chasing the ball and—"

"That's not a vision, silly!" Atticus scolded. He was still lying atop the rock, on his back with all four paws up in the air. Atticus rubbed one eye and rolled over onto his side to face Beauregard. "You're *always* dreaming of chasing balls."

"The dowger is not always." Beauregard stated emphatically, turning to Simon with a perfectly serious look on his innocent face. Simon grinned at him. "Sometimes the dowger dreams about chasing squeels."

"He means *squirrels*, in case you were wondering, Simon-by-the-Way. Dog needs a full-time translator. See what I mean, Caleb and Mary? Now those are no more visions than…well, my dreaming about finding one of those delicious eggs down by the riverbank."

"Atticus! We'll have no more talk about eating eggs," Caleb rebuked him. "You might consider that would be slightly offensive to some of us. And more importantly, remember Beauregard's gift to us, please. Simplicity. Simple thoughts and simple things. The Truth." He stretched out his wings and turned to face Beauregard. "Now, Beauregard, dear friend, what was the rest of that dream?"

"Probably smacked into a tree and drowned in slobber," Atticus muttered under his breath. Simon giggled.

"What was that, Atticus?" Caleb asked.

"Oh nothing, nothing," Atticus responded. "Let's all hear what Beauregard has to say." He'd rolled over onto his belly, with legs sprawled out every which way except for one paw, on which he rested his chin. He stared at Beauregard with mock interest.

Beauregard sat down, closed both eyes and screwed up one side of his face. Evidently he was having a problem remembering the dream. They all waited patiently for a minute or so before Kit finally called out, "Beauregard! The dream!" Mr. and Mrs. Beaver shushed him for interrupting Beauregard's concentration (such as it was), but the prompting at least urged Beauregard to pop open one eye.

"The dowger finks it rolled into sand. No, the dowger needs be clear: not just any sand. *The* sand." And then he opened the other eye too and sighed loudly, letting his head hang low.

All the animals stared at Beauregard, and a tangible weariness seemed to blanket them. One by one they stopped their awakening movements (stretching, yawning, grooming) and proceeded to mournfully sit down again. Even Kit stopped bouncing. Beauregard's dream had obviously meant much more to them than it did to Simon, who could not at all begin to understand the dread that encompassed them now. He gaped at them in curious confusion.

"What's the matter? Why are you all so—afraid, I guess—of Beauregard's dream? It couldn't possibly be merely sand that you're all dreading," Simon stated. Dim memories of sandboxes and trips to the beach flickered across his mind, and there was an unusual hazy sweetness associated with them. He was remembering the carefree times before his father's drinking binges had begun.

"Simon-by-the-Way, I guess that, for many reasons, we've just been reminded of the seriousness of our undertaking." The music filling Mary's voice was subdued and somber, but it was still present all the same. "In the first place, we—" and she looked around at the whole group of animals now, "we have all just assumed you would take your rightful place and go with us. But we've neglected to warn you of the danger." She bowed her head and lowered her eyelids. "We have been remiss to not do so, for this is a very dangerous journey, and you have every right to know that truth. And even to decide not to go."

The silence now was almost unbearable for Simon. It seemed as though no one even breathed for the fear that surrounded them all.

"Dangerous? How?" Simon drew in the fresh air and scanned the beautiful scenery all around him. "I can't imagine anything being even the slightest bit scary here. Not like…well, not like other places I've known."

"Oh, but there is danger where we must go. Physical risks. Hazardous conditions," Caleb warned. "To not respect it is to be the most vulnerable. Simon-by-the-Way, you must understand and respect the perils we will face on our journey."

Simon stared off into the distance, his mind in another place, another time. "I've had to learn to not be afraid of many things. And when I'm scared to face those things anyway." He looked intently at Caleb, a kind of man-to-man look, it seemed. "To protect my sister, Abbey. If I'm supposed to go on this journey like you say, then I think I can face whatever's ahead."

"Which brings us to our second question, Simon-by-the-Way," Mary said, even more softly now. "Your bruises and cuts are evidence that what you say is true. You have faced grave danger." She gazed up at him with deep compassion glowing in her eyes. "What enemy did this to you?"

"It was a most horrible creature, Mary," Atticus interrupted. He waved his paws around in the air as he pontificated, gaining momentum as he accentuated his descriptions. "Two vast wheels that claim the victim who tries to tame it by riding him! And when one tries, it throws the poor soul to the ground…" (Atticus even gnashed his teeth at this point) "… attempting to crush, and dissemble, and decimate, and—"

"Atticus!" Simon choked out, trying desperately hard not to laugh—and embarrass poor Atticus by doing so. But he'd listened to Atticus' diatribe as long as was tolerable. "I fell off my bike, Mary. All of you, I simply fell off my bike. A bike is not an animal; it's a metal thing you ride, for fun. I had an accident, that's all. It's that simple." Simon shrugged his shoulders at them and crossed his arms over his chest.

"Few things are rarely so simple. Beauregard?" Caleb asked, questioningly pointing one wing towards the dog.

Beauregard sorrowfully looked over Simon, and then he suddenly raised his nose into the air, opened that cavernous mouth and howled one long, mournful cry. The haunting sound made them all shiver; Simon hugged himself between crossed arms, Kit hid his face in his mother's soft fur while Mr. and Mrs. Beaver held one another, and even Atticus cowered, covering his head with his paws. When Beauregard finally lowered his head and the eerie sound had stopped echoing across the hills, he glanced at Simon only briefly before turning back to Caleb to answer the unspoken question. "This the dowger finks is not so simple."

Atticus' eyes peeked out at Caleb from between his fingers. "Must Beauregard do that? Honestly, he gives me a fright when he makes that sound."

"Yes, Atticus, Beauregard must," Mary said. "His voice is desperately needed to continually guide and warn us, for there are other dangers we will meet upon this journey. Dangers much more perilous than frightening physical conditions." She stared into Simon's eyes. "Something will try to prevent us from finishing. Something from within."

"Within? What's that mean? From within what?" Simon asked.

"Within us. And this enemy—this evil—is more dangerous than any other we shall meet."

Kit rubbed against one of Mary's legs, and he looked up at her timidly. "My tummy feels fluttery, but I still want to go. Is my tummy the em-e-ny?"

Mary smiled at the innocent beaver, and she leaned her beautiful head down to him, caressing his tiny ear with her nose. "No, Kit, your tummy is not the enemy. But we must be on guard, all of us. And most of all, we must not ever forget that the Father of all Creatures will help us with whatever evil is before us. That great Truth is enough for us to know now. What's ahead of us and what each of us must face is known only in part now, as the Prophecy says. We'll have the strength and courage we'll need when—and only when—that strength and courage is needed."

"Crossing the Great Sand will not be so bad?" Kit asked, climbing up onto the rock with Atticus. "Will the Father of all Creatures give us the courage and strength we need?"

Caleb nodded. "If we are to cross the Great Sand, the Father will supply all that is needed."

"And safety? Will this be given to us also for the journey?" Mrs. Beaver asked, her eyes riveted towards her little one, obviously full of concern for his welfare.

Mary sighed. "What *is* safety, I ask all of you? Is it not to be in the protective hand of the Father of all Creatures? Is it not to be where He asks us to be? To be doing His will?" She gazed far off into the distance, towards where the Great Sand must be, Simon assumed. "We cannot—must not—define what safety looks like other than in those ways. We must trust the Father. We must go to the Great Sand."

Atticus covered his face with his paws again. "I don't want to even *think* about it." He peeked one skeptical-looking eye at Caleb. "Couldn't Beauregard be wrong? Shouldn't Simon-by-the-Way be the one to tell us which direction we're supposed to go?"

"What's everyone so afraid of?" Simon asked. "What's the Great Sand, anyway?"

"It's a vast desert," Caleb explained.

"With no water and we're going to be hotter than…than a fried egg in a skillet!"

"Atticus!" Caleb was clearly put out. "Other analogies, if you please!"

"Sorry. I guess I'm getting a little hungry after our nap. And just thinking about the Great Sand makes me thirsty."

"You're entirely right," Mary pointed out, standing up and sniffing the air and ground. "It's time to eat; we must have nourishment before we set out on our journey. Mr. and Mrs. Beaver, do you need to return to your lodge for bark?"

Mrs. Beaver shook her head. "Somehow Mr. Beaver knew…and insisted we all eat well before leaving the lodge." She looked over at Kit and Mr. Beaver with a smile. "But if we were to visit the riverbank one last time, I wouldn't be opposed to a bit of a snack."

Kit's eyes instantly lit up and he resumed the bouncing. "Me too, Mama. Me too!"

"Sounds as if a trip to the river is definitely our first destination," Caleb pointed out. "Atticus, you also must find something to eat, and I'm sure the riverbank would be your first choice of many favorite haunts," he teased. Atticus nodded eagerly and immediately headed to the spot where he usually did his hunting, scrounging whatever tidbit might capture his fancy at the moment. Atticus was not known for being terribly picky. Food wise, that is. "When flying over here I glimpsed some wonderfully fat berries just waiting— begging!—to be picked. Berries that I think you, Simon-by-the-Way, would find quite delicious." He nodded his head in the direction of the berries. "Care to join me for lunch, my new friend? A feast awaits us!" He fluttered over to Simon, landing gently on his shoulder.

Simon grinned up at Caleb, delighted to have the beautiful bird perched on him this way. "I am pretty hungry. And thirsty. A can of pop would be wonderful, but I don't suppose you have any around. Water will be fine."

Beauregard lifted his ears and tilted his head to one side again. Because he took everything so literally, he was very often in this exact state: totally clueless. "Pops is noises. How can Simon-by-the-Way eat pops?" He licked his slobbery tongue once around his mouth, an action he completed in an amazingly short amount of time, especially considering the size of the mouth and tongue. "Does noises taste good?"

"Oh Beauregard…" Simon began, and then just sighed. "Yes, Beauregard, pop…er, *pops* taste good."

The little group made their way to the river together, knowing an easy companionship as they found food, ate, talked—and laughed a good deal, too. All shared what they found—although, quite frankly, Beauregard and Atticus were the only ones who were the slightest bit interested in their individual "delicacies." Mary pawed the ground for tender roots growing by the old oak, and Simon and Caleb did indeed feast on the fat, juicy berries until Simon's hands were stained red and Caleb's breast feathers were tinged with a color that nearly matched the scarlet on his wings. Mr. and Mrs. Beaver and Kit gnawed on some limbs with a tender, delicious bark (according to them), and Simon found the water from the river to be more refreshing than any can of pop he'd ever tasted. When he shared this with Beauregard, Beauregard agreed he was sure that must be true, but he would still love to taste "pops" some day, possibly the next time he heard some.

Finally the entire group gathered one last time at the base of the old, gnarled tree where Simon had first found himself when he fell through the mirror. Caleb (definitely a leader of the small company, along with Mary), Mr. and Mrs. Beaver and Kit, Atticus, plus the Three—Simon, Beauregard and Mary—all stood assembled together for a few moments, gathering strength from each other, willing courage to be their ninth companion.

"Does anyone have any final words of encouragement or wisdom before we set out?" Caleb asked, letting his eyes roam over the entire group before him. "Mary? Or Beauregard?"

"Seriously?" Atticus scoffed. "I can certainly understand asking Mary. But *Beauregard*? What words of wisdom could he possibly offer, other than to address slobbering, or chasing balls or…?" He stopped in mid-sentence and scratched his head. "Isn't that a contradiction of terms—words of wisdom from Beauregard?"

"Remember, Atticus," Mary reprimanded, but the music in her words made the correction a melody still. "Beauregard's gift is the Truth. And Beauregard himself is a gift to us also."

"Gifts can surely come in some mighty surprising packages," Atticus muttered, rolling his eyes upward and drumming his fingers against his temple.

"The dowger finks this is a true saying," Beauregard whispered softly but with a certain hint of doom, and the sadness in his words became a warning before the second mournful howl arose from the depths of Beauregard's simple soul. When the despairing cry was finished, the little band found themselves instinctively huddled even closer together than they had been before. They gazed at one another now with fear welling in their eyes. Beauregard's howl had drained the courage from them, and as his cry was carried away on the wind, their bravery was scattered to the farthest parts of the earth.

Breaking into the despairing silence—and therefore tearing away its gripping hold on them all—Caleb simply stated, "We must ask the Father for help on our journey. Remember that He will supply all we need to begin, to journey, and to finish." And so Caleb lifted his magnificent wings, flapping them and praying this prayer over them all: "O Father of all Creatures, You alone have called us on this journey. And You alone will provide all that we need to complete what You have called us to do. Give us the courage to trust in You and only in You, and may You be glorified in all! Amen and Amen!"

The little band, including Simon also this time, breathed as one and repeated, "Amen and Amen!"

And then Simon heard faintly, but most distinctly, his mother's anxious voice calling, "Simon! Wake up, Simon!"

The mirror reached and pulled at him, and Simon fell back through the strange portal, landing gently on his own bed.

CHAPTER 4

"Why, if a fish came to me, and told
me he was going on a journey, I should say
'With what porpoise?'"
"Don't you mean 'purpose'?" said Alice.
"I mean what I say," the Mock Turtle replied,
in an offended tone.

"Simon, are you all right?" his mom asked, anxiously feeling his forehead (like mothers tend to do when they're worrying), moving on to touch Simon's hair, cheeks and hand. She grabbed up his fingers, squeezing them between hers. "You don't feel warm, but you were sleeping so soundly."

"Honestly, Mom, I'm fine. I was just dreaming, that's all." Simon rolled his eyes at her. "Boy, was I ever dreaming!"

She smiled at him and distractedly ran her fingers through her hair. "Was it a pleasant dream? One you didn't want to let go of?" Closing her eyes a moment, she mused, "I remember my mother telling me to 'snatch up a dream and put it in a jar.'" She opened her eyes quickly. "For special dreams, that is. Happy, glorious dreams. Those dreams need a dream-catching jar." Shaking her head in the remembering, she added, "I used to keep an old jam jar on the nightstand next to my bed. With a lid right next to it, just in case I'd need it."

"Grandma Williams told you that?" Simon asked skeptically, yawning and stretching his arms over his head. "But she told Abbey that fairy tales and 'happy-ever-after' stuff is silly."

"She did? When was this?"

"Last Saturday. When she was putting Abbey to bed, Abbey wanted Grandma to read her a fairy tale. Grandma said she needed to learn to accept the real world. Wouldn't she think dreams were silly, too? Especially good ones?"

Laura Thompson sighed, remembering too well the argument between her husband, Lewis, and her mother. Instantly her features lost the glint of sweet remembering that had settled over them. In their place, the shadows came back: the ever-present deep crease between her brows; eyes that had reflected a hint of sparkle became just dull again; and the smile faded to a mere memory. Laura had once been a pretty woman, beautiful even. Simon thought of the dusty, faded picture of his mom on her wedding day hanging in their living room. Youth and innocence covered her lovely features, and she smiled happily with trusting eyes. Now pain and weariness clung to her like a veil through which she viewed the world—and through which the world viewed her. That veil was the dull grey of shattered dreams. "Grandma wasn't always so cynical, Simon." She stood up slowly, stretching and rubbing the small of her back. "And God forgive me, neither was I."

"Did you ever really use the dream-catching jar, Mom?"

"Course I did! Tucked many a dream in there as soon as I'd wake up. Screwed the lid on as tight as I could, too."

Simon heard the wistful note in her voice, the longing for something precious that had been lost. "What happened to it? To the jar?"

His mother sighed softly as she reached to open the door. Simon noticed how her hand shook slightly as she took the doorknob in her thin, delicate fingers. "Got broken. Smashed. Like every other fragile thing I once owned. Happened long ago, Simon." She stared out into the hallway, and her unfocused gaze appeared to be glimpsing that painful, shattering past rather than the present. "Maybe your grandma's right. We should all just accept the real world. Can't hardly believe I even remembered such a thing after all these years." She took a deep breath and glanced back at Simon. "Supper's about ready. Best wash up and come quick. Your father's going to be ready to eat soon."

Simon listened as his mother's slow footsteps padded down the hallway. He rolled over onto his side, and, staring out his window, thought to himself, *Accept the real world, huh? Boy, what a fool I can be, actually believing I'm in a world with talking animals! Wouldn't Grandma Williams get a kick out of that one?* He sat up, noting with surprise that his many aches and bruises seemed to feel remarkably better than before his nap. *Maybe I should at least snatch up and keep the good part of my dream about healing*, he thought to himself, and then shook his head at his own gullibility.

But when he moved to the mirror to comb his hair before going downstairs for supper (one of his dad's many requirements—combed hair and clean hands which he inspected each evening—despite his dad's unkempt, dirty condition), Simon froze. And leaned towards the mirror for a closer look. "The scrape on my chin's almost completely healed," he whispered, with awe. "And the bruises are gone!" Suddenly Simon grabbed at his dresser, remembering too well the odd sensation of falling through the mirror. He stared at his reflection still, feeling confused and bewildered. "But that was just a dream, wasn't it? It had to be!" he exclaimed.

"Who you talking to? Yourself? Or maybe Alice?" Abbey asked, poking her head through Simon's doorway.

"Alice? Alice who?" Simon grumped. He was irritated at Abbey in his embarrassment, caught talking to himself, and deflection was always the best defense.

"Alice from *Alice's Adventures in Wonderland*, silly. Mrs. Neely, the librarian, is reading it to our class. Remember Alice is the one who climbs through the looking glass? I just thought maybe you saw her in your mirror or something."

Simon felt a strange prickling sensation at the back of his neck, that odd impression that his hair was literally standing on end. He reached up to scratch around the back of his collar. "Um, no, Abbey, that's kind of, well, you know. Remember what Grandma said about accepting the real world?"

"Uh-huh."

"Yeah, well, those things don't happen in the real world. It's just a make-believe story, okay?"

"Sure. Say, how'd your face get healed up so quick?"

"Abbey! Simon! Wash up and come down to supper! *Now!*" The sense of urgency in their mother's voice immediately ended any further discussion (to Simon's great relief) and sent them both scurrying to the bathroom to jostle for a position at the sink for the nightly hand washing.

"Scrub under your nails real good, Abbey. You know Dad'll check there."
They lathered up a good amount of suds, rubbing their hands vigorously. "Here,
let me run my nail under your thumbnail. How'd you get it so black, anyway?"
Simon worked on her with increasing anxiety, noticing that the dirt—or
whatever it was—still stubbornly clung to Abbey's fingers.

"It's not dirt! Honest, Simon, it's paint. Daddy will believe me, won't he?"
Abbey was alarmed, too, as she noticed Simon's sense of urgency. Tears welled
up in her eyes as she continued to explain, "We finger-painted today at school.
I didn't get muddy. I didn't play in the dirt, honest, I didn't!"

Simon stooped down to look her squarely in the eye. "It's okay, Abbey.
Look, it's mostly come off." He held up both hands before her, firmly and
calmly, hoping to ease her rising panic. "Now let's get rinsed off and run
downstairs before Mom has to call us again. Is your hair brushed? Good. Grab
that towel…let me have one more look at you." She held out the tiny hands
again, and Simon, raising one eyebrow, pretended to inspect them as if he were
wearing a monocle. "Ah yes. Right-o!" he mimicked in a British accent. "Such
lovely hands, my dear. Such lovely hands indeed!" Abbey giggled and Simon
winked. He'd successfully hidden his feelings from her, but to his dread, the
paint was still there. *Please, God, just this once?* Simon begged, silently. *Just
this one time can Dad forget to inspect us? Please?* Out loud, to Abbey, he
authoritatively offered: "You look great."

Her enormous eyes looked into his, revealing the complete trust and faith
she placed in him. He recognized it and felt the familiar weight settle onto his
shoulders. "Honest?"

"Honest. Now, let's go. Quick."

They ran downstairs, remembering to slow down and walk calmly just
before they came into the kitchen. Lewis Thompson did not tolerate his
children acting rowdy or boisterous—which, to him, included laughing,
running, or any of the normal tussling back and forth that siblings
generally do. When he was thoroughly drunk—as he was now—he was
also thoroughly angry, and he demanded total peace and quiet from his
entire family. *Cooperation.* That was a term he favored and therefore used

often. By it he meant everything in life should quickly prove submissive—comfortable—for him.

When he was not drunk, which was extremely rare, and—with the alcohol level that was always in his blood, highly improbable—the hazy memories from his previous binge made it nearly impossible for him to bear looking at his children. At those times, he preferred they be invisible, for to look at them, to hear them, to even be reminded of their existence…any of these things brought the beginning twinges of sobering guilt. *But after all, it was his family that drove him to drink, was it not?* So the endless cycle would begin again as one of them would become an irritation of some sort (*it was always their fault!*), he would notice Simon or Abbey, and the possibility of guilt was not acceptable. So of course the only answer was…another drink.

He was sitting at his customary place at the head of the table, lord of the manner. And then he nodded his head, ever so slightly, only once. It was the signal for them to approach. To be inspected. Once again, Simon felt unrelenting nausea plunge through him. Abbey and Simon both hesitated for just the slightest moment, but it was enough to be noticed. "Now!" he ordered, and Simon knew his dad's anger had already been ignited.

Abbey instantly went stiff in her fear, holding back, but Simon put his arm around her waist and pulled her with him. The two stood before their father, holding hands out: Simon's, firm and stiff in his bluffing resolve; and Abbey's, visibly shaking.

Bending his head slightly, Lewis Thompson peered at them through blood-shot, unfocused eyes. Features once defined as sharp and distinguished had become spongy and soft, hazy in the lines of distinction between mouth and chin, nose and cheeks, forehead and eyes. The typical effects of alcoholism were written there clearly—broken blood vessels, swollen nose, red-rimmed eyes. Where he was once driven to succeed, Lewis now was driven by only one overwhelming desire: to drink and forget how life had failed him. If he could forget, he'd regain a sense of control over this world that had so unfairly cheated him. And when he was in control, then he would have *power*. This very moment, Lewis fingers tingled as he felt the first stirrings of power. It was the other intoxicating addiction, the only driving need rivaling the one to drink. "And what's this, young lady?"

"It's paint, Dad—" Simon began.

"Simon, I distinctly recall saying 'young lady.' Did I not say 'young lady'? Is that not correct?" With each question, his voice rose in intensity and sarcasm. Simon could feel Abbey's body trembling next to his.

"Um, yes."

"Yes what?" with profound emphasis on the *what*.

"Yes, sir."

"Are you a young lady?" He sniggered, enjoying the feeling of manipulating his son, relishing the wounded look that clouded over Simon's features.

"No, sir."

"Well, then. I must've been addressing your sister, huh?"

It wasn't until that moment that Simon, anxiously glancing around the kitchen, realized his mother wasn't there, evidently wasn't anywhere in the house. "Um, yes, sir. Dad, where'd Mom go?" Simon asked casually, trying desperately to mask the sudden panic he felt.

"Seems your mother failed to keep a decent supply of a particular beverage in my house. The one thing I ask her to always have on hand and what does she do?"

Simon didn't know if he was supposed to answer or not, but one thing he did know: keeping his dad's mind off Abbey's hands was a necessity. His stomach tightened, his breathing became shallow and rapid, and he could feel himself beginning to sweat profusely. Because the beatings always, *always* occurred when his mother was not home. "She's been working awfully hard lately, Dad. I guess she just forgot—or maybe she didn't have time."

"You implying she works harder than I do?" The anger was escalating, and Simon realized—with despairing resignation—that maybe there was no possibility of stopping it once it started. It was like riding a roller coaster, really, attempting to please his father. The slow, tortuous ascent was inevitable; they would eventually crest the first enormous hill and his fury would burst forth, running its full course on the track until the rage was spent. But on this roller coaster there was never any sense of thrill. Every second was tense, frightening, and purely despairing.

"Oh no, Dad, that's not it at all. I was just—"

"Yeah, you were just trying to give excuses. Just like you're always tryin' to do with your sister here too." He shifted his sneering gaze, turning his full attention back to Abbey. "Now where were we? What is this disgusting *filth* I see all over your grimy hands?" Obscenities spewed out, filthy words that left the hearers feeling dirty somehow also. "How dare you come to my table looking like this! Well, what do you have to say to me?"

Abbey was so terrified she could barely speak above a hoarse whisper. "It's not dirt, honest. It's paint. I—we, Simon and me—we tried to get it all off…" She began weeping, the tears spilling over her cheeks and dripping onto the floor. Abbey never looked her dad in the eye unless he physically pulled her chin up, forcing her to do so. So the tears dripped at her father's feet.

"You know this isn't acceptable, young lady." His voice was chillingly cold.

Lewis stood up, unbuckling and pulling off the hated belt as he rose. Simon watched as Abbey's entire body shook violently now before him. Too late, Simon realized he was shaking also, and as he tried to move towards her, to protect her, his limbs wouldn't cooperate and he merely stood there, watching the blows find their marks once again. He heard the intake of breath with each one, heard Abbey's hysterical sobs and the unmistakable sounds of his dad's belt hitting tender flesh. And yet, all he did was stand there, unable to move, totally passive. He hated himself nearly as much as he hated his father.

Lewis sat back down, harshly scraping his chair against the linoleum as he pulled it up to the table. Slowly, menacingly, he threaded the belt back through the loops, enjoying the suggestive power of the motion. Nonchalantly picking up his fork, he waved it at them, dictatorially commanding, "Now, young lady, get over to that sink and scour those disgusting hands with the scrub brush. And if you don't get it off this time, I'll help. You want that? No, eh? Didn't think so. Simon, you sit down. When your mother gets here I want us all to be sitting at this table like normal. Nothing happened, do you hear me? *Nothing.*"

They moved to obey him slowly, mechanically, stiffly. Simon wanted desperately to go to Abbey and help her, but he knew doing so would merely incite his dad's wrath yet again, and that Abbey could not possibly endure another demonstration of their dad's fury.

When Laura came home they were all seated at the table, silently playacting their roles. Lewis cynically commented, "It's about time. Gimme one of those cans." Abbey's red and swollen eyes could have alerted her mother to what had taken place, but Abbey didn't look up from her plate, nor did she really comprehend that her mother was home. Barely breathing, moving with little sound, mechanically putting just enough food in her mouth so her father would take no notice of her, Abbey attempted to simply disappear. She escaped to find solace the only way she knew: by withdrawing into herself. Simon watched her with despair and saw her wither away a bit more, right before his very eyes.

The agonizingly long meal continued as Lewis shoveled down his food and barked commands; Laura dutifully supplied his needs, hoping to keep his temper in check; and Simon and Abbey silently ate food that had become tasteless to them, merely placating their father. When Simon and Abbey were at last excused from the table, they plodded slowly upstairs.

Simon waited until he knew they could not be heard before he whispered, "Are you okay, Abbey?"

She looked up at him, the first time she'd looked into anyone's eyes since she and Simon had washed their hands before dinner. What Simon saw reflected there crushed him, filling him with such hurt and intense rage that he clenched his fists. Evidently she had no more tears, for her eyes were empty. Empty—and almost completely hollow in the hopelessness clearly exposed there. "Oh, Simon," was all she whispered, and he led her to her room as if she were blind.

The two sought comfort in each other. Staying in Abbey's room—and moving about with an agreed-upon quiet so as not to attract any attention— they eventually sat next to each other while working on separate activities. Abbey silently pasted construction paper flowers on a project while Simon

read an assigned book for school. Frequently one would purposefully reach
out to lightly touch the other's sleeve, hand, or arm. Such a simple thing, the
need for touch, this access to another's knowing *I am*, the recognition *another
knows that I am*. Yet it was of infinite importance for these two children
struggling to survive.

When Laura came to help Abbey get ready for bed, she looked at Simon
with concern. "Are you sure you're all right? You still look feverish to me."
Once more she put her hand to Simon's head.

"I'm fine, Mom," he replied, jerking his head away. "Honest."

She sighed, still scrutinizing his face. "Simon, did anything happen while I
was at the store? I mean, did your father lose his temper or anything?"

Simon caught Abbey's eye for just a second, and instantly knew her fear.
"Oh, Dad got upset 'cause Abbey had some paint under her fingernails." He
shrugged his shoulders. "She washed them again. That's all."

"Simon, did he just yell? Or did he…did he do anything else, Simon?" For
one fleeting second he considered telling her, desperately wanting his mom's
help and protection. But he knew—just as sure as he knew that eventually
another beating would come—he knew his mother couldn't protect them.
Telling her would merely make his mother a victim, too.

Simon looked her straight in the eye and lied, "He just yelled. That's all."
Brushing a quick kiss on her cheek, he muttered, "Good-night Mom. Good-
night Abbey."

When Simon pushed his door closed behind him, leaving it open a crack
like he always did, he moved immediately to his mirror. Standing there
with his eyes closed, he wished and willed the dream to be true. He would
not pray to God this time; no, he equated God with his father—dictatorial,
unapproachable, even mean. So instead, Simon concentrated on making
the dream true merely because he wanted it to be. Then, with a fierce
determination, he opened his eyes and scrutinized the bottom corner of the
mirror. Amazingly, not only was the oddity still there, it had grown in size.
Nearly one quarter of his mirror looked strange now, and he could vaguely see
movement somewhere beyond in that other world. Once more, Simon peered

into the curious expanse, leaning into it with a heart-pumping yearning, and finally he felt himself being pulled into the depths of the mirror.

Immediately, he felt the boniest, pointiest elbow jab his ribs. "Pssst! I don't quite know if you're praying or sleeping, Simon-by-the-Way," Atticus whispered urgently. "But I do know now is not the proper time for another nap."

"Ow! What do you do, Atticus, grind your elbows in a pencil sharpener?" Simon gingerly rubbed his tender ribs. "I wasn't sleeping, I was…oh, forget it." The indignant look on Atticus's face called for too much explaining, too much remembering in order to explain. Simon wanted to forget everything from home—the real world, whatever that was. Wherever that was.

"Is something wrong?" Caleb asked, eying Simon with instant concern. He fluttered over to land on Simon's shoulder for a close up look. Putting his beak nearly against Simon's nose was too much, though, and Simon started to giggle. "Just wanted a closer look for myself," Caleb assured him, ruffling his feathers and easing farther back on Simon's shoulder.

"Close is one thing," Simon said. "But honestly, having a freezing cold dog's nose in my face, a beaver's whiskers tickling my chin and now you eye-to-eye, Caleb. Or, beak-to-eye, shall I say? Well, I think you all take this being close stuff a little too seriously."

"Possibly," Mary mused, "but possibly not. To survive the Great Sand, we *must* stay together. We will need each other desperately. So staying together is essential."

Beauregard—as was his custom when excited—began whirling in circles again. He started to grab up his ball, thought better of it (after glancing at Atticus and his instantly disapproving scowl), and joyously announced, "Follow the dowger! The dowger knows the way to the Great Sand!" Still furiously wagging his tail, he snatched up the slobbery ball.

"Shall we go?" Caleb agreed. "So, then. Lead on, Beauregard. To the Great Sand!"

CHAPTER 5

Alice attended to all these directions, and
explained, as well as she could,
that she had lost her way.
"I don't know what you mean by your way,"
said the Queen: "all the ways about here
belong to me—but why did you come out here
at all?" she added in a kinder tone.

The group trudged merrily along, laughing, singing comical songs, even attempting a round sometimes. Beauregard had quite a dilemma, though, for as much as he dearly loved carrying his ball, Atticus would not tolerate his singing while he had "that detestable thing" (according to Atticus, at least) in his mouth. So Simon volunteered to carry it for Beauregard when the song was a special favorite of the dog's and he couldn't miss adding his voice to the little choir. Once Simon attempted putting it in his pocket, but when it quickly soaked through (leaving quite a spot, too), he decided to just carry it in his hand.

They crossed over gently rolling hills, following a well-worn path. Simon noted that the vegetation was becoming more and more sparse, until finally all that was left were scruffy looking pines and small, scraggly brushes. Then, cresting one last hill, they looked down onto the greatest stretch of sand that Simon had ever seen. It extended as far as the eye could see before them, and because of the sobering impact of its sheer expanse, they all simply stood there. They'd been singing "Row, Row, Row Your Boat" in round (as best they could, for Beauregard had insisted upon carrying his ball for a while and he kept dropping and picking it up again, throwing off the timing of it all), but one by one every voice dropped out and faded away. The merry singing came to an abrupt end.

Only Beauregard still showed excited anticipation, for he wagged his tail happily. "It's the Great Sand! The dowger told you he knowed the way."

"I understood that it was big," Mary said, in a hushed voice. "But somehow this just…just…well, this seems nearly overwhelming." She had to force herself to pull her gaze from the sand—and it seemed to demand exactly that force, for it was as if the Great Sand kept and held your eyes fast. She turned to them and added, "But all journeys must be taken by small steps." Once again Simon felt the melody in her voice wash over him. She blinked her beautiful eyes once and smiled. "Who shall take the first step on this part of our journey?"

"Me! Oh, let me!" Kit bubbled, and he hopped onto the soft sand in one joyous bounce before anyone else could claim the privilege. "Mama! Papa! It feels so squishy. This is fun!"

Kit jumped from one spot to another, buried his nose and snorted out the clinging grains, rolling around gleefully. Finally, shouting and gathering up as much as his two little hands could hold, the delighted little beaver joyfully threw it up into the air over his head. "Come on, everybody! What're you waitin' for? This stuff's terrific!"

Beauregard could contain his exuberance no longer, and so he bounded onto the sand too. "Frow the dowger's ball, Kit!" he begged excitedly. "Please frow the dowger's ball inna sand!" Beauregard nudged it towards Kit's tail and Kit obligingly whacked it a good distance. Unfortunately, batting a ball in this manner sent a tremendous spray of sand (to Kit's great delight, sending him into fits of laughter). The sand flew into nearly everyone's eyes (to Atticus's great outrage , for he was not one of those who covered his). So while Beauregard happily retrieved his ball, everyone else moved a distance out onto the sand—to stay far away from any more beaver tail sand sprays.

Mr. and Mrs. Beaver smiled at their boisterous offspring and then began to explore the feel of the sand for themselves. Caleb pecked here and there, evidently finding a tasty bug or two, and Simon merely sat down to watch, thoroughly enjoying the sight of a baby beaver and a silly dog playing ball together. And Atticus…well, Atticus was nonchalant. After all, who hadn't crawled around on the wet sand that clung to the edges of Pawprint Bend on the riverbank? Is dry sand so terribly different from wet sand? (Everyone knows that it is, but Atticus was in no mood to admit that just now.) So Atticus sat, sighing loudly, drumming his fingers in the powdery stuff. Unfortunately for Atticus, though, sand does not allow for a satisfactory drumming sound. When you're attempting to be highly dramatic, that is a definite disadvantage. Mary found the sand soft to walk on. But while everyone except Atticus, who was decidedly pouting, was apparently delighted with the new terrain, she was not so easily taken in and fooled by initial impressions.

"Caleb," she called, "we must gather up everyone." Mary squinted as she looked towards the east. "The novelty will wear off all too soon. Call everyone together."

Caleb spread his wings and flew over the company, calling them to Mary with a sense of importance and a call to duty from play. Once again the group gathered—Kit, still giggling, and Beauregard, panting from his several chases. Simon shook his head at the ball which was the soggiest he'd ever known it to be (and entirely covered in gritty sand, too). When Atticus noticed, he pronounced it "the oogiest thing I've ever seen in my whole, entire life." Beauregard grinned. Proudly.

"I know the feel of the sand has been a new and fun experience for you," Mary began.

"I'll say!" Kit gushed. "Squishy is fun!"

Mary couldn't help but smile at him. "Still, you must remember we didn't come here to play. We must cross the entire Great Sand." She looked up and nodded towards the east again, and everyone was reminded they saw no end to the sand in that direction. At least, not that their eyes could see. "It will be very difficult, so we must conserve our energy. Beauregard, you also will need your strength, so you can't chase your ball anymore."

Although Mary's tone was soft and kind—because she knew this would be a great hardship for the simple, fun-loving dog—her words were a sad decree indeed for Beauregard. He dropped the slobbery ball from his mouth and forlornly put his head on his paws. "The dowger unnerstands," he said resignedly.

"Good. But not only Beauregard needs to conserve energy. All of us must be wise and cautious, for we have no water to carry with us."

"But what about when we get thirsty?" Kit asked innocently. "Where's the Great Sand Creek? Isn't there a Great Sand Creek, Mary?"

Mary grinned at his reasoning. "No, Kit. There is no creek here like we have in our forest. But when we're thirsty, the Father of all Creatures will supply what we need."

"Will the Father of all Creatures make us a creek?" Kit asked.

"He will give us water in whatever way He chooses," Mary replied. Or did she sing? For this time the words were so melodious that Simon thought they sounded nearly like the carols of Christmas.

"Remember that we must always, *always* stay together," Caleb warned. "The Great Sand can be a place of great deception. We may think that one of us couldn't possibly wander off and be lost when there are no trees or hills, but telling direction and distance here is extremely difficult because of the sand's tricky illusions. Therefore, we must watch out for each other constantly, and we *must* stay close together."

"If knowing direction is so hard," Simon reasoned, "how can we tell we're going the right direction? And which direction do we go, anyway?"

Caleb stretched out one beautiful wing, pointing towards the east. "That way. It's nearly mid-morning now, but soon the sun will be directly overhead." He gave Simon a solemn look and this charge: "It will be your duty to make sure we're always heading east, Simon-by-the-Way. The sun's position will tell you if we are walking correctly—whether it's overhead, or behind us before it sets. We will trust you for this."

Simon swallowed, looking once more towards the seemingly endless sand stretched out before them. He squinted in an attempt to soften the harsh white glare, but what he really saw was Abbey, the intense love and trust he had seen in her vulnerable eyes. He understood the grave responsibility being placed on him so trustingly, and he hung his head in shame. "But I'm not...I'm just not...well, I'm not worthy of *that* kind of trust," he whispered.

They all came to him—each one touching up against Simon in some way. The Beaver family snuggled against his leg as Kit gazed up at Simon adoringly; Caleb nestled onto his shoulder again; Atticus hurried to grab onto Simon's other leg and stood stroking a knee; Beauregard plopped himself at his feet, promptly putting his cold, wet snout on one of Simon's sneakers; and Mary reached out with her nose to softly nuzzle Simon's hand. Her breath felt warm and comforting. From all of them, Simon felt nourished—almost like he had been physically fed—simply by their touch.

"Don't you understand, Simon-by-the-Way?" Mary questioned, so tenderly that her melodic voice composed a ballad. "*None* of us is worthy."

Simon was quiet for a moment, finding Mary's words difficult to grasp. Tentatively, he asked her, "You'd still accept me? And have faith in me to do this?"

"Yes. Just as the Father of all Creatures accepts each of us. As unworthy as we are."

"But He—"

"Loves us," Mary stated. "Completely, just as we are. And so we give our lives back to Him."

Simon took a deep breath, deciding that, even if he didn't fully comprehend Mary's words, he would simply accept them for now. "To all of you,"—and he looked over each creature before him—"I pledge that I'll attempt to do my very best."

And so it was in this way that the brave little band set out across the Great Sand—determined, with great courage *and* humility, as one. Simon walked towards the front, leading the way, with Mary on one side and Atticus on the other; Beauregard and Mr. and Mrs. Beaver and Kit followed just behind. Caleb sat perched upon Mary's back. In no time at all, little Kit grew weary of the pace, for his little paws needed to travel twice as fast as the others just to keep up. So Simon put Kit on Beauregard's back, where the even rhythm of the dog's pace soon rocked the baby beaver to sleep. There he dozed peacefully on his plump tummy, straddling Beauregard's broad back, with one tiny thumb (does a beaver paw truly have a thumb?) in his mouth.

They sang for a while as they had before, but soon their mouths grew dry and Caleb advised that singing—even unnecessary talking—should be stopped. So they plodded on, silently, into the suffocating stillness of the desert. Mile after mile they trudged across the unmarked sand, leaving a trail of various shapes and sizes of footprints and paw prints behind them.

The sun moved directly overhead and began its slow arc downward. Always before, the sun had been a cheerful friend to Simon. Now it became a relentless adversary. He had to constantly squint his eyes against the bright glare, making his facial muscles sore and tired from the strain. Staring ahead as he concentrated on putting one foot in front of the other was hard work for unprotected eyes, for the sun's rays cruelly reflected off the sand's surface, as off a bright pane of glass. Though Simon realized he wasn't truly glimpsing hazy mirages like he'd seen in old movies, the eerie images of rising waves of intense heat blurred his vision so that he had to blink constantly to see clearly. All that produced a raging headache. How he wished he'd thought to bring along his ratty old baseball cap.

Simon also knew that his face, neck, arms—every tiny fraction of exposed skin the sun's rays could seek out—were being burned. He remembered a terrible sunburn he got once when his family visited the beach, and how the water cooled tender red skin. But there was no water here, no river, not even one small drink. Sweat slipped down the contours of his face, and he licked at the droplets that tickled his lips. Pausing a moment, Simon wiped the sweat from his forehead and cupped one hand over his eyes to survey the sky. "We're still going directly east, best I can tell," he announced.

Everyone paused a moment and Kit, evidently noticing the cessation even in his sleep, shifted positions on Beauregard's back. It was then that everyone really noticed Beauregard for the first time since they had set out in the sand. They were immediately alarmed.

All the animals were panting to some degree, but Beauregard was panting so heavily that his breathing came in rapid, loud bursts of air. He hung his great head so low that his tongue—hanging out as he panted—nearly drug across the sand. Aware of all eyes staring at him, Beauregard took one huge lick with that dripping tongue, instantly sending out a spray of spit. He announced, with great effort, "Black dowgers inna sun not good."

"Oh, Beauregard," Simon said, instantly taking up the poor head in his hands and stroking the soft ears. He was dismayed to feel intense heat radiating off the slick, jet black coat. "Are you all right?"

Beauregard rolled his big brown eyes up to meet Simon's. "The dowger's hot. Yes, the dowger is very hot." He closed his eyes for a moment, but almost immediately popped them back open. "But the dowger doesn't quit. The dowger will cross the Great Sand!"

Simon continued rubbing his ears, knowing how much Beauregard enjoyed that. "Caleb, he's panting so hard. Do you think we should rest a bit?" Glancing around at the entire group, he noted, "Seems as though everyone could use a break." Beauregard, Mr. and Mrs. Beaver and Atticus were already taking advantage of their conversation to sit down for a while. At Simon's suggestion, he and Mary settled into comfortable spots on the sand.

"I agree, but not for long." Caleb glanced up at the sun. "We can only walk until the sun sets; to continue after that would be dangerous, because we would have no way to know which direction we were going. We could even be retracing our steps and not know it."

Kit stirred now, yawning and stretching out his little arms. "Where are we?" he asked. "Are we close to the end of the Great Sand?" Not being one to stay put in any place very long unless he happened to be sound asleep—Kit tumbled off Beauregard's back and padded about. Raising himself up onto his back legs, he poked his nose up into the air, twitching bristly whiskers as he sniffed.

"No, Kit, unfortunately not," Mr. Beaver said. "We still have…well, just how much more do we have to go?" Barton looked at Simon—who quickly shrugged his shoulders and looked to Caleb for an answer. Unfortunately, Caleb then turned to Mary who started the entire process again by looking back at Simon.

"STOP THAT AT ONCE!" Atticus screeched, and it was an amazing yell from someone of Atticus' size. Needless to say, he immediately gained everyone's undivided attention. "Do you mean to tell me we've started across this unbearable, despicable, horrendous (Atticus was a great fan of descriptive adjectives), tortuous inferno and no one—not a one of you!—knows how far it is? Can this truly be what you're implying?"

Caleb and Mary looked at each other and nodded.

At this, Atticus thrust both arms up into the air, palms up, with each tiny finger spread wide apart. "Amazing! Absolutely astounding! Abhorrently astronomical!" (Sometimes Atticus enjoyed using alliteration too, but he had to be especially invigorated. As he was just now, obviously.) He crossed both arms across his chest and raised one eyebrow of white fur just above his black mask, glaring at each of them in turn. Even Kit, who was sitting perfectly transfixed before Atticus, received a stern glance. "Now, let me get this straight," Atticus began. "We're crossing the Great Sand. No one knows how far that is. And we're doing so because a simple dog saw sand in a dream."

Seven heads nodded. Atticus slapped himself on the forehead.

"Not just any dog, Atticus," Simon insisted. "Beauregard is special." Beauregard's panting had finally calmed a bit, and he looked up at Simon with complete devotion.

"Special. Right," Atticus mumbled. "A dog who talks Dowger Talk. A boy with serious wounds from the ferocious bike, whatever that is. A family with a baby, nonetheless. One small bird and a defenseless deer. What a crew."

"Don't forget the raccoon who thinks he's Shakespeare," Simon teased.

"A what? Shake's pear? Never heard of that fruit." Atticus looked terribly insulted. "And whatever would compel anyone with a fraction of intelligence to think that I'm a fruit?"

"Oh, Atticus," Simon sighed, grinning and shaking his head.

"I guess this whole discussion proves what we were trying to explain earlier," Mary pointed out. "None of us is worthy in our eyes. This group would look rather different if we'd done the choosing instead of the Father of all Creatures."

Simon's eyes lit up. "You mean if we'd picked out who should go on this journey, we'd probably choose huge, savage animals? Like a lion or a grizzly?"

"Possibly. Or a big, powerful man instead of one small boy."

"I'm not so small." He didn't mean to take offense, but Simon was, after all, eleven years old. And every boy thinks himself bigger than he actually is.

"Maybe not quite so small. Yet broken. And therefore usable."

"But I don't have any broken bones," Simon insisted. Mary had been staring deeply into Simon's eyes, but he broke away from her steady gaze, knowing again the odd sensation that she could see into his innermost thoughts and feelings. He realized suddenly that he didn't want Mary to know him like that, and especially when Simon himself avoided those depths.

"Brokenness doesn't always refer to bones. Or even bruises of the skin." Simon glanced back at her warily now. Finding her gaze still too intense and too powerful, he turned his attention back to stroking Beauregard's soft head. "It may be a condition of the soul, one that leaves a tender heart pliable and usable," Mary continued, lifting her head and looking off into the distance now. They could barely hear her whisper, "To give one's heart to the Father of all Creatures, to give one's very life—as unworthy though it may be—is the greatest joy. We must guard our hearts carefully, for if we don't trust them to our Father, they belong to another. And then the enemy is within." She stood up, stretching out her lovely long legs and graceful neck. "We must be on our way. I'd guess we have about four more hours of daylight, and we need to make use of it."

The others rose, too, discovering the short rest had really only made them want to sit all the more. But somehow each one found the courage to trudge on, and this time even Kit bounced along beside Beauregard instead of riding on his back. Atticus brought up the rear, and he could still be heard muttering about dogs and dreams and such. But everyone knew this was just Atticus being Atticus. He might grumble and grouch and murmur along the way, but he'd be right there with them all the same.

When the journey was nearly unbearable to them and poor Beauregard was panting almost uncontrollably, a cooling breeze arose from the north. It drifted over the small band, rumpling sweat-soaked hair, cooling tender, burned skin, caressing them with its healing refreshment. It was as if the breeze cajoled and coaxed them forward, teasing them into accepting just one more step, just one more short distance. When the sun finally touched the horizon in the west, they had traveled diligently and well. Though they wearily dropped to the sand, each one knew and felt assured that the group had done as the Father of all Creatures had asked. They had journeyed determinedly and courageously.

Exhausted, they curled up in the sand, cuddling up against each other for a sense of security and protection. And though each one was terribly thirsty and hungry—empty tummies could be heard rumbling piteously throughout the long night—all were too fearlessly lionhearted to complain. Or maybe simply too weary.

So they slept, one small, brave group of friends huddled together in the great vastness of a cruel, unrelenting desert. But they slept soundly, and deeply, knowing the Father of all Creatures watched over them.

⤝⤞

A pesky fly buzzed Simon's nose. Swatting at it and slowly opening drowsy eyes to the glaring, merciless sun, Simon groaned and licked dry, cracking lips. Mary lay perfectly still, smiling at him.

"Good morning, Simon-by-the-Way. Did you sleep well?"

Simon struggled to disentangle arms and legs from various paws and furry tails as he sat up, rousing Beauregard and Atticus as he did so. He rubbed his eyes, immediately finding them too sore to be decently rubbed awake. "Don't really remember going to sleep," Simon sighed. "I can hardly even remember stopping here, or lying down. And it seems like we only slept five minutes." The sun was hot already, and Simon pushed back sticky hair from his forehead. "Mary, how much farther is it? We can't…"

"Can't what?" Kit asked, who, although he had just this very moment awakened, was already jumping from his mother's lap to Atticus's tail (which immediately elicited a testy "Hey!" from Atticus) to Simon's lap. "Can't wait to see the end of the sand? Well, I still think it's squishy and fun, but I'm excited to see what comes next on our journey."

"And that's exactly why we must be on our way," Caleb said, extending and ruffling his wings.

"But don't we gots any breakfast?" Kit asked innocently, glancing around him for any sign of a tree or bark or even a scrap of twig. Unfortunately, there was absolutely nothing to be found except the all-too-abundant sand. Kit sighed. "You always tell me I need to eat a good breakfast for all my wiggling about, don't you, Mama?" He gave her an imploring, expectant look, and stretched out one chubby, dimpled paw towards his mama. But Mrs. Beaver could only return the pitiful look with a despairing one. It nearly broke her mother's heart to not be able to provide for her baby.

She pulled Kit into her arms, where she lovingly caressed his tiny ears—scratching behind them in the difficult to reach places, tenderly tracing the delicate edge from the tip to the base of each one. "Your food today must be trust in the Father's care," she soothingly murmured to him. "That's a type of food, my precious one, that satisfies in a different way."

"But I think my tummy's kinda angry. It's really grumbling, Mama! It doesn't understand how trust can be a food and wants just a *tiny* little bit of bark—"

"Then let's play a pretend game!" Mary interrupted. She leaned down towards Kit and immediately captured his interest by her challenging and excited expression. "Kit—everyone—close your eyes. Now, picture the Father of All Creatures feeding you from his very hand. It's not a food like you've ever known before...not like bark or seeds or berries or—"

"Eggs?" Atticus asked. With a bit of teasing sarcasm, it must be noted.

"Atticus!" Caleb peeked open one menacing eye to give Atticus a much deserved disapproving stare. Atticus shrugged his shoulders innocently.

"Will the Father's food make the dowger's tummy feel better ickity spit?" Beauregard dutifully kept both eyes closed, but the look on his face was still definitely hopeful.

At this question, Atticus just had to pop open both eyes, rolling them dramatically for the greatest effect. "I do believe the phrase is correctly pronounced *lickety split*." (He drew out the words, making even the word *split* sound like it had two syllables.) "That is, for someone with a *normal* vocal-berry."

"Vocabulary." Simon corrected.

"That's what I said."

"No, you—"

"No one's concentrating, Mary!" Kit reached up to grab at one of Mary's legs, cheating a little as he peeked at her. "I'm trying, Mary, and I can almost taste it, almost feel it making my grumbly tummy be quiet. Tell us more!"

"You're so right, Kit," Mary said, nuzzling him again as she evidently loved to do. "We're not trying hard enough. And your great faith, little one, should be a lesson to us all. Everyone, close your eyes now—no peeking! Concentrate on the Father and what He has to give to each of us. He will give us what we need for this day."

Slowly, the miracle unfolded before the mind's eye of the trusting little band. For though not one of them received a drop of water or the tiniest morsel of food, each somehow felt refreshed. Satisfied. Sufficient to face the day and whatever struggles lay ahead of them in the seemingly endless sand, the interminable heat. One by one they stretched stiff muscles, easing up to open renewed eyes that gazed out across the expanse of the Great Sand. And then they pressed on, having feasted on the unlimited supply of trust in their Father and His miraculous provision.

But even such a glorious beginning for the day couldn't stop the desert from being a place of great suffering, and all too soon, Simon was forced to scoop up Kit and carry him in the crook of his arm. Beauregard could not bear the little beaver today. He suffered mercilessly, his sides heaving in and out with such grievous panting that Simon worried Beauregard's lungs would burst from the throbbing, laborious spasms in his tortured body.

The sun peaked in its upwards climb, and the brave group trudged along more and more slowly, until, though they were still walking, their pace was equal to a crawl. Any exposed skin—even the tiny, fragile places on the animals' ears—was terribly burned, and their thirst became all-consuming. It was all they could think about, the only thing now that drove them on. Soon they would be too spent to even do that.

Unfortunately, the terrain had changed gradually, so that there were now small hills to climb over. They didn't notice the small changes at first, but soon their aching legs revealed that another cruel twist had been added to their task. Even the smallest uphill climb caused great pain, and with the pain came even greater thirst. Finally, they looked up to see a hill that was the highest yet, and their courage floundered. Beauregard lay down.

Caleb anxiously looked over the exhausted, disheartened group before him and stated, "There's only one thing to be done. I must fly ahead and scout out the lay of the land. Once I find out how much farther the Great Sand extends, I'll come back and tell you." He desperately wanted to sound encouraging. "It can't be much farther. It can't!"

But Simon looked up at Caleb with alarm. "You said we should never separate! Didn't Caleb say that, Mary? It's too dangerous—the sand's too deceptive, you said so!"

Mary could barely speak. Even her deep, liquid eyes seemed dry in the searing heat. "I'm afraid it's the only choice we have, Simon-by-the-Way. We must have some hope and guidance from Caleb as to how much farther…" Her voice broke as she glanced at Beauregard, and in her eyes Simon saw for the first time the true danger of what they faced on this journey. He'd assumed the task would be somewhat difficult, that he—that they all—would be tested in their ability to be brave. But in Mary's eyes Simon saw something he hadn't expected, and it filled him with sudden, excruciating pain.

Beauregard appeared to be dying.

He lay on his side, and his rib cage rose and fell in horrendous bursts as the exhausted dog gasped for air. For the first time, the ever-wagging tail was still and limp, and the adored ball lay abandoned at his feet. Mary glanced with desperation at Caleb and nodded; he alighted from Simon's shoulder, circling once around them. Simon could see the intense concern in Caleb's eyes as he watched him fly away, slowly disappearing from sight as the black bird was absorbed by the vast white sky.

Glancing from the empty sky to the prostrate Beauregard, Simon's eyes filled with unbidden tears. He immediately wiped them dry with sore, rough hands. Just that tiny bit of saltiness burned his tender skin. "Mary," he whispered softly, "Caleb could get lost. And Beauregard could..." Simon paused a moment, unable to utter the dreadful words. "Mary, I'm afraid."

She nodded. "I am also, Simon-by-the-Way." She anxiously glanced up towards the sky, already searching for Caleb. And then they all watched as one single tear formed and slipped from those loving eyes to the sand below her.

Atticus crawled over to Beauregard, tenderly placing one paw on the soft head. "Mary, will Beauregard be all right?" he asked. The rakish look was gone, replaced by deep sorrow as his ears and black mask hung low.

But Mary merely continued to search the sky. She had no answer, no promises which she could make. And for the first time, her music was silent.

"Mrs. Beaver, let's turn our tails towards dear Beauregard and wave them back and forth like fans," Barton suggested. "If we could provide just a bit of a breeze, maybe that would help some."

"The rest of us could gather around Beauregard too," Atticus offered, "forming something like a tent to shield him from the sun."

To this Mary agreed, so each of them moved to circle around the beloved dog, Mr. and Mrs. Beaver fanning desperately while the others blocked the sun's sweltering rays as best they could. This was how Caleb found them when he returned: huddled in a circle, desperately trying to save their companion.

"I have joyful news!" Caleb shouted excitedly, and he arched his beautiful wings before landing on Mary's back. "The Father of all Creatures has heard our cry. The Great Sand ends just over this last hill. You have done it, you brave, dear ones! Just a little farther. He has also provided a clear, cool spring. Do you hear me? Water is just a short ways, just a little farther!"

Kit wiggled in Simon's arms, awakening at the enthusiasm in Caleb's voice. "Mama, I'm so thirsty," he said, giving her a piteous look.

"My darling," she answered, "the Father of all Creatures watches over us. You will have a wonderfully cool drink soon."

"Is it a trust drink again?" Kit mumbled, rubbing sleepy eyes.

"No, sweetest, not this time. Caleb says the Father has provided us with real water—a beautiful spring!" She looked over at her husband and smiled, and Kit, in his child-like faith and innocent trust, climbed out of Simon's arms to begin walking—even bouncing some—up the hill.

"Come on everybody! Watcha waitin' for?" and he waved them on to join him with one pudgy arm and paw.

So they stood, still feeling the tremendous weariness but believing relief was just within reach. Their belief was enough to make the thirst and pain and nearly overwhelming fatigue bearable for one last hill—just a few steps more, and only a few steps more. Until they noticed Beauregard.

He hadn't moved a muscle, nor had his eyes registered Caleb's return— hadn't registered he recognized or saw any of them. He didn't even blink, but merely stared straight ahead through cloudy, unfocused eyes. Simon knelt down before him, putting his red, singed nose next to Beauregard's great black one. For once, Beauregard's nose was not cold, but instead was burning like Simon's. Simon instinctively knew this was a frightening sign. "Beauregard," he whispered, "you hafta get up. It's just over the hill. Water. Cooling water! Come on, Beauregard, *please?*"

Beauregard continued to lie there, convulsively panting and completely unresponsive, tongue draped limply on the scorching sand. Fine grains clung to it, but he was oblivious to the irritation or pain. The animals gathered around him, totally at a loss what to do, and Simon was near panic as he pleaded, "You've got to get up, Beauregard. Now!" He glanced around frantically at Atticus and Mary, directing all of them, "Help me lift him up. I'll carry him. I can do it!"

Immediately, Atticus, Mary, and Mr. and Mrs. Beaver pushed and pulled at Beauregard, nudging him with noses and paws, attempting leverage with heads and backs. Caleb flew just above them, calling out directions in a frenzy. Even Kit worked at lifting the pitiful tail. Finally they all managed to wedge Beauregard's sweltering body into Simon's arms, but as Simon attempted to stand, he collapsed under the weight. "I will get up!" he hissed through clenched teeth, for Simon saw the looks of despair on their faces. But as he tried yet again, his feeble and too weary legs buckled beneath him.

Exhausted from their efforts, they all sat gasping now. And then Mary put her nose onto Simon's shoulder. "It is no use, Simon-by-the-Way. Beauregard wouldn't want us all to give up now. He'd tell us to go on without him, you know he would. He'll be…safe in the Father's hands. We must climb the last hill. We must continue on."

Simon merely hung his head, finding no words, no answers, no defense. Once more he was paralyzed and immobile before an enemy. He stared at Beauregard with dry eyes, seeing not just a simple dog, but Abbey too. And once more he hated himself for his inability to defend and protect one that he loved so fiercely

Everyone except Simon knew hot tears on tender cheeks. They wept before their simple friend, bowing heads in silent grieving, realizing only now how much wisdom and depth of character could come from one who asked for so little in return. Simon couldn't take his hands away from his dear friend, couldn't bear to think of pulling them away until Atticus, pushing and grunting in his urgency, wedged his way in between Simon and Beauregard. "Hey. I've got an idea. What if…what if we threw Beauregard's ball? You know, this simple dog just might…well, he just might rouse himself to chase that oogey ball."

Simon looked up, feeling the beginnings of hope stirring within. "Mary? Caleb? What do you think?"

They both shrugged and Atticus added, "Well, it certainly can't hurt. And I just think…no, I believe that it *will* work. That dog has never, ever refused to chase his ball." Atticus pointed towards the last hill. "Throw it up the hill, Simon-by-the-Way. Throw it!"

"Yes! Throw it!" Kit echoed, and he hopped up and down in excitement.

So Simon picked up Beauregard's ball—surprised to find even it dried out from the scorching sun—and tossed it just a few steps up the hill. "Beauregard," he lovingly whispered into one ear. "I threw your ball. Fetch it, Beauregard. Come on, go get your ball!"

They waited, anxiously, for any sign from the unresponsive dog. Finally, the previously unfocused eyes sluggishly blinked once. Dark pupils appeared to perceptively sharpen, centering on the ball lying just ahead of him. He wiggled his nose, twitching wiry whiskers a few times, and then lifted his great head just a fraction of an inch off the ground.

"Atta boy, Beauregard. Go get it!" Simon cheered him on, and all the other animals joined in too, coaxing the dog to stand—pushing and pulling quite indignantly at his backside, but who noticed such a thing now?—and then to inch up the hill towards the waiting ball. After Beauregard slowly stooped to pick it up, he chewed it (just one pitiful chew) before dropping it at Simon's feet. So Simon threw it just a short ways once more—and so on, again and again—until the simple dog with an enormous heart faithfully followed his friends up the hill.

In this way the brave little band crested the last hill—and could finally glimpse the cooling water glistening invitingly in the sun just below them. "See it, Beauregard? See the water now?" Simon asked, stroking his head.

"The dowger sees the water. The dowger will get there too. Ickity spit," he panted, and with one last burst of effort, he lumbered down the hill towards the spring with Simon following behind, laughing joyfully at Beauregard's waggling tail.

CHAPTER 6

"I wish I hadn't cried so much!" said Alice, as
she swam about, trying to find her way out.
"I shall be punished for it now, I suppose, by
being drowned in my own tears! That will be
a queer thing, to be sure!"

Anyone watching the unfolding scene certainly would have exploded into fits of laughter, for each member of the little company jumped or plopped quite unceremoniously into the cooling spring. Mary's graceful leap gave off almost no splash, but the beaver family demonstrated no such grace—or desire to. They smacked their tails in wild, gleeful joy, sending sprays of water high up into the air—and onto everyone else. Even Atticus lost any pretense at nonchalance or dignity, for he immediately climbed in and proceeded to paddle about, activity altogether unusual for a raccoon, who usually avoids immersion in the water at all costs. Atticus even aimed return volleys at the beaver family, with a definite disadvantage in equipment and skill, however.

Caleb's uncoordinated landing was a sight to behold, and after taking in a much-needed drink, Beauregard executed a glorious belly flop—complete with all four legs sticking straight out. The sight nearly sent Simon into hysterics, he laughed so hard; then, not to be outdone, he launched himself from an old log that stuck out over the water and performed his favorite jump: the cannon ball. Which of course became a challenge that everyone accepted gleefully. Dozens of creative jumps and dives were executed (more hilarious belly busters, front and back flips and twists, can openers, even swan dives—or maybe blackbird dives) until the exhausted performers lay spent on the little beach.

Any swimmer knows that one is most ravenous after cavorting about in the water, and these swimmers were no exception. So they scouted about, finding food plenteous, nourishing, and delicious. Many even discovered their very favorites to be at hand; Simon located some wonderfully sweet blueberries (he would choose blueberries above every other fruit) and Atticus was elated to find an abundance of crayfish—delicacies to him, disgusting creatures to everyone else. Once their hunger and thirst were satisfied, a gentle darkness began to drift down upon them and they returned to the little beach. One by one they bedded down for the night in the soft, cool sand. A gentle, hazy glow of moonlight highlighted the sleeping friends' outlines against the whiteness of the beach, outlines which showed some cuddling together for warmth, some merely for the comfort of being next to another.

There by the spring that had been their salvation, the group once again received the gift of healing sleep. It was a sleep so peaceful and deep that even though the Father of all Creatures reached out a hand and tenderly touched each of them, they didn't stir from their dreaming. His strong and gentle fingers moved among them much like a mother stroking her ailing child, much like Simon's mother had lovingly touched him. They weren't fingers like we know them to be, but more a hint of wind, a caress, a whisper that soothes and nourishes. And yet still they had more form than we would know a wind or whisper to have, for the Father did indeed touch each one of his children. He felt them, He knew each by name, and He left His mark upon each one.

When Kit awoke first the following morning—immediately eager to further explore this new world—he didn't notice the Father of all Creatures had touched him. As the others awakened (soon after Kit, for once Kit was awake, *all* were awake) the others didn't notice either. Except for Mary. She sniffed at the air as she lifted her lovely head, closing her eyes and splaying long lashes across her cheeks. It was as if she were remembering something—a smell from the past, the favored scent of a blooming flower, the fragrance ever associated with a loved one. "He was here," was all she said, and smiled contentedly.

"He was?" Caleb asked, amazed and obviously delighted.

"Who? What are you talking about?" Simon stretched out his arms and legs, and bent over the spring to wash the sleep from his eyes.

The entire beaver family, Atticus and Beauregard sniffed at the air now, evidently seeking the same scent Mary'd discovered. But while the others nodded in agreement and delight, Beauregard sighed in discouragement. "The dowger nose is too sore to snuffle," he announced sadly.

"Sniff," Atticus corrected.

Beauregard shook his disappointed head. "The nose won't sniffle neither."

"No, it's *sniff*, Beauregard."

"Hey!" Simon was definitely getting frustrated, wanting desperately to sniff at the air (or sniffle or snuffle or whatever it was they were all enjoying) like everyone else, but instinctively knowing it would do him—a mere human with an insufficient tweak of a nose—not one bit of good. And besides, it would also look terribly silly. "*Who* was here? Let me in on the secret, will you?"

"It's no secret, Simon-by-the-Way," Kit said, happily clapping his tiny paws together and looking up at Simon in surprise. "Don't ya know? The Father of all Creatures was here!"

Simon stopped splashing his face for a moment, turning to Mary with a bewildered look on his face. "Do you mean *God*? Was God here while we were sleeping?"

"I've heard some creatures call Him God. We refer to Him as our Father since He is just that—our Creator, our Provider, our Protector!" Mary exclaimed.

"And yes, Simon-by-the-Way, the Father of all Creatures did visit us while we were asleep. Isn't it wonderful how He's watching over us? That He takes care of us and delights in His creatures so much that He touches each one of us tenderly?" She closed her eyes again, as if able to recall the feel of His touch.

"He's not my father," Simon announced stubbornly. "And He didn't touch me either." He pulled at his shirt as if he were about to remove it, but after glancing nervously at his stomach, he quickly tucked it back into the waist of his jeans. He plopped down, dejectedly, hiding his face between his knees, wrapping both arms over his head. Willfully withdrawing from them all.

Beauregard immediately came to his new adored friend, pushing up beside him and nudging at one of Simon's hands with his deficient nose.

"Go away, Beauregard," Simon said flatly.

But simple dogs don't give up so easily, and Beauregard continued pestering to be noticed until Simon finally relented and began stroking the dog's head with jerking movements which were less than tenderly applied. He kept his face hidden between his knees. "Doesn't Simon-by-the-Way love the Father of all Creatures?" Beauregard asked, insistently poking his nose at Simon's arms still in an effort to expose his face. Beauregard could be frustratingly persistent. Or persistently frustrating. "The dowger does," he whispered. "The dowger knows and loves His touch best of all."

"His touch isn't loving."

The animals had been somewhat absentmindedly listening to Simon and Beauregard, but now the glaringly obvious pain in Simon's voice captured and held their attention—almost like a cry in the night. The clipped response exposed what Simon had vainly attempted to hide: his apprehension in even speaking the words, and his fear of the Father.

Mary placed her nose on Simon's shoulder, closing her eyes so she could concentrate on his hurt and know it as Simon did. She sighed deeply, and pain moved across her features, clearly etching its harsh marks upon her sweet face. Mary had many gifts, among them the ability to sometimes know others' inner thoughts and feelings, as well as the gift of empathy. Her empathy moved to the hurting one's heart and dwelt there, meshing and entwining until one could allow oneself to accept the beginnings of healing, and ultimately, to accept the Father's love. But these gifts were not without cost for Mary, for knowing another's inner thoughts and feelings can be a tremendous burden, a weight that can make one weary and lose heart. Taking on the pain of one she loved so dearly—making the pain her very own—could nearly break her tender heart.

So Mary cried, sobbing out the pain for both of them, and the tears came as if there would be no end to them. All the other animals gathered around too, huddling up next to Simon and Mary, attempting to soothe and comfort. Soft weeping could be heard amongst all the animals, for they had bonded as one, and what one felt deeply, *all* felt. When one member hurt, each one carried the pain. Friendship, the little friends knew, meant a sharing of joys and sorrows. So they all wept for the pain Simon carried within his heart. Everyone, that is, except Simon.

When at last Mary's tears ceased, Simon lifted his weary head and gazed at each of them. And then he reached out to touch each one—caressing Beauregard's satiny ear, Atticus's tiny paw, tweaking Kit's whisker, rubbing Barton's tail and Mrs. Beaver's tummy, brushing against Caleb's wing and Mary's nuzzling nose. Not one of the little company knew or saw the reality: the very same unseen hand that had visited earlier returned, and He directed Simon's hand now. Guided Simon to touch the very places He had gently touched earlier, leaving His mark upon them. Simon felt those same marks with his hand, but he didn't realize that. Nor did he notice that, after touching Mary's nose, he placed his hand over his own heart—where his mark from the Father had been lovingly seared forever.

Wisely, Mary said nothing more to Simon, understanding that their tears and loving touch would represent the Father's, telling—*living*—for Simon much more than her mere words could say. But she rose with a heavy heart, for she knew Simon's pain now. She had confronted the enemy which had produced that pain, and it had been a terrible thing.

"You're all becoming my very dearest friends," Simon said to them. He glanced away, avoiding looking any of them in the eye. "But honestly, I'm okay. You don't have to worry about me." He shrugged his shoulders. "So I don't much want your Father of all Creatures to touch me. Doesn't hurt anything. Certainly doesn't hurt *me*."

Mary gave Beauregard a sorrowful look, and once again Beauregard lifted his noble head to the sky and released a woeful howl. This time the poor animals couldn't even turn to huddle together, but instead were so instantly paralyzed by the wretched sound that they visibly trembled, attempting to cover eyes and ears with quivering paws. Simon suffered, too. The first time Beauregard wailed, the sound had echoed across the hills. But this time, it seemed to be trapped within Simon's own head, cruelly echoing back and forth until it finally cut deep into his heart. The place where he had laid his hand on his chest—where the Father of all Creatures had touched Simon first—now felt hot to the touch, as if a brand had been centered right over Simon's heart.

When Beauregard finished and stood with head hanging low, Atticus was the first to catch his breath and mutter, "I would rather prefer that your sniffer worked and your wailer did not, Beauregard. My, but that is a disheartening sound!"

"Yes, Atticus, that's exactly what it is," Mary whispered. "Disheartening. For it is like a poor mirror cruelly reflecting and magnifying our flaws and brokenness. But someday…someday the mirror shall be worn away and replaced with clear glass. Then we shall gaze upon Him unhindered, and see face to face!"

"Mary, you're speaking in riddles," Kit said, looking up at her with wonder in his tiny eyes. Simon, too, watched her with a look of awe, for the musical quality of her voice was more distinct than he'd ever known it to be. If she spoke any longer, Simon was sure he could almost grasp the melody itself, could repeat it and hum the haunting strain. Kit hugged one of Mary's legs. "What does the riddle mean, Mary?"

She nuzzled her nose against him lovingly, and Kit closed his eyes in the sweetness of this moment of intimacy. "It's not meant to be a riddle, but is part of the revelation from the Father of all Creatures. And it means, little one, that we must be about our journey." Mary shifted her gaze up towards the beautiful sky, and she closed her eyes in the pleasure of what she knew and passionately longed for.

"Which brings us back to the purpose of our being here," Caleb said. He flew to a limb which hung just above the little group and gazed down at them as a proud father would look at his children. "We have successfully completed the first part of our journey, my dear friends. We have crossed the Great Sand!" This was a cause for great rejoicing, and so they responded with cheers and clapping—especially Kit and Beauregard, who couldn't contain their bubbling-over joy. But Caleb was not done, and he gained their attention by stretching out his magnificent wings. A hush quickly fell over them all, for they sensed and embraced Caleb's infectious excitement for the announcement he was about to make. "All the Father's Creatures listen to this word. The three who image the Way, the Truth and the Life have completed the first part of the journey from Knowing in Part to Knowing Fully. The Father of all Creatures is glorified! Let us worship Him now and forever. Amen and Amen!"

Each member of the brave company lifted jubilant voices, shouting, "Amen and Amen!" Even Simon—who initially viewed this time of worship with skeptical hesitation—soon joined them, for the wonder in Mary's and Caleb's voices was enough for him to respond to the Source of their awe. Their own familiar voices weren't the only ones which the happy group heard, however, for a chorus rose from above and around and below them—rustling voices, husky voices, soft and loud voices, even unrecognizable sounds from all nature which could not be likened to a voice at all. All the sounds combined and flowed together to compose and perform a melodic composition, perfectly in tune, with harmony and rhythmic accompanists!

When the chorus had ended—coming to a close gradually, like the sound of a chirping bird flying into the distance until one can only hear it in his memory—Atticus turned towards Mary and Caleb with paws on hips. "Clearly we're to continue this journey. So where do we go now?" He wagged one tiny finger back and forth at Caleb. "And don't even think of asking Beauregard."

Mary grinned at him. "Now Atticus. You know as well as I do that Beauregard was perfectly correct in leading us across the Great Sand…"

"You could ask me. I'd tell everybody!" Kit interrupted. He bounced from the decaying log he'd just climbed, back down to the ground, managing to jostle Beauregard (who merely happily waggled his tail in response), Atticus (who was being dramatic once again, stretching both arms up into the air and asking no one in particular, *Why me?*) and even his own papa, as he tripped over Mr. Beaver's tail in his excitement.

"Kit, you mustn't be rude," Mrs. Beaver scolded, but not very sternly. Even Mr. Beaver found it hard to hide his smile, for the youngster was overflowing with infectious enthusiasm.

"And where would you tell us to go?" Caleb asked, looking down at Kit from Simon's shoulder. The stiff beak was miraculously molded into what looked like an affectionate smile.

"We should follow the stream," he announced. "Let's see where it takes us!"

"I think that sounds like a marvelous idea," Mary agreed. "Kit, you shall be a leader of beavers one day." Mr. and Mrs. Beaver beamed. And Kit...well, Kit bounced. Atticus? He loudly smacked his poor forehead again, causing Beauregard to worry about his dear friend's head.

"Jsha jsdow…" Beauregard attempted to talk with the ball in his mouth. One might wonder how Beauregard could forget not to talk with his mouth full, but simple dogs tend to forget things—in a matter of seconds, really. Seeing Atticus' scornful glare, Beauregard dutifully dropped the ball. "Sorry. The dowger was trying to say he finks Atticus will get a forehead ache."

Atticus sighed. "It's called a headache, Beauregard, and the only reason I'd get one is from trying to communicate with you."

"Ha! That's the way I feel about trying to talk to you, Atticus," Simon teased.

The little group began to make its way alongside the cheerful stream that bubbled from the spring, enjoying the gentle sounds it made. It was like hearing from an old friend, as it reminded them of their beloved stream at home. Caleb perched on Simon's shoulder and Mary trotted easily along beside Mr. and Mrs. Beaver.

"Is forehead aches catching?" Beauregard asked. Kit pranced along beside him, proudly carrying the oogey ball.

"Nah, I don't think so," Simon answered. "Unless it's the flu or something like that."

"But the dowger likes catching a ball what somebody frew!"

"That's *flu*, Beauregard," Simon corrected him.

"No, it's *hopeless!*" Atticus fumed. And then he hit his forehead again.

CHAPTER 7

They hadn't gone much farther before the
blade of one of the oars got fast in the water
and wouldn't come out again
(so Alice explained it afterwards), and the
consequence was that the handle of it caught
her under the chin, and, in spite of a series of
little shrieks of 'Oh, oh, oh!' from poor Alice,
it swept her straight off the seat, and down
among the heap of rushes.

The day's journey was like a pleasant stroll for the contented little group; the terrain was easy to cross (there was almost a path for them to follow, since the low-lying brush was nearly worn away from other animals' treks to the stream) and whenever one was thirsty or hungry, cool, clear water and plentiful, delicious food were just a step or skip or hop (or in Kit's case, a bounce) away. They followed along beside the meandering stream, calling out titles of favorite songs and then singing them with bravado (even Atticus, who swung his arms and marched in step to each tune) and innocent joy.

By late afternoon, they noticed the stream's gentle gurgling had begun to change to a steady rushing sound. After climbing through some brambles to check on the winding water, they discovered two surprises: first, the little stream was no longer little nor a mere stream; and second, the now wide stream ended abruptly when it joined a wide river dotted with dangerous rapids.

They all climbed onto a tremendous rock which sat at the intersection of the two bodies of rushing water. They stood, gawking in wonder and fear, for there was no bridge, no shallow water, and, as far as Simon could tell, no boat.

He didn't know if his animal friends even knew what a boat was; but though one would have been helpful, there was no boat to be seen anyway and no available means to make one.

"We must look like a giant monument," Mrs. Beaver said, suddenly giggling. "Each of us standing here on this huge rock as if frozen, staring with eyes wide and mouths hanging open!"

"However will we get across it?" Simon asked with concern, looking about the group and realizing that for some, the journey would be easy. For others—like himself—it seemed nearly impossible.

Kit tapped Simon's knee. "Swimming's great fun. Why, I could cross this little puddle with my eyes closed! Can't you swim, Simon-by-the-Way?"

Simon plopped down on the rock and allowed Kit to scramble up into his lap. "Well, I've taken a few swimming lessons."

"Why would anybody need to go to school for swimming?" Kit asked, his face a picture of puzzlement. "Haven't you always known how to swim?"

Simon smiled down at him while Mr. Beaver explained, "Kit, beavers are born knowing how to swim. But Simon-by-the-Way's not a beaver, you know; he's a human. Baby humans are born knowing how to walk and talk instead. Isn't that correct, Simon-by-the-Way?"

"Well...not exactly," Simon answered, chuckling at Mr. Barton's assumption and Kit's continued look of genuine amazement and blatant pity. Kit couldn't even begin to imagine not being able to swim and felt a good deal of sympathy for Simon's inadequacy in this area. "Actually, the only skills my mom's ever mentioned me being born with were crying, eating, and filling diapers!"

Atticus made a "*bphff!*" sound and gestured a wave of dismissal with one paw. "I don't even care to hear what a diaper is. But that all seems rather off subject." He looked out over the raging waters, twitching whiskers and rubbing his paws together nervously. "The point is, how are we to get across? Or rather, are we to cross in the first place? Going north is not an option since we're quite hemmed in here, so maybe we should just continue following this river southward." The idea of taking the easy route seemed an inspired idea to Atticus. He didn't relish the thought of being completely submersed in the dangerous looking rapids, and he was well aware that raccoons can succumb to treacherous rivers such as this one. "Isn't that a possible and reasonable course of action, Mary? Caleb? Why not just stay on this side of the river? Who says we need to cross anyway?" Atticus stared into silent faces for only a split second, before Beauregard piped up.

"The dowger does."

Atticus shook his head, dramatically putting a paw across his eyes. "I swear I'm getting simpler by the minute. Why on earth didn't I think to silence him by putting that oogey ball in his cavernous mouth before I even asked that question?"

"Now, Atticus," Mary attempted to calm him. "Beauregard, why are you so sure we should do this? Have you had another dream? Another vision?"

"Another sporting illusion of chasing balls and running head first into trees?"

"*Atticus.*"

"Sorry."

Mary turned her attention back to the thoughtful dog who sat with head cocked to one side and floppy ears stuck out as he concentrated deeply. He squinted his eyes, scrunched up one side of his face (which exposed moist jowls and a few nasty-looking teeth), and his tail moved slowly, swishing back and forth across the rock. Thinking was a thorough physical exertion for Beauregard. After several moments (while Atticus impatiently drummed his fingers on the rock), Beauregard finally announced: "The dowger finks so because it's *there.*"

Atticus flopped right over onto his back, staring up at the sky and shaking his head back and forth. "I've heard everything now. Absolutely *everything*. We should cross the Great Sand because a dog dreamed of sand and now we should cross this river—not because of a dream. Oh, no. That I could at least somewhat understand. But no. We should ford a raging river because it's there." He thrust one extended finger straight up into the air. "It exists; therefore we cross! Makes perfect sense." Beauregard grinned and bounded over to Atticus, where he proceeded to lick Atticus' entire face. "Aargh! Stop that this instant, you brute!"

Though Atticus convinced Beauregard to cease this unwanted display of affection, Beauregard continued to gaze at him with devotion. And still waggling his tail, he announced, "The dowger says (Beauregard always pronounced *says* so that it rhymed with the word *days*) fank-you."

Atticus sat up, wiping furiously at his drool-coated face. "You are purely impossible. I was being facetious."

"How can Atticus be Fa-see-shush? Atticus is Atticus."

Their banter had been a temporary distraction to Simon, but now he looked out over the intimidating water, instantly feeling the hot flush of fear fall upon him. "Do you agree with Beauregard, Mary?" he asked. "Should we attempt it? And how?"

Mary looked at Caleb. He nodded. And then she did, too. "I always assumed we would eventually go to the other side. I just didn't know where. Or when."

"Hey! Hey—how 'bout this? I suggest we go *back*," Atticus said, diplomatically holding up one index finger. "It's a great idea, actually! Logical and perfectly practical." Glancing from face to face, Atticus sought their approval for what he was convinced was one grand solution to their dilemma. "We could simply walk back to where we started this morning. The water was calm there!"

But not one of the little band registered agreement. Kit sighed. Simon frowned. Mary looked extremely doubtful, and Beauregard shook his head, vigorously.

"I'm sorry, Atticus," Mary said to him, attempting to gently handle his sudden enthusiasm for changing course. "The prophecy calls for us to trust our Father at every part of the journey. Turning back—for any reason—just doesn't seem to be what He'd want us to do." She looked around the group, catching everyone's eyes. "Do the rest of you agree?"

Everyone nodded at her query—except Atticus, of course. He flopped back down on the rock where he proceeded to sulk, pout, and glare at anyone who dared glance his way.

"I could go on a quick scouting excursion," Caleb suggested. "Look for the best crossing point—where the river's more shallow and calm."

"Somehow I just don't believe there's going to be any good place," Simon offered, his voice sounding weary and tired.

"It's true I can't guarantee a good place," Caleb said, "but I can look for the best one available. Does everyone agree I should fly over the area?"

They all nodded (except Atticus, who was still being intentionally difficult and so merely shrugged his shoulders) and once again Caleb flew from Simon's shoulder to examine unknown territory. Every eye watched him diligently, and when they could see him no more, each one felt suddenly so small, and therefore most vulnerable.

They fidgeted a good deal, switching from sitting or lying on one side to the other. In Simon's case, he shifted from sitting cross-legged, to pulling his feet up underneath him, to lying flat on his back, to flouncing over onto his stomach. None of them could find a comfortable position, and especially not when Kit, in his nervousness, was even more squirmy than usual.

After Caleb had followed the river a good ways south, he flew back towards them and into their sight. Kit—having the youngest and sharpest eyes—first saw the beautiful wings against the bright blue sky and pointing, shouted excitedly, "There's Caleb! See him, Mama and Papa?" They waved at Caleb and welcomed him back with great relief and joy, feeling a sense of safety merely because they were together again.

Caleb landed on the rock and sat perched in front of them. His look, however, was a grave one. "Unfortunately, you were correct, Simon-by-the-Way. There is no good place to cross the river. The easiest one is right here." He shook his head. "The rapids continue all the way downstream, and the farther south I flew, the more they raged and hit up against tremendous rocks, even greater than this one. The sound was nearly deafening from the force of the water." Caleb stopped for a moment, seeking the right words to express what he'd seen and felt. There was awe in his voice when he added, "It was a power unlike anything I've ever heard or seen before." And then he whispered, "A power that I want none of you to experience."

Simon swallowed. "But if any of us has a problem swimming, we'll be caught up in the strong current, and pulled right down into those very rapids!"

He looked around at them, gauging to see if his friends' faces reflected the fear he knew shone in his own eyes. Caleb and the beavers all appeared to be entirely confident, but he also saw respect for the river's power; in the others' eyes Simon recognized fear—but whether it was for Simon or themselves, he couldn't tell.

"I have a proper and practical solution," Barton Beaver announced. He strolled out in front of them all, standing upright with paws clenched behind his back and tail dragging across the rock. Slowly pacing back and forth, he proceeded to state in a calm, business-like voice, "To tell you the truth, I've been wondering why the Father of all Creatures would have us—an insignificant beaver family with a baby in tow—come along on this miraculous journey." He took a deep breath before continuing. "And now I believe I understand why."

"Why, Papa?" Kit asked. "Why are beavers 'insigfant'? And what's that?"

Mrs. Beaver leaned over to pull Kit up against her. "It means not necessary for the journey. But now's not the time, Kit. Hush—"

"Oh, but it is," Mary interrupted. "Each and every one of us"—and she turned to indicate everyone in the little company—"is necessary and needed and important. And now Mr. Beaver will explain why he believes his dear family has been chosen to travel along with us."

"Exactly," Mr. Beaver replied. "It's quite simple, really. We shall build a partial dam. Not like the complicated structure we have back home, mind you. The current is much too swift here and quite frankly, we haven't the time. But we'll block the flow enough so that one huge tree—which we shall fell and anchor as a bridge across the river—will be a safe passageway for those of you who cannot swim." He glanced over at Atticus. "Or are slightly uncomfortable with this current."

"Mr. Beaver, that's a tremendous idea!" Mrs. Beaver gushed. The love and pride she felt were evident in her eyes, and obviously everyone else saw the wisdom and insight in Mr. Beaver's creative solution, for there were immediate pats on the back all accompanied by excited discussion.

"Truly, it's a wonderful plan," Mary added. "Let this be a lesson to every single one of us: there shall be no more talk about anyone being unnecessary.

Agreed? Each one here has a very significant—" (Mary looked directly at Kit when she said this) "—and important contribution to this journey. The Father of all Creatures himself has certainly made this clear by calling each one of us! Now, Mr. Beaver, Mrs. Beaver, Kit, how shall the rest of us help you build this miraculous dam?"

They soon learned why beavers are indeed considered to be nature's greatest engineers, for Mr. and Mrs. Beaver seemed to instantly design and go about implementing an ingenious plan. While Caleb scouted for fallen branches and tree limbs, Simon and the other animals began dragging them towards the point on the river where the project would begin. Then, after chipping away at several smaller trees, the three beavers began gathering all the materials that would be used to construct the dam itself.

Once their wood gathering was finished, the group—minus Mr. and Mrs. Beaver and Kit, of course—once again sat on the huge rock. This time, however, rather than watching the waters in fear, they followed every fascinating movement of the industrious beavers with great admiration and respect. Slipping gracefully and efficiently through the water, the three built— out of nothing but a pile of brush and timber—a safe pathway to continue their journey.

Finally, all was complete except for the final tree which would become their bridge across the dangerous current. The beavers hadn't completely blocked the river. Instead, they had altered the normal flow by hindering the current's force a good deal so that the large tree would stay firmly anchored in place. This would then allow them all to cross safely. Mrs. Beaver and Kit continued to parole the dam, scanning for any possible weaknesses and shoring up places here and there where the current was eating away at their structure. Mr. Beaver, meanwhile, climbed out of the river to find a suitable tree for the bridge.

"You all can help me with our choice," Barton said. "These are the main considerations: First, it must be adjacent to the river. And second, it must be wide enough for all of you to walk upon, but not so large that I can't fell it. Fan out a bit and let me know which trees seem suitable for our needs. Then we'll decide upon one."

"Sounds easy enough to me," Atticus offered. And it did sound terribly easy.

But after traipsing up and down a small stretch of the river for a good long while, they still couldn't agree on any one tree. Mrs. Beaver and Kit climbed out of the river to discover what was taking so long. They soon heard how every tree was either too far from the river, too far from the dam, too narrow for easy crossing, or too wide for Barton to cut down. Tired of the delay and eager to be safely across the frightening river, everyone was becoming restless and frustrated. And some had even begun to issue vague ultimatums, insisting that *this tree* or *that tree* was obviously the only legitimate choice. They weren't simply trees anymore, but instead had suddenly become "*my*" trees. Each member of the group was beginning to take the choice of tree personally.

Atticus leaned against a particularly huge pine. Even Simon couldn't begin to stretch his arms all the way around the trunk, it was so great in size. It was, however, right next to the river and the closest to the dam. Atticus crossed his arms over his chest and glowered at them all. "You're just not being reasonable," he insisted. "My tree's the best. Anyone with two eyes and half a brain can see that. Which excludes Beauregard, of course."

"The dowger gots two eyes," Beauregard said, plopping down in front of Atticus. He looked terribly confused. "And the dowger don't gots half a brain."

"I stand corrected. You have *less* than half a brain. And this is the perfect tree. Discussion over. Choice made." He threw both arms up in the air before then planting both paws on his hips.

Mary sighed. "But you know Barton said it would take him hours and hours to chew enough for it to come down, Atticus. And it's so large that if it doesn't fall in the exact direction we need it to, all of us together could never move it. Not an inch! If that happens, poor Barton would have to begin all over again!"

Atticus stubbornly shrugged his shoulders. "So we'd start all over again. We'd help pick another tree."

"But the dowger can't help Barton chew it down," Beauregard said, shaking his head sadly. "The dowger chews the ball. The dowger can't chew the tree."

"Then Barton must be overjoyed," Atticus smirked. "At least it won't be all slobbery from your assistance!"

Simon pointed to a maple adjacent to the pine. "I think this one looks like the best choice. Its trunk isn't nearly as wide, it's close and it has a lot of limbs we could hang onto while we're walking across it."

"But those limbs are so large they could break the dam itself," Barton pointed out.

"Exactly." Atticus wasn't about to give in, and thus proceeded to resolutely argue for his choice. "My pine's branches are smaller and softer. They wouldn't hurt the dam at all."

Poor Barton stood glancing dismally from one to the other, ringing his hands and sighing loudly until Caleb interceded and called them all to order by flying onto a low-lying limb and spreading his wings.

"Children of the Father of all Creatures, listen and heed my words! We've lost sight of the reason for our journey; we've been distracted from the goal which we strive to obtain. Instead, let us keep ever before us what we desire to achieve: to complete this wondrous journey. The Father has promised to guide us, to keep us safely in His hand, to help us do what He has asked us to do. We must plan and execute to the best of our abilities. But ultimately, *we must trust the Father for our safety—no matter how that looks, no matter how scary it appears, we need to recognize that He's still in control.* Let us not allow anything—especially vain attempts to guarantee security when this is not our responsibility—to keep us from striving to do His will. Let us have the courage to do our part. And the courage to trust the Father for His!"

Silence followed. There was no joyful chorus of 'Amens,' no sounds of worship from nature around them, no emotional responses stirred by the power of Caleb's words. Instead, they looked deeply within their hearts and saw a gnawing, unrelenting fear. Oh, they'd known times of uncertainty when they had set out on their journey. The thought of crossing the Great Sand had given them pause. But now they realized they had set out with incomplete faith—an untested faith, one that hadn't yet known the touch of searing pain.

Until Beauregard nearly died.

Now the idea of death was no longer a mere concept. To have the courage to trust with naïve ignorance is one thing; to demonstrate strength of character by believing Him when tremendous danger and pain are a reality is another. One is misleading and incomplete, like a child who merely clutches his mother's skirt. The other is to stare into the frightening center of the flame… and willingly step in. *This* is true faith.

"What will you decide?" Caleb called out, and each one knew he was asking for much more than merely choosing a tree. This was the time to choose to trust.

"I believe Barton is the expert," Mary said softly and yet firmly. "Therefore, he should choose which tree." She was quiet and pensive for a moment before continuing. "I don't know if each of us will safely cross the river. But I do know each of us has been touched by the Father and that we rest in the palm of His hand. That is the only true place of safety." Slowly, so slowly, Mary lifted her head, and as she did she whispered, "Amen and Amen!"

Suddenly the whole earth became a chorus that joined in with the melody lingering around Mary, and the music rose and began to swell in enthusiastic waves of unstructured joy. It was so powerful that it reached out and drew in every member of the little band, and they became a part of the choir that lifted voices of praise to the One who was the reason for the song, the One who truly was the song itself!

One by one, Like a glimpse of a melody that repeats itself throughout a symphony, each of the animals stepped forward to stand by Mary. All repeated, "I am in the palm of His hand. There I am safe!"

Until Simon was the only one left standing apart, looking very alone.

Beauregard looked at him with his great soft eyes. "Won't Simon-by-the-Way come, too? Doesn't Simon-by-the-Way trust the Father?"

With shoulders slumped, he hung his head in complete despair. "You don't understand…*none* of you. I can't trust Him! And I can't *ever* because He's just like my father!"

Mary walked over to Simon and gazed up into his ashen face. "What is your father like, Simon-by-the-Way?" she asked softly.

He blinked twice, to suppress the tears that threatened. They barely heard Simon say, "He's mean. So awful mean I wish he was dead! He…" Simon shut his eyes against the all-too-real image of his father, hoping for the courage to speak. "He beats my little sister. Sometimes he hits her, so hard! And no matter how hard I try, I can't stop him. I *hate* him and I hate what he does, but I just can't stop him."

Mary glanced away from Simon to gaze sorrowfully into Beauregard's eyes, for she knew once again he would howl despairingly for the boy, for his pain, and for the love they all felt for him. The dog lifted his head, and this time his disconsolate cry competed with the sounds of the swirling river, and it was carried away downstream as surely as the twigs and leaves and grasses. As always, they clung to one another until Beauregard ceased and hung his head in anguish.

"Simon-by-the-Way, this will take great courage for you to believe." Mary's voice was soft and yet authoritative at the same time, for there was not one hint of doubt in what she would say. "The Father of all Creatures is *not* like your father. He is good and loving and desires to show how much He loves you."

Simon flinched physically from the impact of Mary's words and answered defensively, "But He can't love me. I'm not worth loving."

"Oh Simon. It's not a matter of worth. He gives his love freely."

"But it's so hard to accept when you feel unlovable."

She nodded. "Oh, I know, Simon-by-the-Way. Often I feel unlovable too because sometimes all I see are my imperfections."

Simon gaped at her. "You? Imperfections? But you're wonderful, Mary... you're..."

"Far from what I should be." She hesitated a moment, weighing and measuring her words. "Shall I tell you a story about a young one so selfish she caused her parents' deaths?"

Simon turned from her in obvious anguish. "I don't want to hear this—"

"Oh, but you must, Simon-by-the-Way. You must hear how that one *demanded* food when there was a great drought and famine in the land. And so the loving mother and father gave her all they had until they were weak and dying from their lack. Completely blind to their pain, the young one so haughtily ordered them to provide more that her parents ventured to the Forbidden Land. Where they soon died. *For her!*"

Barely above a whisper, Simon begged, "Mary, don't…please."

"That young one was *me*, Simon-by-the-Way!" Her commanding voice was a chorus of emotion. "I caused my own dear parents' death, for only moments after they left, the Father of All Creatures sent relief from the drought and famine. Rain fell! Plants once again grew and flourished, miraculously. There was no need to disobey Him. But only then did I recognize that. Only then did I know my unworthiness and finally begin to know His forgiveness and love. So do you believe me now?" She moved to stare into his brilliant blue eyes with her liquid ones. "Do you understand when I gaze into the brook by our home to view myself, I see only the flaws, the weaknesses, the defects I am sure make me unlovable before the Father? But someday, someday we'll know *fully*, Simon-by-the-Way. We won't be gazing into mirrors, but clear glass instead. For the first time, we'll truly see ourselves. And Him! And we'll be able to accept and know His forgiveness and love *completely*. Can you understand that just a little?"

Beauregard pushed at Simon's leg with his nose. "The dowger finks Simon-by-the-Way's very lovable."

Simon smiled at him and looked back up into Mary's lovely eyes. There, too, he saw only love and acceptance. And finally he let his gaze wander over the remainder of the animals in the little group which had become so precious to him—to Atticus, Mr. and Mrs. Beaver, Kit, and Caleb. They didn't say anything. And yet they said everything with their eyes. Finally, Simon nodded. The little band became a united group once more.

Having overcome the obstacles of their disagreement, they appointed Barton the "chief chooser of the tree" and he picked out one which none of them had initially chosen. Immediately he set to work—chewing away with powerful, sharp incisors—and all watched his skill and determination with fascination. Mrs. Beaver and Kit headed back into the water, already needing to replace and repair sections of the dam. Obviously, the current was still strong, maybe even too strong. As they were working, they detected dark clouds moving in just to the north of them.

Caleb was the first to call their attention to the imposing clouds, having noticed a change in the force and direction of the winds. "Look, Mary," he said, pointing towards the darkness. "A storm's gathering. Evidently heading this way."

She nodded, immediately looking concerned. "It will make the river rise, pushing the current against us with even greater force." Glancing towards Barton, she added, "I'll tell Barton he must hurry. You warn Mrs. Beaver of the impending danger. She may want Kit to swim to shore."

Simon watched the gathering clouds with rising anxiety, too. He'd never cared for thunderstorms, although he would never have admitted that to Abbey. She needed him too much when lightning struck and thunder boomed, almost demanding he be calm and reassuring since she was terrified of the storms herself. So Simon had always hidden his own fears as he allowed his frightened sister to cling to him while they sat indoors and waited for the bad weather to eventually pass. Now, however, he was outside, and the storm was an entirely new challenge for him.

Barton called to them, instructing and directing how to help push the tree towards the river as he finished chewing at the now precarious base. Finally, with a great crash, the tree fell almost exactly where it was needed and the entire group sent up a great cheer. But their celebration didn't last long, for they felt the first drops of rain—cold spatters which made them shiver. As they maneuvered the tree up against the dam, a steady downpour began.

Mrs. Beaver had sent Kit to shore, where he sat dejectedly, waiting for his father. "Mama said I must get out of the water, Papa, but I didn't need to. Honest! It's just a little bit of silly old rain!"

"I know, Kit," Mr. Beaver explained, "but your mama understands the danger better than you do. A little rain here could be a great storm just upriver. The water can rise quickly and become dangerous in a moment's time." He sat up on his haunches, sniffing at the air. "The storm is just north of us, and it's heading our way! Quickly now, we must get across the bridge." His voice was not panicky, but it held a sense of urgency and conveyed the force of a command to be obeyed.

The wind was noticeable now; it rippled hair and fur at odd angles and branches of trees swayed back and forth. Clouds moved with it, too, rushing and pushing up against each other in their hurry to move south. The darkness from the storm had slowly inched its way to nearly cover them—an eerie darkness that only a daytime storm brings, an ashen grey clinging to whatever it touches, ringing the outlines of everything with a sickening, jaundiced yellow. The rain stung their skin as the wind whipped it against them, forcing the little group to huddle together, cowering and hugging up against one another in a vain attempt to keep warm and dry. There they stood, paralyzed with fear by the storm that gradually edged its way towards them.

Caleb quickly took command. The fierce wind hit against him forcefully as he attempted to fly in place just above the little group, but he fought back and began shouting out instructions. "Mr. Beaver, I want you to walk across the tree first. Show all the others how easy it is. All of you now, watch Barton!"

When the great tree had fallen, it had broken just where Barton had chewed so capably. But just before it gave way, the pull of the tree brought up the entire root system. Now those immense exposed roots became the band's ladder, albeit a muddy one. Barton proceeded to climb the nearly five-foot-tall barricade, but the mixture of rain and soil had created a slippery mess. As he struggled to reach the trunk, his feet slipped out from beneath him, and mud caused the branches he used as handholds to pull right out of his little grip. It seemed that for every four inches Barton gained, he slipped back at least three. Finally, after climbing about half way, Barton rested, panting with frustration.

Caleb had hoped Barton could climb the roots and cross the entire river without any assistance, but he now wasted no more time on what would not be. A beaver's feet were made for paddling in water, not for climbing slippery tree trunks. "Simon-by-the-Way, we're going to need your height and strength—and great courage!—to get us all across the river. Give Barton a boost, will you?" The storm was gathering more intensity, and Caleb had to shout at the top of his lungs to be heard above the gusting wind.

Simon had been huddled with the others, and he hesitated for a moment before leaving the security of the little group. Summoning all his courage and looking once to Mary for a nod of belief in him—which she gave whole-heartedly—Simon hurried over to Barton and pushed against the beaver's bottom. They both struggled and grunted and *"oomphed!"* a great deal (completely covering Simon in mud from head to toe in the process), but at last Barton reached the highest root and safely pulled himself to the top. There he rested for a brief moment to catch his breath, and then he jumped up onto his feet and quickly scampered all the way across the tree trunk to the other side of the river. He waved his arms and shouted encouragingly to them, "See! I'm safely on the other side. It's easy!" Then he dove into the water to help Mrs. Beaver repair the dam—the temporary, tenuous dam which was being eroded away by the rising water with every passing moment.

Caleb watched them both frantically working on the structure and noticed that it was only a matter of time before the unremitting current would overtake their harried repairs. He realized their time to cross the bridge was dangerously short. Barking out orders again, purposefully hiding from his trusting friends the panic he felt inside, Caleb called out, "All right, who's next? Efficiently now! Mary, how about you?"

Mary approached the mound of roots with great apprehension, for unlike Barton, she had no fingers or paws with which to grab and pull herself up. Hooves were nearly useless in situations like this. She took a deep breath, nodded at Simon, and then began the slow work of climbing the intimidating mountain of roots. Simon pushed with all his might until Mary reached the top. She stood there, panting, trembling, and looking out across a river which seemed to stretch on for miles before her. "I am safe in the palm of His hand," she whispered to herself. "Safe in the palm of His hand." After taking one last breath and slowly exhaling, she stepped gracefully and lightly across the tree, constantly repeating, "Safe in His hand, safe in His hand, safe in His hand." When she reached the other side, she called out, "Barton's right. It *is* easy! Come on, Atticus!"

Atticus stood exactly where he was, shaking his head slowly back and forth. Beauregard nudged him on the backside. "Come on, Atticus! It's the raccoon's turn now. The dowger finks it looks like fun!"

Atticus frowned sarcastically at him. "The *dowger's* not crossing yet, is he?"

Caleb was finding it increasingly difficult to fight the wind, and his wings were quickly tiring. He was about to lose his temper and give Atticus a great scolding when a flash of lightening and a clap of thunder reverberated across the sky. Almost instantly, Atticus managed to frantically scramble up Simon's back and perched himself right on the very top of Simon's head, clutching with all his might. He had tufts of Simon's hair clenched tightly between every single finger, and there he sat, staring wildly about him.

"Atticus, this is ridiculous, *you hafta get off.* I remember desperately wanting a raccoon hat when I was little, but Atticus—ouch!—that hurts!" Simon fussed at him. It felt most embarrassing to have a silly raccoon perched atop your head, but when he was pulling your hair out by the roots too, well, that was entirely too much. "Atticus, get off my head this minute and climb up onto the tree trunk. Do you hear me? *Atticus!*"

But the terrorized Atticus continued to sit there, holding on for dear life, staring unblinkingly at the sky above him. Once again, Caleb quickly sized up the situation and realized drastic measures were called for immediately. He flew at Atticus, pecking at the bushy, ringed tail. "Atticus! Do you hear me?" Caleb shouted at him, straining to be heard clearly above the fierce sounds of the storm. "I promise you I'll peck out every single hair on your precious tail if you don't get across that tree now! Your tail will be bald, do you hear? Stripped naked!" And he pecked at Atticus again, pulling out a good-sized chunk of thick fur.

Finally, Atticus blinked—as if waking from a deep sleep—and after grumbling "Honestly! Horrendous happenstance!" at Caleb (he was at the alliteration stage again), he wiggled off Simon's head and up to the top of the roots. Then he looked down at the raging waters below him and his fear increased. Though Mr. and Mrs. Beaver continued to work feverishly, the dam was being steadily broken apart, and the intense pressure of the water pushed at and flowed under the dam, rising in more fearsome power with every passing minute.

Caleb fluttered down onto the middle of the tree and landed there. "Don't look down!" he ordered Atticus. "Look at me, Atticus; come to me. *Just don't look down!*"

Atticus took one hesitant step and then another before he glanced down at the water again. And stopped.

"Atticus, Beauregard is right behind you and quite ready to go. I can assure you he will scamper across here with the greatest of ease. Are you going to let a simple dog make a fool of you? Look at me and come to me. Now!"

Caleb's challenge was simply inspired, for Atticus not only finished his walk across the now terribly slippery tree, he completed it quickly and without even so much as another glance down at the river. Atticus assumed Caleb was exaggerating about Beauregard's being right behind him. Beauregard, however, was indeed already at the top of the roots and stood eager and willing to take his turn, with his ball clenched tightly in his mouth. Almost as quickly as Atticus hopped off the tree onto the wonderful safety of the ground on the other side of the river (where Atticus dramatically bent down and kissed the mud), Beauregard was right beside him, offering excitedly, "Wasn't it fun, Atticus? The dowger liked it! Say, Atticus, wanna do it again?"

The only two now left were Simon and Kit, but Kit had been instructed to join his parents once everyone else was safely across the bridge. Then Mr. and Mrs. Beaver would make sure Kit—and they themselves, too, of course—were safely on the other side. Simon had helped everyone else up the slippery mess of roots, but now he had to go it alone. He was nearly to the top when the lightening and thunder struck again and startled him. He jerked, lost his grip, and fell nearly all the way back down to the ground again. His hair clung to his forehead and rain constantly trickled into his eyes, making it nearly impossible to see. He was reaching a point of desperation when Mary called out instructions to Caleb. "Tell him to say it, Caleb! Tell him to say that he's safe in the Father's hand!"

Caleb flew over to Simon, knowing this must be his final flight. His wings were exhausted, and any further attempts would be disastrous for him. Working furiously against the powerful winds, Caleb fluttered erratically above Simon's head and shouted, "Mary says to tell you to say it!"

"*What?*" Simon asked, totally bewildered by Caleb's request.

"Say out loud that you're safe in the Father's hand! Come on, Simon-by-the-Way, do it!"

Simon sighed, feeling extreme frustration at the seemingly useless exercise. Sudden anger rose within him because, while he'd offered physical and practical help to everyone else for safe passage, now all he was to receive was a silly bunch of words.

"Simon-by-the-Way, please listen to Mary. She understands things, you know she does. Trust her. Trust the Father of all Creatures! Do this and cross the river!"

Simon closed his eyes a moment, gathering courage to say the words. But even more so than saying them, he was trying to summon the courage to *mean what he said*. Simon despised the untruthfulness of his father, the way he lied to himself and everyone else around him. Time and time again Simon had vowed he would never be like him or trust him. As he concentrated on the words, he breathed the first real prayer he had ever prayed. "God, help me to believe. I can't by myself. I need you!"

Not one member of the little company really saw what happened—not even Simon, although he surely must have sensed it. For the giant, omnipotent hand reached out and gently scooped up the angry, terrified boy and placed him on the trunk of the great tree. As Simon crossed, slowly putting one foot in front of the other and mumbling over and over to himself, "I'm safe in the Father's hand, safe in the Father's hand," that hand was indeed over and under and around him, protecting him from the ferocious storm, the blinding lightening, and the deafening thunder. The storm reached its peak of fury while Simon walked across the tree. He crossed unscathed, untouched by the storm—but touched by the invisible hand of the One who held and guided him so tenderly.

When Simon finally reached the other side and Caleb landed on Mary's back, totally exhausted but safe, the little band cheered and clapped once again. They'd succeeded in overcoming a mighty obstacle and had done so by supporting each other and working together. So they laughed and hugged and continued to get drenched in the merciless rain, not noticing any previous discomforts. The river had symbolized a grave and deadly enemy and they had defeated it. They had won!

"Hey everybody, look at me!" a small voice called, a voice nearly lost in the wind and rain. Kit had somehow climbed up onto the tree trunk all by himself (he was indeed squirmy enough to get anywhere), and he began to edge his way across the precarious bridge. Mr. and Mrs. Beaver had been frantically searching for their dear baby, and had just now joined the group, hoping Kit was already there.

"Oh, Barton, look!" Mrs. Beaver cried, and the fear in her voice had the intensity only a mother's could hold. "The dam won't last, Barton! Oh, Kit!"

And even as she uttered the fateful words, the dam began to break apart with wrenching tears and crashing logs and timber. In the blink of an eye, the entire dam was caught up in the surging current and swept away, leaving the exposed tree all too vulnerable. It heaved back and forth a moment, and in that instant the terror was clearly recognizable in Kit's little eyes. The tree groaned loudly and then gave way, dumping Kit into the foaming waters. His head bobbed up once, twice—and then disappeared into the rapids.

Father and mother immediately dove into the violent river, while Mary grabbed at Beauregard and Simon, instinctively sensing they would attempt to give their lives to save the dear little baby beaver. But no one would ever have suspected the courageous, dear heart that lived and beat beneath the breast of Atticus, for he also intuitively jumped right into the turbulent current.

"Atticus!" was all Mary could cry, and then he was gone, too—swallowed up immediately by the ravenous river.

CHAPTER 8

*"Don't let us quarrel," the White Queen said
in an anxious tone.
"What is the cause of lightning?"
"The cause of lightning," Alice said
very decidedly, for she felt quite certain about
this, "is the thunder—no, no!" she hastily
corrected herself. "I meant the other way."
"It's too late to correct it," said the
Red Queen: "when you've once said a thing,
that fixes it, and you must take
the consequences."*

They all stared down into the churning water, waiting and straining their eyes for any glimpse of their dear friends. Tossing leaves and moving shadows fooled them, giving false hope and bitterly frustrating them each time. And then *finally* Mr. and Mrs. Beaver's heads popped up at the riverbank, dragging a thoroughly drenched and bedraggled Kit. The three of them lay spent, panting and coughing up muddy river water. "We caught him just before he was thrown up against a terrible rock," Barton finally managed to choke out. "We must thank the Father of all Creatures that we're all safe."

"But we're not all safe!" Simon frantically ran from where the beavers lay to the place where Atticus had jumped in. Pointing to the exact spot, he shouted, "Atticus jumped in right here! You've got to find him!"

Feeling responsible for each one's safety, Mary attempted to caution the courageous yet exhausted beavers about the considerable risk. But again, there was simply no time for any discussion. Barton gave Kit one stern look of warning and calmly but firmly ordered, "Stay put!" before he and Mrs. Beaver dove right back into the churning river.

Once more, the remainder of the little company anxiously paced up and down the riverbank, painstakingly scrutinizing the water for any signs of the beavers or Atticus. "Shouldn't we move downriver a ways?" Simon asked. "The current would take them that direction anyway, and we may be able to somehow help Mr. and Mrs. Beaver find Atticus."

Caleb glanced quickly over to Mary, as if silently seeking her opinion. Mary—ever so slightly—shook her head 'no.' "I'm concerned about leaving this particular place, Simon-by-the-Way," Caleb said. "We're separated now, which is a very dangerous and vulnerable position for us to be in. I think by staying here—the last place we were all together—we have the greatest chance of being reunited. When Mr. and Mrs. Beaver return…" (he conspicuously left out Atticus's name, and Simon noticed) "…they will come back here. If we move elsewhere, they may not be able to find us. Do you understand, Simon-by-the-Way?"

Simon nodded slowly, accepting Caleb's reasoning, but not the reality of what it might mean for Atticus. Certainly Atticus was nowhere near them now, having undoubtedly been carried a good distance downstream. All Simon could picture in his mind's eye was his dear raccoon friend, stranded upon some rock in the middle of the river, cold, frightened and injured. He shivered and was instantly aware of Beauregard's leaning heavily against him.

"The dowger misses his Atticus."

Simon stroked the dog's head absentmindedly, continuing to watch the river. The storm had passed over them by now, but a steady drizzle continued, hampering their efforts to see. Simon wiped the aggravating rain from his eyes and cupped one hand over his brow. Attempting to move closer to the river, he nearly tripped over Kit. The poor little beaver sat huddled at Simon's feet and was, for once, completely still. Kit, too, stared into the foaming water, knowing intense fear for his mama and papa and Atticus—and deep shame for the fact that *he* was the reason they were all in danger.

Caleb still rested on Mary's back, but he tested his wings now, finding them recovered enough to fly a short distance. "I'm going to fly downstream a ways," he stated. "I can't stand just waiting here any more." Simon continued to pace back and forth as Caleb spoke, completely understanding the need to do something, anything. "Maybe I can at least spot them and bring back some good news. It could be they're all resting on the riverbank, waiting to regain sufficient strength to come back." The words themselves were encouraging and hopeful, but the tone of Caleb's voice didn't disguise the fear he felt at what might have happened to his friends. He shook the rainwater from his wings and said, "I'll return shortly. My wings are still weak and the rain is enough to weigh me down even more. Take courage, my dear friends. Our Father is with us!"

So it was with ever-greater despair that the frightened little band watched yet another member of their group separate from them. Those remaining—Mary, Simon, Beauregard, and Kit—stood side-by-side. They didn't even notice the steady drizzle, feeling too worried about their dear friends to be bothered by a simple thing like rain.

They continued to frantically watch the water for signs of the beavers and the raccoon; then, suddenly, they'd remember Caleb and awkwardly jerk their heads up to search the dismal, dreary sky. Simon could not remember ever feeling so forlorn, so heartsick and empty. Even through all the painful experiences with his father he had never felt such an aching hollowness; in those times, his all-consuming anger was like a companion he clung to, harbored, and nourished as his *right*. Somehow, that anger became an accomplice and friend that never left him completely vulnerable before the one towards whom he directed his rage.

Images of Atticus filled his mind—the first time he spotted the melodramatic creature lounging across a limb, the sight of him teasingly arguing with Beauregard, the many mannerisms which would seem overacted by anyone else but merely became an endearing part of Atticus's imaginative personality. Simon realized these creatures had truly become his friends and to lose one would be unbearable for him. For the first time, Simon understood why he always avoided making friends until now, why he skillfully evaded allowing himself to become attached. For to be this close—to love a friend this much—made him feel all too vulnerable. Fleetingly, he wished he'd never come here, had never met any of his new companions. Rather than love these creatures in a way that would only bring him pain, he almost wished he could hate them.

With one hand Simon continued to absentmindedly pet Beauregard's head and with the other he stroked the baby beaver. Kit hadn't spoken since his rescue, and Simon sensed his overwhelming guilt. Beauregard attempted to soothe the baby beaver's fear and shame. "The dowger knows Kit didn't mean anyfing bad to happen," Beauregard said softly. He nuzzled Kit's back. "Everyone else does, too."

Kit looked up at him with pain-filled eyes, but remained silent.

They heard Caleb's approach before they saw him, for a dense fog was settling in, covering everything with its murkiness. He landed on a rock before them and they could tell instantly that the news was not encouraging. "Kit, I saw your mama and papa and they are safe. They were resting a moment on the bank."

"And Atticus?" Simon asked hopefully. "Any sign of him at all?"

Caleb hung his head before answering, "A great tuft of hair from his tail was wedged between two rocks. Barton and Mrs. Beaver pointed it out to me, hoping it might be a clue to his whereabouts. But it didn't help any and that dear bit of hair was just like the one I so spitefully pulled out when I was angry with him about crossing the river…" Caleb fell into silence, sitting with his head so low that his beak rested limply on the rock. His tiny little body heaved one great sob before he was still again.

"You didn't intend it to be unkind, Caleb," Mary said softly. "You did it to save his life."

The rain eventually dwindled away, but the encroaching fog continued to gather and move in around them until they could no longer see any distance at all, not even across the river. The sounds of the river and forest were magnified and distorted until the swirling rapids seemed to be sneaking closer, seeking them out to snatch them the way they had Atticus. They huddled against each other in their fear, exhaustion, and confusion. It felt as though the vaporous mist was slowly swallowing them all, and they felt doomed to be pulled into the stealthily encroaching water.

Finally they heard a splash. Eagerly running towards the noise, they watched as Barton and Mrs. Beaver literally dragged themselves up onto the bank, their limp tails now cumbersome dead weight. The little group gathered, anxious for any glimmer of hope concerning Atticus, terrified to hear their worst fears may indeed be true. Mr. and Mrs. Beaver lay panting and exhausted, unable to do anything but gasp for air. Simon instinctively sensed the glaring difference between the exhilarating exhaustion of defeating an enemy—and the weary fatigue of failure. The beavers' faces registered only utter defeat.

When she was finally able to regain some strength, Mrs. Beaver sat up and bundled Kit into her arms. Her eyes puddled with tears as she hoarsely whispered, "We must sing Atticus's praises to the Father of all Creatures, Kit, for it is the greatest sacrifice to give one's life for another. Atticus would not want you to feel regret, but only gratitude that he could show his love for you—and therefore the Father of all Creatures—in this valiant way." She stopped for a moment, choking back tears. "We must make sure the magnificent name of Atticus is never forgotten!"

"Why would it be forgotten? Isn't Atticus still swimming? Won't he be coming back?" Kit questioned her, gazing up into his mama's face with complete trust.

"No, Kit, he's not swimming. And he won't be coming back."

"Why? Is he tired of our journey? Doesn't he wanna be with us anymore?"

"Oh, no, Kit. It's neither of those things. Atticus *can't* come back to us."

Kits eyes grew wide. "Is he hurt, Mama?"

"I promise you Atticus will never hurt again."

Kit continued to stare into his mother's gentle eyes, still not grasping what she obviously didn't want to put to words. They all knew that to clearly say a thing—especially a hurtful thing—is to give it form, and therefore believability. So all of them waited tensely, fearfully, hoping Mrs. Beaver would not say the dreaded pronouncement, even though they knew in their hearts that they were just deceiving themselves now. "Mama, is Atticus safe in the Father's hand?"

"Oh, yes, Kit. He is." Tears slipped from her eyes onto Kit's dear little face.

He was quiet for a moment before whispering, "Mama, did Atticus die?"

She cuddled him tightly to her, stroking his head and face and ears, allowing the tears to fall freely wherever they would. "Those rapids are *so* treacherous that I can't imagine how…and with Caleb not able to find him *anywhere*…" Her voice trailed off, and as she closed her eyes and shook her head, one tear dropped onto Kit's face. Mama Beaver took a deep, shuddering breath before continuing, "Yes, darling Kit, I'm afraid Atticus died. And just as I am cradling you tenderly in my arms just now, the Father of all Creatures holds dear Atticus in his. For Atticus is completely safe now, as he will forever be."

"Oh, Atticus!" was all Kit could cry out into the mist, and the distraught baby clung to his mama, sobbing piteously, finding little comfort in the caresses she so compassionately gave. Their tears flowed and mingled together, completely blending as one, before the droplets continued their silent journey to the soaked ground beneath them.

The rest of the anguished, heartbroken group watched, stunned and so shocked and unbelieving still that there was no immediate response except for an almost uniform intake of breaths. Simon couldn't contain his mounting wretchedness any longer, however, and suddenly cried out, "No! I won't believe it—he can't have drowned. We've got to search some more!"

Barton, tears spilling from his eyes, merely shook his head. "I'm sorry, Simon-by-the-Way, but the current is too fierce." The despondent ache in his words was nearly unbearable. "We did our best—I promise you we did. Mrs. Beaver and I barely survived the pull of the current *ourselves*. We searched downstream for a great distance, finding those pitiful bits of Atticus' tail here and there until…until we reached rapids that were beyond anything we've ever known or seen." His voice was barely audible now. "And then there were no more signs. There was…nothing."

Their hopes now completely dashed, the little band bent beneath the weight of a devouring pain. And just like the fog that hovered above everything, this smothering, suffocating grief covered them now. The beaver family continued to desperately cling to one another and they wept bitterly. Great tears fell from Mary's eyes; she hung her head until it lay piteously on the muddy ground. Caleb's small body jerked erratically in convulsive sobs and poor Beauregard howled out his despair uncontrollably. Time after time he lifted his head to the heavy fog, mournfully crying out, "Atticus, the dowger's friend! Oh, dearest Atticus, the dowger's friend!" The mist surrounding them caused an eerie distortion that made the plaintive wail sound as though it came from everywhere, from all of nature, from the very core of the earth itself.

Simon intentionally stood apart. He watched the little band with dry, suspicious eyes, feeling his ever-present companion temptingly beckoning. Anger swelled and raged within until he finally hurled his fury as if throwing piercing knives, harshly screaming at them all, "You can't just give up on him! *How dare you do that.* I'll show you—I won't give up, ever. You…you *cowards.* I hate you all!"

Mary immediately fell all the way to the ground, as if fatally wounded by Simon's words. The rest merely stared at him in complete shock, except for Beauregard: he submissively crawled on his belly to Simon's feet, where he rested his head. Rolling his tortured eyes up to Simon, Beauregard said simply, "The dowger understands. The dowger aches for Atticus, too. Won't Simon-by-the-Way comfort the poor dowger?"

Simon hesitated for just a moment before tentatively reaching out a trembling hand to touch Beauregard's soft head. He let it rest there for only the briefest moment before he jerked his whole body around, sneering at them, "I'll find Atticus if none of you selfish cowards will. Just go ahead and cry and do nothing! I hate you, do you hear me? I hate you, and most of all, *I hate your horrid Father of all Creatures!*" And then Simon lunged forward, taking one great leap out into the surging waters below him.

It seemed an eternity passed as Simon dropped through the air, an endless falling through nothingness while he clenched his teeth and tensed every muscle, waiting for the sudden shock of landing in startling, icy water. But after floating and struggling in mid-air, he found himself merely floundering in hot, rumpled sheets and blankets upon his own bed. And instead of being soaked from a jump into a cold, raging river, he found he was drenched with his own sticky sweat.

He stared up at the ceiling in his bedroom. Grabbing his pillow and with all his might, Simon whipped it against the now hated mirror.

CHAPTER 9

"What matters it how far we go?"
his scaly friend replied.
"There is another shore, you know,
upon the other side.
The further off from England,
the nearer is to France.
Then turn not pale, beloved snail,
but come and join the dance.
Will you, won't you, will you, won't you,
will you join the dance?
Will you, won't you, will you, won't you,
will you join the dance?"

Simon lay in his bed for some time, attempting to sort out the total confusion he felt—where he was, the time of day and the day itself, how real life and this world beyond the mirror existed. He finally pieced together that it was Sunday morning, meaning only one night had passed since he had left "home" and had gone—where? Away? Or merely to an imagined, warped dream? Still, he clearly recognized at least one thing in an overwhelming flood of emotion: grief. Unbearable pain. Simon rubbed his pounding head, hoping to ease at least some of the aching grief inhabiting every single inch of his body, throbbing against his temples, and flowing from his heart. But no simple massage could begin to dispel this pain, and when Simon shut his eyes in frustration, the image of Atticus in his memory was enough to make him groan out loud.

Abbey was immediately at his door. "Simon," she whispered urgently, knocking softly. "Are you all right? I heard you groan and…well, are you hurting, Simon? Please, can I come in?"

He turned over on his side to stare through the crack in the door. "I'm all right, Abbey. Go away." Rarely did Simon deny his sister access to his room, and she responded with instant concern.

Inching the door open a bit further and seeking to make eye contact, Abbey pleaded again, "Simon, I need to come in. Please?"

Simon sighed, knowing there was no sense arguing with her, that eventually his father would hear them and then neither one would win. "All right, then!" he said in a clipped tone. "Come on in. But you'd better be quiet— shut the door behind you and don't talk above a whisper. I've got a headache."

Abbey tiptoed in and gently shut the door. After crawling up onto his bed, she peered at Simon's red-ringed eyes. "You look terrible."

"Thanks. That helps." He continued to stare up at the ceiling, willfully ignoring her.

"Are you sick or something?"

"Something." Simon knew he was being intentionally difficult. But he just couldn't seem to care right now.

"What?"

"You asked if I was sick or something. Well, I'm not sick. So it's something else, isn't it?"

"Oh." She looked over his bed, noting the knotted, disheveled bedclothes and his pillow on the floor. "Were you having a bad dream? Your covers are a mess!"

"Yeah, a bad dream. Which gave me a rotten headache. And now my little sister is making it even worse." Abbey immediately glanced downward, biting her lip. Finally Simon felt a softening towards her, and he reached out a hand to cover one of her delicate ones. "Hey, I'm sorry, okay? It was a long night."

"Did you know Daddy's not home?"

"What?"

"He never came home last night. I heard Mommy call the police in the middle of the night." Her voice revealed no sense of panic, just relief.

"Are you sure he's not home by now?" Simon sat up and reached for his jeans. He knew his mom would need him, that a trip to the police station was inevitable if indeed his dad had not yet returned. They'd done this routine many times before, the two of them. Abbey would stay with a neighbor while he and his mom went to the jail to bail out his dad. The smells there—the decay, mustiness, and rank urine—were quite familiar, as were the looks the policemen gave him each time. Embarrassment. Undisguised repugnance. Pity. Simon despised every single one.

Abbey shook her head. "Nope. I heard Mommy calling the police again this morning, asking if they'd seen him." The city cops all knew their dad by name, a fact Abbey simply accepted, and one Simon noted with disgust.

Simon continued to get dressed, grabbing a clean t-shirt out of his dresser and pulling it over his head. He quickly ran a comb through his tousled hair. "How did she sound?"

"Worried. He's not at the station, I'm sure. 'Cause she kept asking them where they thought he could be."

"She tried the usual bars first?"

"Uh-huh. I think he was at one of them last night and then left."

For just a moment Simon stared deeply into the mirror. In his mind's eye he saw no reflections, but instead peered into a land far away, a place which aroused such a mixed-up jumble of feelings that he felt exhausted just thinking of it all. And then he saw his friends. Mary. He smelled her wildness, heard the music which always hovered about her, saw the love in her eyes. Caleb. Beauregard. *How could such simpleness be so endearing?* Simon wondered. Mr. and Mrs. Beaver. Kit. So precocious and adorable. And Atticus. *Do I truly hate them?* he asked himself. *Do I want to hate them? Oh, Atticus, I do know that I don't ever want to go back if you're not there!* Grief threatened to swallow him until Abbey broke into his thoughts again. "Do you think he could be...well... hurt or something?"

"What?"

"Daddy. Do you think he could be hurt?"

Simon hesitated for only a moment, and the vision of the other land completely vanished. Along with it went Mary's eyes of love, her insistence that God loved Simon, too. His companion returned, strengthened now by the despair of Atticus's death. "I hope so," Simon whispered to his own reflection in the mirror now. "I hope he's *dead*."

The phone rang, startling them both. Simon turned to Abbey and gestured towards the door. "That's probably Dad now. Needing us to come pick him up at some other police station or crummy bar. Come on."

They hurried across the hall and down the steps towards the kitchen, straining to pick up any snatches of their mom's conversation. But there were no words to hear, none of the usual excuses given, no embarrassed apologies made once again for the man who would never think to utter them himself. Their mom merely stood motionless before them, phone to her ear, mouth hanging open, eyes wide with a stricken look across her ashen face. Simon and Abbey stared up at her. "I see," was all she uttered, and, "yes, I'll come as soon as possible." Mechanically, she replaced the phone on its cradle without ever taking her eyes from the children who stood trustingly before her.

Laura put a hand on her children's shoulders. "It's about your father," she said softly. "There's been a terrible accident and…they're quite sure it's him. They say he…they say he must've died instantly."

Simon felt Abbey tremble and their mother pulled her into her arms. Laura stroked Abbey's hair, whispering softly, "It's all right, Abbey. Everything will be okay. I promise you, *we'll* be okay." She glanced over to Simon, concern written all over her features now. "Simon? Are you all right?"

He stared out the window through narrowed eyes, looking at but not truly seeing the rusty swing set in their backyard. The swings swayed gently in the breeze. "I hated him, you know. I'm glad he's dead."

"Oh, Simon." His mother pulled him into her arms, too, but Simon only submitted to her clinging embrace for a moment before he stiffly pushed away.

"What do we need to do?" Simon was calm, businesslike, the man of the house now. And Laura, sensing his need to cope in this manner, discussed with Simon the unpleasant task which awaited them: a trip to the morgue and identification of the body.

She insisted they eat some breakfast first, so they sat around the kitchen table in a numbing silence, eating cold cereal from faded plastic bowls. Then they climbed into the old rusting station wagon which resisted starting, as always, grinding and whining a good bit before finally turning over. *Of course Dad couldn't have wrecked this useless junk heap*, Simon muttered to himself. *No, he had to make sure he accomplished one last, giant hassle for Mom—taking the decent car, the only dependable one with him for his last drunken drive.*

They traveled in silence, absentmindedly staring out of the dirty windows, watching a world go by that seemed unreachable, certainly not relatable. The familiar four-lane highway bustled with cars full of people, some off to work; others enjoying a day of fun; and a good number driving to churches scattered across town. Simon glanced over at the road they would normally take to church and realized he wasn't at all disappointed they weren't headed there.

In fact, he was pleased that it wasn't a normal Sunday morning when he would endure a lesson and a long church service with its old-fashioned songs and boring sermon. Nor was Simon up to the old men's 'amens' during the service (how different those sounded from the animals' amens) or the awkward 'hellos' to patronizing people with plastered-on smiles. Especially when they always seemed to look down at him, his mom, and Abbey with disdain—as if his family carried some dirty, infectious disease, and was definitely not good enough to be around church people. But the worst part, which he suddenly understood colored over all the others, was the worship of a God that Simon wanted nothing to do with. A God Simon would never love the way Mary did. He glared towards the church. And then clenched his fists in defiance.

Laura turned the old wagon onto the road to the hospital, another all-too-familiar destination. For if their husband and father wasn't in jail, then he was either at a bar, passed out stone cold on the floor, or at the emergency room getting patched up from some brawl he'd either caused or joined. When they pulled up to the imposing structure with gleaming marble columns and shiny windows this time, however, they followed the directions Laura'd been given to the morgue

The wagon sputtered a bit and wheezed to a stop, and Laura turned to them with a palpable anxiety. "I'll take you in with me," she began nervously, "but you're to stay in the waiting area. Obviously, you can't…well, you'll just have to wait for me there. Okay?"

Abbey agreed to their mother's directive, but Simon, deliberately saying nothing in response, reached for the door handle and climbed out. *I'm not a baby anymore. I'm the man of the house now*, he thought to himself. *No one's gonna stop me from seeing my dad, if that's what I need to do…*

Laura grabbed Abbey's hand and they all walked resolutely through the automatic doors. The morgue was in the basement, so they waited for the elevator, staring unblinkingly at the closed door, willing it to open and take them to the lowest level. The elevator dumped them out onto a sterile, nearly colorless hallway where they followed overbearing signs with stark arrows. Their footsteps echoed off the bare walls and the smell—a distinct, sharp odor Simon knew he would never forget—repulsed each one. Abbey glanced up at her mother, wiping at a suddenly runny nose.

"Need a tissue?" Laura asked. She dropped Abbey's hand a moment to fish around in her purse. "I know. The smell's nasty, isn't it?"

Finally they reached the end of the hallway. To the left was a stark, dingy waiting room with scattered chairs—dirty plastic tan seats on thin metal rod bases. Two faux-wood end tables held torn, aged magazines. All the walls were bare except one, and that one merely contained a window to an adjacent office. Instructions and various signs were tacked across most of it, but not enough to hide the dirt and numerous smudged fingerprints all over the now-closed window. Florescent lighting glared, buzzed, and blinked overhead, creating an annoying atmosphere. The room was cool and damp, ugly—and entirely fitting for this particular wing of a hospital.

To the right was another one of those boldly printed, domineering signs. **MORGUE**, it simply said. But Simon read much more there, sensed coldness behind the letters. He sneered back at it.

Laura stooped down to look Abbey in the eye, and as she did so, she grabbed Simon's arm. "I want both of you to stay right here, okay?" Her fingers tightened on Simon's arm and she shifted her weight, allowing one knee to rest on the linoleum floor. "Simon, look after your sister. Wish I'd thought to

have you bring along a book. You'll just have to read a magazine or something."
She glanced at the end tables and their collection of assorted periodicals,
sighing, immediately surmising they'd be practically useless. "I shouldn't be
long, though."

The window scraped open and a pinched face peered out at them. "Can I
help you?"

"I'm here to identify someone." Laura stood up, nervously clutching at her
purse with one hand and rubbing at the slim wedding band with the other.
"Um, will it be all right if my children wait here while I go on in? The police
said I should just—"

"That'll be fine," the face said. "You go ahead. Don't worry; we'll keep an
eye on them."

"Thank you." Laura smiled, but the tension she felt made her expression
jerk into existence and disappear in a fraction of a moment. "You sure you'll be
okay?" She glanced at Abbey and Simon, a sense of needing to depend on him
clearly being communicated to Simon. They both nodded.

"Go ahead, Mom," Simon said quietly. "Let's get this over with and get out
of here." He shivered slightly. "This place gives me the creeps." Abbey took his
hand and he felt her quivering response. "But it's no big deal, really," he added,
attempting to calm his sister's fears. "Come on, Abbey. Let's see what we can
find to read."

Simon guided her towards the chairs and settled Abbey into one. Her
petite feet, clad in worn sneakers with a gaping hole in one toe, dangled several
inches above the floor. Simon noted again how small she was, how the room
nearly swallowed her tiny form and subdued personality. *He'll never hurt her
again*, he thought triumphantly, protectively. *Never again.* He turned to his
mom—who hesitated still to leave them—and gestured towards the entrance
to the morgue. Simon and Abbey watched her stare at the morgue entrance
a moment, noticeably take a deep breath, and then push a small button —
producing an irritating buzz—before disappearing behind the opening door.

Simon thumbed through several magazines until he found a suitable
article on nature, and he read out loud to Abbey for exactly five minutes—

watching every minute tick by on the black-and-white clock mounted above the window. Then he stood up, stretching his arms above his head. "I need to go to the bathroom, Abbey. I'll tell the receptionist so she'll know where I am," Simon whispered to her. Abbey's dangling feet anxiously swung back and forth, back and forth. Though Simon's statement was certainly understandable, somehow she felt wary. She watched him rap softly on the window until it slid open and the face reappeared. "I'm going to the restroom for just a minute," Simon informed her, deliberately keeping his voice perfectly calm and even. "Can you keep an eye on my sister for me?"

"Of course. The men's room is just down the hall to the right. You'll notice the sign on the first door." She closed the window only halfway this time, thereby fulfilling her obligation to Simon's request, he assumed.

"Be right back, Abbey." Simon pointed to the magazine. "Why don't you see how many words you can sound out on your own?"

Abbey nodded, still not taking her eyes off of Simon. She instinctively knew he wasn't heading for the restroom, but she hadn't the slightest idea where he was going until Simon suddenly reached for the button to the morgue.

The buzz alerted the face at the window, and instantly the resisting pane screeched open. "Who's there?" But Simon had already slipped through the door and was running through another hallway to find his mom, and more importantly, to locate his hated father.

It was the smell that directed him, telling him more than signs or pointing arrows ever could. Simon heard a voice or two calling after him, and a hand came up empty as it tried to grab his t-shirt. Racing towards the door that he knew was the right one, Simon could hear his mother's soft weeping and strange men's voices murmuring. And suddenly—all too suddenly—he was in the room.

A table stood in the exact center, and on the metal table lay a body with a plain white sheet over it. Simon hesitated for only a second—enough for his mother to cry out—and then lunged towards the sheet to grab it up and reveal the horror that lay underneath.

The sight before Simon was hazy and indistinct, as if from a dream. *Was that Dad?* Or was it *Atticus?*

Simon sunk to the floor, crying out from the pain which stabbed through his entire body. "*No.* Oh, no. My hate killed him! *I* killed them *both* and I didn't mean it! How could you do this, God?"

Laura was there instantly, pulling him into her arms, protectively clutching him to her breast. "No, Simon, you mustn't think that way, son. It was your dad's own doing, his own fault for driving drunk, just like always. You didn't kill your father, you didn't!"

"You don't understand—I killed them…I killed him, I know I did, 'cause I *wished* it so. I hated him and I wanted him dead!" Simon cried out. "Just this morning I said it to Abbey. I did Mom, I did!"

"Wishing doesn't make things happen, Simon," she soothed him, gripping him more tightly. Mother and child sat on the cold linoleum floor, rocking back and forth. "He hurt you, I know he did, Simon. Of course you wanted him dead—anyone who's been hurt like you have would wish that." She pulled his chin up so he had to look her in the eye. "How much did he hurt you, Simon? Tell me."

But Simon closed his eyes to her and lay his head wearily against her chest. "He never loved me, did he?"

"Oh, my darling, yes, he did. In his own way. He just…he just couldn't love anybody else because he hated himself so much."

Simon opened his eyes again, staring at the frightening table as if his father could hear them even now. "I need to look at…I need to see once more, Mom. Please? And then I want to get away from here."

Laura glanced up at the policeman and saw him nod his head. The two stood slowly, weakly, while someone pulled down the sheet one last time. Only this time, Simon clearly saw what he knew was actually there on the metal table—the lifeless form of his now powerless father. "Are you ready now, ma'am?" the policeman asked softly after giving them a few moments.

"Simon?" she whispered.

He sighed once and nodded.

"Yes. Thank you," Laura answered, and taking Simon's hand firmly between hers, she led him gently, protectively, from the frigid room.

CHAPTER 10

The Unicorn looked dreamily at Alice,
and said "Talk, child."
Alice could not help her lips curling up into a
smile as she began: "Do you know, I always
thought Unicorns were fabulous monsters,
too? I never saw one alive before!"
"Well, now that we have seen each other,"
said the Unicorn, "if you'll believe in me, I'll
believe in you. Is that a bargain?"

T he next few days were a blur as friends and relatives descended upon them. Simon, Abbey, and even Laura were amazed at the droves of people that came to pay their respects, and they were even more bewildered as to how everyone insisted on talking about Lewis as if he had been some kind of saint. Insurance representatives, lawyers, funeral directors, and salesmen pushed decisions upon Laura at a furious pace. Although Simon had initially reacted with skepticism towards their pastor's offer to help with this stressful load, he was amazed to discover this man was the one person who finally— and practically—gave his frazzled mom direction, wise counsel, and genuine assistance. Even more amazing to Simon was the fact that the pastor did so without an open palm, not asking for or taking anything in return.

Simon absolutely dreaded attending the funeral, but when the day arrived, he listened in astonishment to the pastor. Instead of an uncomfortable, even nightmarish message centered around his dad's miserable life, the minister spoke of him in a way that didn't gloss over, glorify, or dismiss him; he merely made Lewis sound incredibly sad. A life wasted. The focus, then, was upon God the Father and His Son, Jesus Christ, and the relationship these two share. That all men and women have the opportunity to know forgiveness because of

God's redemptive love. His unfailing love. The pastor's sincerity in his belief was real, just like Mary's, which made the love seem almost real, too. Almost.

Laura, Simon, and Abbey sat front and center, first row, the dutiful mourning family there to grieve the loss. Laura even cried a bit, wiping her eyes on a freshly laundered handkerchief; but whether she mourned the loss of a husband or a life that could and should have been wasn't revealed through those tears. Abbey sniffed once or twice, too, but not enough to require a hanky from mom, and Simon was, of course, completely dry-eyed. They wore dark clothes, befitting the occasion. Laura's hat and accompanying awkward veil looked totally foreign to Simon and Abbey. They'd never seen their mother in any kind of hat except a baseball cap, which she usually wore backwards to poke fun at Simon.

Their mom's veil seemed to function like a protective screen which they wanted to hide behind, blurring their perceptions so they could make it through the nearly intolerable situation. Laura sifted through a myriad of emotions, choosing only to allow what she wanted to feel. Abbey protected herself out of sheer necessity in the way she always did, blocking out her feelings entirely. She was nearly catatonic in her withdrawal from the world. Simon felt two emotions collide within him at the same time: his hate for his dad—and his conflicting desire for love and acceptance. Forced to choose, he reached for what was less confusing: hate won. It was readily available, a shroud to cloak all the other feelings, and it was so much easier. Simon was comfortable with his hate.

All the conflicting feelings Laura, Simon, and Abbey knew that long day were disguised to everyone else, locked deeply inside, each one concealing the past hate and fear and disgust in various ways. Their father's alcoholism was the family secret as it is for so many families, the "problem" which everyone either ignores, rationalizes, or even denies exists to anyone outside the family. The townspeople knew, of course, as did relatives and friends. The secret was still kept by all this day, however, complete with condolences, flowers, tears, and a dutiful family, front and center, first row, there to grieve the loss.

Even the weather was a willing participant in the drama, for it was a fresh, sweet-smelling spring day. Nature appeared new and full of promise when it should have reflected the actual mood of this funeral: dark and gloomy. Still, Simon felt a twinge of hope in his heart when he watched his dad's casket being lowered into the soft, dewy ground—hope for peace in his home now; hope for a reawakening, emotionally and physically, for Abbey; hope for his mom; hope for himself, too. Simon held onto this fleeting hope…until they arrived back home and the pastor approached Simon in the sanctuary of his own room.

Simon had just retreated there, and, after those four long, tension-filled days, was just now gathering enough courage to approach his mirror when he heard the gentle knock at his door. Certain it was Abbey or his mom, Simon quickly answered, "You can come in."

The face of the pastor registered Simon's surprise. "Sorry if I startled you, but I'd like to talk with you for just a few minutes. That okay?"

Simon hesitated and moved to stand by his window. He stared out into the backyard where relatives and friends were gathered in small groups. They annoyed him, and his curt tone evidenced his aggravation. "Sure. No problem."

"Are you okay? I mean, how are you doing?"

Simon smiled, redirecting his annoyance away from the irritating scene below towards this interfering man. The pastor was attempting to get too close, and Simon thought to himself, *Not a chance, mister!* Aloud he replied nonchalantly, "I'm fine. Just fine."

"Your mother told me what happened at the morgue."

"She had no right to do that." He clenched his teeth, feeling his stomach muscles tighten, too.

"I'm sure she didn't mean it as a betrayal of your confidence. She only wants to help you, Simon."

"Like you do." Simon intentionally spat out his sarcasm, lifting his eyebrows and then slowly, dramatically, turning away from him.

There was silence for a moment as the pastor measured the boy's cynical response. "Yes, Simon, I do. I care about you. But even more so, God cares about you."

Simon smirked. "Right. I've heard that line before."

"What is it that makes you doubt God's love? Can you share that with me?"

Simon shook his head, rolling his eyes. "Like you could make it all go away?"

"I suppose not. But maybe I can help—by helping to take your *misunderstanding* of God's love away. That's possible."

"I doubt it."

The pastor waited a moment, wisely giving Simon time to consider the worth of what he offered. Very softly, and with tenderness filling his words, he asked, "Did your father hurt you, Simon? Did he ever hit you?"

Simon watched the crowd hovering around his mother and Abbey. He hated the way they fawned over and pawed at his sister, forcing Abbey to withdraw even further by cowering behind her mother's skirt. She was just too shy for all of this…this fiasco. In a monotone, Simon responded, "It's like this. My dad beat Abbey. Only Abbey. I tried to protect her, but I couldn't stop him. And I hate him for that." Flippant answers, intentionally so.

"Abbey says he beat *you*."

Simon whipped his head around to glare at him, feeling even more protective of Abbey now. Through clenched teeth he hissed, "*Just leave my sister alone.* You don't need to talk to her. I can help her and *I* can take care of her just fine." Simon narrowed his eyes at the man he now considered an adversary. "She didn't tell you the truth, anyway. Abbey doesn't—well, she doesn't remember what happened because…because she's not strong enough. Like I am. And I tried to protect her! I almost did, but he always…He was just so much bigger and did whatever he wanted to, no matter how hard I tried." Simon hesitated a moment, adding, "Mom says I look just like him when he was my age. Same blue eyes especially. Maybe he didn't hit me 'cause of that. I don't know."

"You have to know there was nothing you could have done, Simon. Absolutely nothing."

Simon glanced away from him, gazing out the window once more. The people gravitated away from his mother and Abbey to a table piled high with food, filling cheap paper plates, grabbing flimsy plastic utensils, stuffing themselves. "I wished him dead, didn't I? I did do something."

"You know as well as I do that your wish had nothing to do with your dad's death. He was an alcoholic."

"An *alcoholic*? He was a mean ol' drunk."

"He was a sick man, Simon—an alcoholic. But whatever he was, the fact remains that he essentially killed himself."

"Are you going to try to convince me now that I shouldn't feel guilty? Because you think I feel guilty?"

He hesitated, searching out Simon's motives. "If you do feel guilty, then yes, that's what I'm trying to do. I want to help you let go of that."

"Ha! Well, I don't. I hated him, and like I already told you, I wanted him dead!"

The pastor sighed resignedly, and reached for the doorknob. "Simon, you have every right to be angry at your dad. I know his alcoholism kept him from being the dad he should've been to you and Abbey. But if you continue to cling onto this anger inside of you," he paused and shook his head, clearly searching for the right words. "It's…I'm afraid it could eat away at you like a cancer until there's nothing much left of the loving person God's created you to be. Simon?"Simon looked up at him, and the pastor's intense gaze captured Simon's attention. "You need to separate out your feelings about your earthly father from your heavenly Father. Because your hate for your dad obviously spills out onto God when they're nothing alike. Did you hear that, Simon? Your father and God are *nothing* alike!" He stopped again, collecting his thoughts, choosing his words carefully. "And one more thing: You despise your dad so much—but the irony is, as long as you cling to that hate…" (and he drew out these wretched words slowly and deliberately) "*…you are in grave danger.* Sometimes, when we don't learn to forgive, when we cling to our anger until it becomes a deeply rooted bitterness, we can become like the very thing that hurts us the most."

Now Simon convulsively jerked towards him, his entire body trembling with visible anger. "How dare you say that to me? I'm nothing like him, *nothing*! I wouldn't ever hurt my mom or my sister…ever!"

The pastor leaned slightly towards Simon, and when he spoke, his voice was soft and full of concern. "Simon, whenever you're ready to talk, I'll be here. I want you to know God's love, and I want to help you recognize and release this destructive hate. The rage in you will be like a mirror of your father's own anger. Don't you see how it hinders and distorts your view of God? You'll only know in part…and you can never know Him fully until you meet Him and His love face to face!"

The familiar words hit up against Simon like a physical blow, intermingling with the memory of Mary's past longings until he was certain that he heard Mary's music, smelled Mary's scent, looked into Mary's eyes. The door closed. The pastor was gone. The only two living things remaining in his room were Simon himself…and the mirror.

He inched cautiously towards it now, noting that fully three-fourths of the mirror was shrouded over with the curiously fuzzy, shifting images. Only the top of Simon's head (showing the stubborn cowlick which always caused him such aggravation) reflected back at him; the portal, taking up the rest of the mirror, beckoned to Simon with a forceful intensity. He leaned backwards, away from the pull, stiffening his arms and tightly gripping his dresser with one hand, his bed with the other. As he continued to resist, Simon glanced outside…at the cloying friends, the nosey relatives, the insensitive strangers. Suddenly, he changed his mind. He closed his eyes, pleading, "Forgive me, Atticus," and leaned into the mirror.

"Umph!" Simon cried out, landing roughly on spongy, muddy ground while Beauregard, Mary, Caleb, and all of the beavers—even Kit—pounced on his flailing limbs.

"Hold him down. Don't let him get up!" Mary commanded. "We can't let him attempt another jump, can't risk losing someone else. He's far too precious to us!"

Simon looked up at Mary in total confusion. "What're you doing? What's happening?"

"Don't you remember?" Caleb asked, responding to Simon's bewilderment with confusion of his own. "You tried to jump into the river, to rescue Atticus!"

He pointed towards Mary, adding, "But Mary stopped you...tripped you up, she did. And you should thank her for that, Simon-by-the-Way. She saved your life!"

Simon attempted to sit up, which caused the animals to redouble their strenuous efforts to hold him down. "Look, I promise I won't try to jump again, okay? Honest—I promise you. Can I sit up now?"

Beauregard snorted, exhaling a fine spray across Simon's cheek. (This caused Simon to wrinkle his nose in disgust—affectionate disgust, but disgust nonetheless.) "The dowger won't let go 'til Simon-by-the-Way promises again. Simon-by-the-Way frightened the dowger. Yes, Simon-by-the-Way did."

Simon smiled at him, recognizing how much he'd missed this simple dog and his unique, funny language. How much he'd missed all of them. "I promise I won't jump, Beauregard." He glanced around the entire group, grinning at Kit, who had both of his tiny arms wrapped around one of Simon's ankles and was huffing and puffing from his rigorous efforts. (And, who probably couldn't have held down a pygmy gnat.) "I promise all of you," Simon assured them.

Slowly they released him and backed away a bit to catch their breaths. All except for Kit, that is. He bounded into Simon's lap and took a terribly exaggerated deep breath, arching his rounded little shoulders to a tremendous height before finally dropping them quite dramatically. It was too reminiscent of Atticus, and caused Simon a quick stab of pain.

Mary moved around to face Simon, peering deeply into his eyes and obviously attempting to read his thoughts again. "I don't understand," she began, "because you were so angry and now—instantly!—you're calmer, completely changed somehow." Her eyes seemed to grow even larger as her pupils darkened. "I see just vaguely...you've been home, faced a loss of some sort. Are you all right? What's happened, Simon-by-the-Way?"

"I was home. It's my father..."

"Did he hurt you?" Kit asked, protectively placing his tiny hands against Simon's tummy.

Simon smiled down at him. "No, Kit, he didn't. And he won't hurt my sister ever again either. 'Cause he died. In an accident."

They all watched his face, waiting for his mourning to show, realizing suddenly that none would come. Still, even without Simon's acknowledgment, they understood the trauma it must've brought to Simon and his family, and they huddled closer to him. All of them felt the pain especially tenderly, as they were reminded of the other recent death, reminded of the one who was absent now from their little company.

"I know I've only been gone for a blink of an eye here, but back in my world, it's been several days." Simon paused a moment, searching for the right words. "Is Atticus still, um, missing? You see, I promised myself, promised Atticus also, that I wouldn't ever go through my mirror again if he was…gone. I just didn't want to come back at all if Atticus wasn't here." Simon stopped for a moment, swallowing down the lump in his throat, gathering courage to ask what he must. "Is Atticus really dead, Mary?"

She looked down, letting the long lashes rest against her cheeks. And then she nodded.

Simon remembered—much too vividly—the spiteful words he'd hurdled at them and the wounded looks he'd elicited. He whispered, "I'm sorry. Sorry for what I said about all of you. I didn't mean it…any of it." Kit stretched his arms across Simon's tummy, giving him a beaver hug, and Beauregard rested his clammy yet endearing nose on the other side of Simon's lap. Mr. and Mrs. Beaver held hands and cuddled together by his feet; Mary (with Caleb perched on her back) curled up next to Simon on the side opposite Beauregard. Finally, Simon lay down, too, with Kit wedged tightly between the warm softness of his tummy and the crook of his arm. They lay quietly, each one silently mourning.

"The dowger finks Atticus was the bestest friend ever," Beauregard whispered into the silence.

Caleb stretched himself upwards again, and in the muted twilight the brilliant scarlet seemed to flame and glow against the background of those wings all the more. "All creatures of the Father, listen to this word!" Caleb's words rang with triumph, joy, and deep sorrow all at the same time. "The name of Atticus shall forevermore be known as a name of great valor, great sacrifice, and great love! Remember him always, and do not let his story be forgotten. He journeyed long and well, and now…now he is fully known! Amen and Amen!"

They whispered together, "Amen and Amen!" and were quiet once again.

"He shall indeed be remembered," Mary breathed into the darkness. "For we carry him in our hearts."

Mary's music was a lullaby, and the exhausted little company drifted peacefully—yet sorrowfully—to sleep.

Whiskers rubbed against Simon's nose, tickling and immediately bringing forth a mighty sneeze. "A-choo!" Simon slipped opened one eye, drowsily peeking at the irritant. It was Kit. "Geez, I really should've known better than to let you sleep next to me. The instant the sun comes up you're flouncing around, waking up everyone and—"

"Shhh!" Kit insisted, putting one tiny paw to Simon's lips. "I had to crawl up to your face, Simon-by-the-Way. You see, there's a monster rustling around in the forest. I heard it and it's huge and ferocious and probably terrifically hungry!"

Simon rolled his eyes. "Kit, there are no monsters here. You know we were all up and down this riverbank just last night. We saw nothing and noticed no strange tracks, either."

"But I heard it. Listen!" Kit put his other paw to his ear, cupping it there and tensing his entire chubby little body into frozen preparedness.

"I don't hear anything."

"Shhhh!"

And then there was a noise—just the slightest one, to be sure—but definitely a noise of leaves being trampled, and twigs being snapped. With the faintest little groan. "Is that your ferocious monster?" Simon asked. "Kit, that doesn't sound much bigger than a mouse. Or you!"

But Kit's eyes were enormous and filled with absolute terror. "It *is* a monster, I tell you! Only monsters sneak through the forest like that, on the lookout for something to eat, something yummy like *us* and—"

"Oh, Kit, honestly."

The rustling reoccurred then, only a bit louder, since whatever it was had clearly moved closer.

Now Beauregard's head popped up. Both ears perked upwards and he tipped his head to one side, listening intently. "The dowger heard somefing." He raised that great snout, sniffing the air. "What did the dowger hear?"

"Kit's monster," Simon answered, shaking his head incredulously.

Beauregard turned to look at Simon, obviously totally perplexed now. "Kit has a monster? Kit never told the dowger he had his very own—"

This time the branches of a small tree rattled back and forth, as if someone had twitched it intentionally. Two small leaves fluttered lazily to the ground, one floating back and forth (they watched every glide, loop, and airy spin) until it eventually landed only a few yards from the tip of Beauregard's tail, which he immediately thumped, curiously. All three of them—Simon, Kit and, Beauregard—stared at the leaf as if it were...well, not a monster, certainly, but at least as though it were alive. Voraciously hungry. And therefore after a nip of Beauregard's tail.

Just to be safe, Beauregard tucked his tail beneath him and whispered huskily to Simon, "Does Simon-by-the-Way fink Kit's monster is as big and ferocious as the bike?"

"What monster?" Mary had been awakened by the commotion and rubbed sleepy eyes against a leg.

"The one in the forest!" Kit exclaimed, now squiggling and squirming over everyone, rousing his mama and papa, too. He caused dozing, unsuspecting Caleb to topple off Mary's back and plop unceremoniously upon the ground.

Simon sat up and retrieved poor Caleb. His feathers were definitely ruffled, both physically and emotionally. "A bike? What are you talking about, Beauregard?" Simon asked.

"The horrible bike. What hurt Simon-by-the-Way!"

"Beauregard, I already explained that a bike is not a monster and—"

Suddenly, a twig snapped, definitely just beyond the clearing in which they rested. Kit immediately raced for safe refuge between Mr. and Mrs. Beaver (but then courageously peeked out from behind his papa's back), and Beauregard jerked up into a defensive, knight-like stance with legs stretched out stiffly, nose held low to the ground, and ears back in a threatening position. He leaned forward ever so slightly, ready to pounce on whatever moved towards them. He even lifted his jowls in a nasty snarl, and a low growl resonated from deep in his throat.

Mary stood behind him, sniffing the air as Beauregard had earlier, and Simon moved to intentionally place the beaver family behind them all for the greatest protection. He stood next to Beauregard, putting his arm around the dog's neck. In this formation, ever so slowly, they inched cautiously towards the noise that was now only a few feet away.

Beauregard kept his nose to the ground, alternating a curious sniff with the throaty, rumbling growl. Suddenly his ears shifted forward as he came to an instantaneous stop. Simon jerked to a halt with him since his arm was still around Beauregard's neck. But the remainder of the little company—Mary, Caleb, Mr. Beaver, Mrs. Beaver, and Kit—were like dominoes, bumping and stumbling into the rump in front of each one. Several "oomphs!" were heard until all could regain their composure (and dignity) enough to question why Beauregard had ground to such a sudden and unexpected halt in their dashing advance towards danger.

"What is it?" Mary whispered. "Is it too big? Too frightening? Too savage?"

In answer, Beauregard's tail began to wag furiously. Frantically sniffing the ground (a dog on the scent of something can be tenaciously single-minded and intent, as Beauregard was just now), he sprinted across the remaining short distance of the clearing into the edge of the forest, where he immediately came to another dead stop in a nasty thicket. The rest of the group, however, could only see Beauregard's behind…and his still feverishly wagging tail.

They waited for what seemed like forever, frightened nearly out of their wits for poor, dear Beauregard until they could stand waiting no longer.

"Beauregard," Mary whispered—although a rather loud, raspy whisper it was—"what *is* it?"

He turned to them, finally, with transparent ecstasy: ears nearly straight up, jowls spread in a huge smile, eyes alight, and his tail wagging at a speed they'd never seen before. "Not them other fings!" he cried out. "No, it's too wunnerful!"

"What? The *monster*?" Kit asked.

"No! Atticus!" Beauregard rang out with joy.

CHAPTER 11

Did you say 'pig,' or 'fig'?" said the Cat.
"I said 'pig'," replied Alice; "and I wish you
wouldn't keep appearing and vanishing so
suddenly: you make one quite giddy!"
"All right," said the Cat; and this time it
vanished quite slowly, beginning with the end
of the tail, and ending with the grin,
which remained some time
after the rest of it had gone.

There was a mad tumble forward, arms and legs and paws and hands hopelessly entangled, as everyone attempted to dash forward willy-nilly into the thicket. The possibility of Atticus's being there was such an enticement that there was simply no way any sort of orderly advancement would do. So they grunted and fussed, floundering and blustering on the still soggy ground, until they finally managed to arrive where Beauregard lay.

There, between Beauregard's big paws—and currently being licked from one end to the other by the dog's gigantic, rough tongue—rested their dear Atticus. He was a terrible mess, to be sure, but it was indeed him. Several exclamations of 'Oh, Atticus!' and 'You're alive!' rang out. Everyone reached out a hand or paw to stroke him, touch him, feel him for themselves—to be sure he truly had returned, that he was alive, a fully alive Atticus! He, of course, proceeded to prove his vitality immediately.

"I hate to ask a favor so soon, but will one of you kindly inform this simple dog I've had enough water over me, around me, in me, and throughout me for some time to come? And that I definitely do *not* desire another drenching?"

Beauregard stopped for merely a fraction of a second—long enough to point his nose to the sky and joyfully shout, "The dowger's dearest friend! Oh, the dowger's dearest friend is alive!" And then he immediately returned to his determined licking.

Poor Atticus was manipulated quite easily; he was obviously too weak to stop Beauregard. The dog's strong tongue wedged the raccoon's matted, muddy fur this way and that, slowly nudging Atticus himself across the ground as Beauregard changed directions with his medicinal cleansing.

Mary finally came to Atticus's rescue. "Beauregard, I know your licking has wonderful healing benefits—and you've only the sincerest of intentions to help our friend—but I do believe he's too weak for even this right now. I'm sure you've helped him quite enough already." Beauregard looked doubtful, but he gave Atticus a great, serious sniff and one last giant lick before ceasing. Mary continued, "Simon, why don't you pick up Atticus and carry him to the clearing? By any chance, Caleb, did you happen to spot any crayfish while you were flying along the river? Certainly Atticus needs nourishment. Immediately."

Caleb nodded. "As a matter of fact, I did notice some. And I remember exactly where they were, too, because I thought about Atticus when I saw them. With great sadness, I might add, which is now replaced with such joy! I am quite delighted to fetch as many as I can carry." He stretched out his wings, preparing to fly. "I shall return as quickly as possible, Atticus. With a feast, I promise you!"

Atticus gave him a weak smile and sighed.

Simon felt terribly privileged to be able to help Atticus, who lay stretched out on the ground, completely still and limp in his exhaustion. Simon crouched down, moving his head low to the ground in order to look Atticus in the eye. "Does anything hurt especially, Atticus? Should I be careful of any sore places when I pick you up?"

"Not one specifically," Atticus said, drawing out the words slowly. "Just every…single…inch."

Simon tenderly reached underneath him, and as he lifted the precious bundle in his arms, he realized why he was so overjoyed to be chosen to do this small act. He paused a moment, gently pulling Atticus close. Burying his face in Atticus's fur, Simon hugged him, caressed him, feeling and displaying emotions he'd never allowed himself to experience to this depth before. "Oh, Atticus," Simon whispered. "I've missed you so! To think we'd lost you was—" But the boy could not finish. Nor was there any need, for Atticus put his tiny nose to Simon's cheek, his small way of returning the intense hug. When Simon finally raised his head from the soft fur, his eyes were dry, but Atticus's coat glistened with the drops of Simon's tears.

Simon carried him to the clearing with all the other creatures right at his heels. Each one's nose—all five of them—was glued to either his shoulder (Mary was this tall), elbow (Beauregard), knees (Mr. and Mrs. Beaver), or ankle (Kit, of course, who was not about to be missed simply because he was the smallest). Simon sat down slowly so as not to jostle Atticus too much, carefully placing the pathetic, fragile raccoon in his lap.

Mary immediately lay next to Atticus; Beauregard plopped on the other side, insisting on putting his nose on one of Atticus's paws. It seemed that he was simply compelled to touch his dear friend in some way; he evidently only felt secure if there was physical contact between the two. Simon noticed, and understood completely. He winked at the tenderhearted dog and gave him a quick pat on the head before fulfilling this same need for connecting touch by smoothing the fur on Atticus's back. Mr. and Mrs. Beaver moved to stand in front of Atticus, holding hands and nervously glancing downwards. They were silent for a few seconds until Mr. Beaver gathered enough courage to speak.

"Atticus, we're so terribly sorry. I promise you, we diligently searched, but—"

Atticus weakly lifted one paw to stop them. "I know your valiant and selfless character. You would have given your very lives for me, if Mary had permitted it." He gave Mary a quick glance of understanding, too. "Don't fret another moment. You did your best, I'm certain of that. But it was the Father of All Creatures who could rescue me, and none other."

Mary's eyes were alight now, and her music swelled like a crescendo when she exclaimed, "Oh, Atticus! As soon as you're refreshed, you must tell us this story so we may praise and worship the Father for all that He's done!"

Atticus nodded, smiling, and for the first time it was a true, vibrant Atticus smile. "I shall, Mary. And we shall indeed lift 'Amens!' to the Father this day!" And then Atticus noticed poor Kit, hanging back, hunkering behind an old rotting stump. He furtively peeked out at the raccoon, saw Atticus staring at him, and immediately jerked back behind his cover. Just like any young one, he thought he was invisible once out of sight, and assumed his guilt was, too. "Kit," Atticus said softly. "Please come here to me."

Kit peered around the stump. But he did not move a muscle. Except to pop a thumb into his mouth.

"Kit," his mama said softly "Atticus wants to speak with you."

He pulled out the thumb, making a little *"thup!"* sound. Kit was obviously feeling insecure. "But I did a bad thing, Mama." The thumb went right back in.

"Yes, you did, indeed. Fortunately, though, Atticus is safe. But there are always consequences to our actions, Kit. And part of growing up and being responsible is to face the consequences for what we've done." Mrs. Beaver moved over next to Kit and put one paw on his bottom, giving him a gentle push forward. "Go to Atticus, Kit. Ask for forgiveness. And then we shall see what happens next."

Kit sighed and took a deep breath, trying to gather courage. He inched his way towards Atticus, no bounce to his step now. Eyes downcast, deliberately placing one paw slowly in front of the other, Kit looked as though he were walking towards the gallows. Simon was having a terribly difficult time keeping a straight face; an adorable baby beaver dragging himself towards his imagined death was just too much. Finally Kit halted, still several feet away from Atticus.

"Closer," Atticus insisted.

Kit inched forward a bit more and took another quick peek at Atticus. The stubborn raccoon was shaking his head 'no' and obstinately pointing one small finger downwards, indicating a spot a mere inch from Simon's sneakers. Again the poor little beaver sighed, and the inching began again. (The tot was truly astounding; either he could cover distances in just a few bounces— managing to jostle everyone else in the process—or he plodded along for what seemed like decades.)

Finally Kit was just next to Atticus's nose. With head still low, he rolled his eyes up to meet the racoon's gaze. The thumb was still firmly planted in his mouth. "Thi'm thorry," he whimpered.

Simon did giggle now and Beauregard's head shot up, complete with a proud, wide grin that expanded from ear to ear. "Kit talks like the dowger! The dowger is frilled. Isn't Atticus frilled too?"

"I'm overwhelmed with the news," Atticus said cynically, giving Simon a sharp look too—which silenced his giggling (for the moment, at least)—and turned back to the baby beaver before him. "Kit, Beauregard's simpleness— and even more so, his complete acceptance of that simpleness—makes his ability to learn and change a total impossibility." Atticus slowly changed positions (grimacing with each and every movement), and planting his chin on his palm, he propped himself up by an elbow. Simon found it necessary to squirm around just a bit, too, finding Atticus's elbow as sharp as ever. "But for you, Kit, I at least have hope. It is insolently, insipidly impolite" —he was revving up again—"to talk with your mouth full." He wrinkled up his nose in disgust and added, "Now, take that thumb out of your mouth. What was it you were trying to say?"

Kit made the "*thup!*" sound again. By now he was totally mortified and unable to even peek up at Atticus at all. He cowered even more, staring down at the ground and speaking barely above a whisper. Drawing circles in the wet ground with one small toe, he mumbled, "I'm really sorry, Atticus, and I—"

"You are totally and completely forgiven, my dearest little friend." Atticus's voice was warm, and more tender than Simon had ever heard before. "I'm just overjoyed to see you're alive and safe! There's simply no way I could be angry with you." Mary smiled lovingly at him, noticing that a change had occurred in Atticus. The raccoon reached out one of his hands, and laid it upon Kit's head. Finally, Kit knew enough courage to look up.

"You mean you're really and truly not mad at me?"

Atticus smiled. "Not in the least."

"And I don't have any conse-quenches?"

Caleb interrupted just at that moment, landing with a great *flop!* as he dropped the huge leaf he was carrying like a satchel in his bill. The makeshift container's contents spilled across the ground, revealing several good-sized crayfish. "Breakfast is now served!" Caleb declared proudly, and he bowed before Atticus, pointing to the delicacies.

"Just one moment," Mrs. Beaver said, coming forward and putting one arm around her son. "*Consequences* (she sounded it out slowly and correctly for Kit's benefit) are terribly important for a lesson to be learned, and to be learned properly—so one won't ever forget. Kit, what was it that you did wrong?"

He gazed up into his mama's face, wrinkling his brow thoughtfully . "Um, I disobeyed my mama."

"And?"

"I did a dangerous thing."

"Which put others in danger, too." Kit nodded up at her. "It seems to me that, because of his weakened state, Atticus will need assistance in readying these crayfish. I think it quite fitting for Kit to shell them for you, Atticus. And, he should continue to help you find food until you're quite recovered. As a matter of fact, I believe Kit should be available to help you in whatever way necessary, whenever you need something. Agreed, Atticus?"

Atticus nodded, but the doubtful look on his face—left eyebrow pulled up comically high along with his top left lip—proved he was thoroughly thinking through all the ramifications of this particular promise of…"help." He resolved right then that his healing would need to be a quick affair—for *his* continued health, that is.

Kit sniffed at the crayfish and immediately wrinkled up his tiny nose. He sat back on his heels and stated emphatically, "*Disgusting.* They're really oogey, Atticus."

Beauregard smiled smugly, assuming Kit meant it as a compliment. "Oogey's good. Oogey's very good to the dowger!" He picked up his ball and gave it several good chews.

"Makes no difference," his mama replied, with not one hint of sympathy in her voice. "Atticus needs nourishment. Proceed."

So Kit shelled the crayfish, and with each and every one could be heard muttering beneath his breath, "From now on, I will always obey my mama. I will *always* obey my mama," which, of course, is sweet music to any mama's ears.

With each bite, Atticus' strength returned just a little more until finally he was quite content. Feeling much more able to move about, he stretched out cramped legs and finally crawled—slowly, but deliberately—off Simon's lap. Which immediately caused a unified gasp from the entire company.

Atticus's tail—which they had failed to notice before now since Atticus had kept it tucked beneath him—was completely bald, stripped naked except for one pitiful-looking little puff on the very tip.

"Oh Atticus, your poor tail!" Simon cried out.

For once, Kit was speechless and Mary wailed, "Oh, how awful! What happened, Atticus?"

Beauregard, of course, had to add an encouraging comment, creating a major stir after he uttered an unbelievable observation: "The dowger finks it looks beautiful. It looks just like a poodle's tail. And the dowger likes poodles!" There was a literal eruption of voices. Mary attempted to soothe what she assumed must be crushed feelings on Atticus's part because of Beauregard's seemingly incredibly calloused remark. Thinking major damage control was needed, Mary was heard exclaiming how "unique" his tail was now...or something to that effect.

Blustering and flustering were heard all around, and Caleb flopped about in his embarrassment for Atticus. Kit had dissolved into a fit of giggles (to his mama and papa's great dismay; they were "a-hemming" and elbowing Kit something fierce) and although Simon was sorely tempted to laugh, too, he knew that was absolutely unacceptable. So he merely covered his mouth with both hands—very tightly, lest any chuckle should inadvertently escape.

Then Atticus began to talk—or sputter, maybe.

It began as the teeniest "*mmph!*" which seemed to escape unbidden from his throat. In between an intake of breath and a surprising snigger, Atticus uttered, "He said...(gasp, snicker)...he said...I looked...(hiccup, chortle)... like a...*poodle!* (wheeze, snuffle, snuffle, chuckle)." Chaos was still at a feverish pitch, but somehow everyone managed to hear Atticus choke out once more, *"He said I look like a poodle!"* just before he completely dissolved into a puddle of laughter. So hard was Atticus carrying on, as a matter of fact, that he fell over onto his back and clutched at his tummy. Rolling back and forth like he'd completely lost his wits, he kept repeating, "A *poodle*! He says I look like a poodle!" in between uproarious, totally out of control bursts of laughter. All the time he was thrashing about his hilarious looking tail, too.

Obviously, Atticus's reactions were the end of any attempts at order and dignity or soothing of tender feelings, for Kit was rolling on the ground now with Atticus, completely giving in to his fit of giggles. Simon could contain himself no longer, either…and then Mr. and Mrs. Beaver began chuckling at the sight of Atticus and Kit tossing about like two rollicking pups. (With Beauregard creating even further pandemonium, whirling in delighted circles and tossing his beloved ball up in the air.) Caleb at least attempted to stay in some control, but soon he and Mary also were caught up into the absolute joy of it all…the relief and release of so much pain and tension into the wonderful healing effects of pure, joyful laughter.

And though the little company could not see it, the Father of all Creatures also joined in on the merriment, delighting in His creation of laughter—a gift of delicious pleasure, given back to the Father as a blessed offering. For the sound of joy-filled laughter is a delight to His ear, a sweet taste to His mouth, and a balm to His eye. Worship…through a chorus of giggles, chuckles, and jubilation!

Finally Mary could contain herself no longer, and she turned to Atticus with anticipation in her sparkling eyes. "Oh, tell us now, Atticus. Please share the story of how you were saved!"

Atticus sat up, and, since he had collected a good deal of grass and leaves in his rolling around, first (dramatically, of course) dusted himself off. Then, throwing his palms up and out with a giant flourish, he began, "Well, first I jumped in. You were all obviously aware of that fact." He glanced quickly around the group, noting that he had everyone's undivided attention. Taking center stage, Atticus positively *launched* into a possibly Oscar-winning performance. "I can't tell you how spitefully frigid the water was. Brrrr! Babbling, bothersome brook! How I refrained from instantly freezing into an icicle, I have no earthly idea."

"The dowger didn't know aminals could turn into icicles. Can aminals be icicles?" Beauregard asked.

Atticus glared at him. "Yes, indeed, *animals* can be icicles. Especially dogs who've been given an *icy glare*. Now where was I? Oh, yes. Well, after I collected my wits, I began frantically paddling about in search of Kit. But he was nowhere to be found and soon I couldn't tell which direction was which anyway. I was at the complete mercy of the raging, riotous, rampaging waters!" Atticus flung an arm across his forehead and gave a great sigh. "Great goose feathers, what a perilous predicament I was in. By that time, there was certainly no deciding which direction my nose would travel, either. Downstream it went. In a trice!"

"Didn't the rest of you go that way, too, Atticus?" Kit asked innocently.

"Indeed it did. Directly. Immediately. At an expedient velocity, I might add."

Kit looked up at his mama with a puzzled expression. "Does that mean fast, Mama?"

"Yes it does, Kit. Don't interrupt."

"Well, before I knew what was happening, I was being tumbled about in the surging current. I could barely gasp for a bit of life-giving air." Atticus threw his arms about in every direction now, tumbling them in circles and tossing them high above his ears. "My head was sucked under, I was pitched about in numerous tumultuous somersaults until I thought my poor distraught lungs might burst for lack of air—"

Mary gasped at this point, mumbling, "Poor Atticus...poor, dearest Atticus," and shook her head back and forth.

"And then somehow, mercifully, I was able to just get my head above water and catch a quick breath, only to be sucked under those treacherous currents yet again." He put both hands on his hips, matter-of-factly. "All things considered, it appeared rather hopeless at that point, I must say."

"It must have seemed like forever," Caleb said.

"Oh, yes. That it did. Until what happened next."

"What?" Kit asked. He sat transfixed at Atticus's feet, enthralled with his story.

"I came into the most dangerous of rapids. Oh, my friends, you have never seen anything like this…this *abyss* of despair before."

"We saw them also," Barton put in. "But we didn't experience them. Atticus, however did you survive?"

"I began hitting up against the jagged rocks. And the rocks were what stripped my poor tail, grabbing at me so that I became wedged between more of them than I could even count." He gave them all a pompous look. "And I can count up to ten, mind you."

Beauregard was simply awestruck in his admiration. "Ten! The dowger can't count past four." He leaned towards Simon, stating profoundly, "That's how many feet the dowger has."

Simon smothered another giggle.

"My pitiful tail would get caught and there I would be, struggling, fighting like mad to keep my head above water and catch my breath. And suddenly I'd pop loose, nearly drowning the very next moment, only to get wedged between more horrendous rocks and have more fur ripped from my tender tail. It seemed a relentless, endless cycle until I finally was mercifully washed atop the most ferocious rock I'd encountered yet. Evidently the current was so strong there it just swooshed me right on top of the thing."

"Swooshed?" Kit asked.

"Definitely swooshed," Atticus answered.

"The dowger was once swooshed," Beauregard put in. "The dowger's ball fell inna river and—"

"Beauregard, not now," Atticus instructed emphatically, giving him a glowering look. "As I was saying before I was *interrupted*," he rolled his eyes upwards and shook his head, like he was shaking off a menacing insect, "here I was on this ferocious rock."

"Mama, can a rock be ferocious?" Kit was determined to understand every single bit of Atticus' story, no matter how dramatically exaggerated it was.

"Hush, Kit."

"As I was saying," and this time Atticus glared down at Kit, "I was marooned on this *ferocious* rock, completely exhausted, out of breath, my tail was as you see it, and I was totally surrounded by swirling, ravenous rapids. There was literally no place to go."

"No place?" Kit asked. (He just could not keep quiet to save himself. Maybe his mouth had to be moving because his naturally wriggly body was being so still.)

"Absolutely. No place."

"Is that when the Father of all Creatures came?" Mary asked, and she leaned forward eagerly as she posed her question.

"Not immediately. I just sat there for some time, quivering with fear and uncertainty and exhaustion. And then I remembered, Mary, what you taught us to say when we were frightened."

"I'm safe in the Father's hand?" she asked.

"Exactly. And so I began repeating it, over and over. I can't tell you all what a comfort it was as I sat there, staring about me at the frightening situation, looking over the hopelessness of it all. Suddenly I realized—with His Hand right there—nothing is hopeless. Absolutely nothing!" One great tear slipped from Atticus's eye, a tear formed in sincerity and love for the Father of all Creatures. For this one moment, there were no dramatics from Atticus. Mary sniffed loudly and Mrs. Beaver wiped away a tear, too.

"What happened next?" Kit was spellbound, and there was awe in his voice.

"Amazingly, I fell asleep. Sound asleep. And had the most wonderful dream I have ever had in my *whole entire life*. For in my dream, that great Hand came and picked me right up, cradling me in His magnificent palm, and gently carrying me to safety on the riverbank." Atticus looked around the whole group, his eyes glistening and wide with wonder. "When I woke up several hours later, there I was. On the riverbank."

"It was no dream," Caleb whispered.

"No, Caleb. It indeed was no dream."

They knew it would happen then just as sure as they knew Atticus had experienced a miracle: Caleb stretched out his wings, exposing the always-startling scarlet, and his voice rang out with deep emotion, "All the Father's Creatures, join in this praise! For He has brought the Three together to complete the journey from Knowing in Part to Knowing Fully! He has rescued Beauregard, the Truth, from the Great Sand. He has delivered Atticus from the Raging River. And when the journey is complete, the three shall be Fully Known and the Father of all Creatures will be glorified. Let us praise Him with uplifted hearts. Let us praise Him with joyous voices. Let us praise Him with all the earth, for He alone is worthy to be praised! Amen and Amen!"

They all jumped spontaneously to their feet, for the little company could no longer contain such praise. Their worship was like a flowing fountain—a bubbling fountain which sends sprays leaping into the air. Hands clapped, little paws stomped, tails thumped and waggled, and cheerful, glowing faces were upturned to capture the sun's rays. Even Simon sang out, lifting his hands to the sky, for he knew overwhelming happiness now that Atticus was alive. Their worship continued, changing from joyous laughter to wondrous story to joyous praise, and the Father was glorified in all!

When they were finally still—from a bit of exhaustion, to be quite truthful—they discovered all their rolling and jumping and praising had drained each one, leaving them very hungry. So they searched for food, finding an abundant supply by the riverbank once again. Atticus found even more crayfish, to Kit's misfortune. The conscientious baby beaver, however, peeled them dutifully, and even earnestly asked if Atticus would like more of the crayfish or any other type of food. Though Atticus insisted he felt ever so much better and that Kit need not bother about him any more, Kit had taken his mother quite seriously—and literally. He was, therefore, at Atticus's feet constantly, tripping him up frequently, too. He was a terrific "help" already, just as Atticus had predicted.

Mary and Caleb decreed that, though Atticus was much recuperated, a day of rest was warranted. So they rested for a while after breakfast, urging Atticus to tell them more details about his adventure. He didn't disappoint, adding descriptive details which almost seemed a bit imaginative, like the fish with great, sharp teeth and a mouth the size of a cavern who was intent upon swallowing Atticus for dinner. Then they played games for the remainder of the beautiful, sunny day. This, of course, included Beauregard chasing after his precious ball and Kit happily obliging by whacking it over and over again with his tail. Their active play did at least one great measure of good: the baby beaver was worn out for a bit, and he took a short nap, which meant a needed rest for Atticus, also.

It wasn't until after dinner when they were all lying around, knowing contentedness, with a head resting on a furry tummy here and a foot or paw draped casually across an arm over there, that Caleb broached the subject of where their journey should take them next. Atticus immediately jerked up and grabbed Beauregard's ball. He had no intention of throwing the oogey thing (it was incredibly slobbery from the day's activities), but instead plopped it right into Beauregard's mouth. Like a plug.

"There. Now someone else can answer Caleb's question," Atticus stated emphatically, obviously pleased with his imaginative solution.

"Bwth zthz szwdow—"

"Beauregard, surely you know better than that by now," Atticus whined, tragically slapping a hand across his furrowed brow.

Simon chuckled at them both. "It's never stopped him before. And certainly you know *that* better by now too, Atticus," Simon teased.

"Can you believe I was the goose who said nothing was hopeless—nothing? I had forgotten to include this simple dog. Woe to me for uttering such a foolish thing." Atticus fell over backwards, landing on his bald tail and covering his eyes with both hands. But unfortunately, the effect was entirely lost on Beauregard, who would still have his say.

Dropping the ball at his feet, Beauregard simply stated, "The dowger knows what to do next."

Atticus groaned. "Here it comes. Intelligence at its best."

"The dowger says—" (remember that he pronounces it to rhyme with *days*), Beauregard began most seriously, but then he stopped abruptly. "Who is Integents?" he asked. He was most confused as to whom Atticus was referring to.

"That's my third cousin removed on my father's side, a very bright little thing—had kind of an unusual cute stripe to her tail—who advised me never to listen to black dogs who—"

"*Atticus!*" Mary scolded.

"Sorry."

"What do you think, Beauregard?" Mary asked him.

He was evidently still chewing on Atticus's reply about a third cousin, but he shook off his bewilderment and replied, "The dowger says *up.*"

"Up?"

He nodded his great head and jumped to his feet, waggling his tail frantically again. "Follow the dowger and you'll see!"

Beauregard dashed around in a circle in his exuberance as he waited for everyone to stand, and then he took off at a gallop, jumping fallen branches, brush, and old stumps as he loped along the riverbank. When he came to a great pile of rocks, he climbed on top, shouting excitedly, "Up! Come see up!"

Mary arrived first, followed by Simon. Atticus was detained a good deal, since his ever-present shadow, Kit, was at his feet, causing him to stumble constantly over his "helper." Mr. and Mrs. Beaver followed along behind, and Caleb flew just above them, keeping an eye on the little band and wondering what—or where—on earth Beauregard could be leading them. Once they all climbed up on the rocks, their questions were answered immediately. For just a short ways off in the distance arose a spectacular mountain.

The very highest point had a hint of snow upon it—a pure, lovely white which seemed to glisten and sparkle in the sunshine. Obviously the vegetation was thick, for a rich, dark green covered most of it until vanishing near the top. The majesty of that mountain! It was a monument to the Father's glory itself—so magnificent, so emblazoned with power, so grand as it simply rose to the highest heavens right before their eyes. They stood gazing upon it with sheer awe, attempting to drink in and absorb the amazing beauty.

"Isn't it magnificent?" Mary whispered, her voice filled with reverent awe. "And do you all realize what lies there, within sight? Why, we're staring at the completion of our journey. Oh, I realize we still have a long trek before us." She pointed upwards with her nose. "But our goal is right before us, my friends!"

They all stood still for a moment, feeling challenged by Mary's words, yet dumbfounded by the sheer expanse of the mountain. The reality of climbing—and the very real dangers that entailed—lay starkly before them. As each one scaled its vast reaches with curious eyes, they were also developing fear for the daunting task.

"Will we all climb safely to the very tip top?" Kit asked in a hushed, spellbound whisper. "Will we meet the Father of all Creatures there?"

Mary was silent for a moment, and then she turned from Kit to stare up at the highest reaches of the mountain again. "Yes, Kit, on this mountain we shall meet the Father of all Creatures, face to face." She closed her eyes again, breathing deeply. An intense desire settled over her immediately—a yearning which formed a deep line between her eyes and put a firm set to her mouth. She turned to face Simon and her glowing eyes bored into his bright blue ones. "Are you ready, Simon-by-the-Way?"

He nodded, searching for the meaning in her words, wondering why she'd asked him—and him only—this question.

"You will meet your Father God there." Her amazing eyes pierced his now, causing Simon to step backwards from their deep scrutiny. "But you will also meet *yourself*. Will you finish the journey, Simon-by-the-Way?"

Simon glanced away, looking to the others for explanations and help. He was totally perplexed by Mary's question and what she expected of him. "Of course I will, Mary," Simon reached out to touch Beauregard and Atticus, patting Mr. and Mrs. Beaver and Kit on their heads too. "We've come so far. I wouldn't leave you…I wouldn't desert any of you. *Ever!*"

By now, however, they knew each other far too well. They knew the hint of a scent in the air, sensed a changed pattern of the wind, recognized what was coming before it even began. Beauregard lifted his head, and on that great pile of rocks before the glorious mountain that would bring an end to their journey together, he howled forlornly into the winds. Though Beauregard's cry was frightening enough by itself, the answering "*Ooooooooo!*" from the mountain was a horror which sent a stabbing chill through every listener's heart. It sounded almost like an echo—oh, how they wished it were only that!—but they knew it was not. No, it was some unknown and malevolent animal that purposefully answered Beauregard's woeful wail. This reverberating howl, however, was not forlorn in tone like Beauregard's. This howl was *evil*.

CHAPTER 12

"Of course they answer to their names?" the
Gnat remarked carelessly.
"I never knew them do it."
"What's the use of their having names," the
Gnat said, "if they wo'n't answer to them?"
"No use to them," said Alice; "but it's useful
to the people that name them, I suppose.
If not, why do things have names at all?"

They spent the night huddled together at the base of the rocks, but this was the first time since beginning the journey that their rest was not peaceful. Every member of the little band tossed fitfully, knowing dark and distressing dreams—nightmares which they couldn't sufficiently recall in the morning in order to relate a simple story which would have helped dispel the aura of terror and dread. Instead, the dreams were without form, beyond description, devoid of places or characters. They were just dark and frightening, enveloped in a confusing fog, and filled with that ghastly howl which floated hauntingly across their minds. Everyone recognized they were only dreams, and yet they seemed entirely too real.

Even though no one attempted to describe them the next morning, each knew the others had shared the same experience. For they had felt each other's tossing and turning, they'd heard the shared sighs and soft cries throughout the night, and they'd all awakened with tense and tired bodies. The weary look on each face—on child, dog, deer, bird, raccoon, and beaver—was the same.

Mary's gaze shifted around the little group. She realized something must be done; they couldn't begin this last and most important leg of their journey without some encouragement and hope. "Caleb," she said, "please call everyone together."

They were eating breakfast, mechanically chewing with little to no appetite, when Caleb stretched out his wings. "Come everyone!" He flew around the clearing and along the riverbank, summoning the scattered weary travelers. "Mary wants us to gather together. She has something important to say!"

Mary leaped up onto the rocks and they all settled before her, waiting expectantly, hoping she could lighten the weight pressing against their hearts and minds. She looked over the dispirited group, smiling affectionately at each of the dear friends. "Before we can set out on this last part of our journey, we must talk. Unspoken fears grow so swiftly and threaten to overwhelm us. We must set them out before us and see them for what they are. Only then are they less ominous. Now, tell me, tell us all, what frightens you the most? Who will be first? Atticus?"

He shivered—a great tremor beginning with the bit of fluff at the end of his tail and subsequently traveling all the way to the very tip of his nose. "The dream that came to all of us. None of us has dared to mention it—but it happened!"

Caleb nodded in agreement. "It was so terrifying…and yet so indescribable. What was it, Mary?"

"A mere reflection of our unspoken fears. That's why the dream had no faces, no form, nothing we could tangibly describe. All we carry still is the hazy recollection of a haunting fear."

"But dreams aren't real, are they, Mary?" Kit asked.

Mary glanced over at Simon before she answered, "No, Kit. Dreams aren't real. As I said, they're merely reflections—poor reflections, like in a mirror."

Kit screwed up his nose, which made his whiskers twitch in his deep concentration. "A mirror? Whatsa mirror?"

"Oh, you know what a mirror is, Kit. Atticus found one not long ago by the creek bed, remember?" Mary turned to Atticus and he responded with an exaggerated nod, obviously still considering it one of his most momentous discoveries. "Remember how we all took turns looking into it, seeing our faces reflected in its shiny glass?"

"Yeah, now I member that. We called it the looking glass. That was fun!" Kit held up his little hands to his face, mimicking the adventure of seeing his whiskers clearly for the very first time.

Atticus raised one eyebrow and folded his arms akimbo. "You'll also clearly recall that Beauregard *sat* on the looking glass, pulverizing my treasure into bits, smooshing it to smithereens, resting his horrendous haunches on my fragile, fine, um…" He had to search a bit for another *f.* "…famous…" Atticus was revving up again.

"Famous? How can a mirror be *famous?*" Simon exclaimed, who was nervous about any discussion of mirrors in the first place.

"Well, it belonged to *me*. At least it *did*, until Mister Coordination plopped on it!"

"The dowger didn't see it," Beauregard explained to Simon, shaking his great head back and forth, his snout nearly touching the ground. He sighed. "Such a little bottom to break the pretty looking glass."

"Little? You're calling that big, bulky behind *little?*"

"Atticus. I do believe we're just a bit off the subject here." Mary was determined to bring a bit of decorum back to the discussion, even as Beauregard was at that very moment straining to look at his behind, going around in circles as he failed to catch up to his intended goal. "Beauregard? Leave that inspection for later, okay? Good. Now, where were we? Oh yes. We were discussing mirrors—or looking glasses—whatever you choose to call them, and how their reflections can distort what we see. Seeing something face to face—with our own eyes—is ever so much better. But do you know what's best of all? Can you imagine the clearest, most revealing way to truly see what's real?"

Kit drew his little brows together, and even Beauregard stopped staring at his backside to concentrate by closing his eyes and clamping shut his big mouth. Mr. and Mrs. Beaver looked at each other and shrugged their shoulders, while Atticus attempted to act disinterested, since he didn't know the answer. Caleb rubbed the tip of one wing against his beak, completely drawn in by all Mary was teaching them. And Simon…well, Simon was nearly spellbound by this discussion of the looking glass and mirrors and reality.

"Only when we see the Father of all Creatures face to face will we truly know what's real. For only then are we fully known!"

"But what does that *mean*, Mary? Being fully known?" Simon wanted a reply he could understand and yet, at the very same moment, he dreaded what Mary might say. Somehow he knew without a doubt that this discussion was directly related to why he'd come here—through the mirror—and how this journey would end.

"I don't know, Simon. I don't understand all of the prophecy—not yet. But since being fully known is indeed part of the prophecy, I know without doubt that it's good and wonderful and what I desire." Mary glanced around the entire company. "I think we simply must trust the Father of all Creatures for this also. He'll reveal it to us. When it's time."

They were all quiet for a moment, reflecting, when Simon interjected into the calm, "Sure. It's easy to *talk* about trust. To discuss what's real and what's not. But the dream I had last night—that's what feels real now. Way too real!"

Mary nodded to murmurs of agreement around him. "I know, I know. It was awful. But let's get the horrible thing out in the open where we can fight its effects. What do we think caused the nightmare in the first place?"

Mrs. Beaver reached out to Kit, and she hugged him to her fiercely. "The very real danger we've faced, that's what! Beauregard, Kit, and Atticus were all near death." She turned to gaze up at the intimidating, powerful mountain, adding, "I'm frightened of what awaits us there, Mary. That horrible animal sound we heard—" (Mrs. Beaver visibly reeled, and Barton quickly moved to support her in her shaky unsteadiness) "—it was *unearthly*. Only a ghastly creature could make such a sound. I'm beginning to wonder if it's truly wise to continue on."

"I've had the very same thoughts and concerns," Barton interjected, and he stretched his arms protectively around his entire family. "As a husband and father, I'm responsible for their safety. How can I knowingly put them at such great risk yet again?"

A silence fell over them all before Mary finally asked, "You would go home, then?"

Barton hesitated, indecisive and struggling with his response. Then he nodded. Mrs. Beaver leaned heavily against him, dabbing at a suddenly runny nose, but Kit grunted and squirmed out from beneath his parents' arms.

"But I don't want to go back!" Kit insisted, and he quickly scrambled up beside Mary, grabbing onto one of her legs and gazing up at her with naïve longing. "I want to finish the journey. We've come this far…please, can't we keep on 'til the end?"

Simon couldn't contain his fears any longer, and he added his voice to the unsettling discussion. "That's *my* greatest fear—the end. I don't want our journey to *ever* end 'cause I don't want to go back to my world. How about this, Mary? Everybody, why can't we just stay here? That creature—whatever it is—is way up on the mountain. So we're safe if we just stay put, right? Mr. and Mrs. Beaver, that would solve your dilemma, too. It's the perfect answer, and it's such a perfect place. Just look." Simon turned in a circle, motioning towards the beauty all around him. "We'd all be happy here, living at the foot of this beautiful mountain. Let's just stay here!"

A weariness fell over Mary's features like a mask: her head swayed, her eyelids drooped, and her usually smiling mouth went slack. "Beauregard? Have you anything to add?" she asked.

Beauregard lay down—flopped was a better description—and as always, tilted his head to one side in contemplation. He gave one great lick all the way around his mouth before slowly stating, "The dowger doesn't want to live at the bottom of the pretty mountain. The Father didn't send the Three there, and the dowger unnerstands that." At Beauregard's profound wisdom, Mary perked up, lifting her head just a bit. Then Beauregard continued, shaking his head in sadness. "But the dowger is afraid, too."

Mary breathed heavily, sagging again. She had counted on Beauregard, and the possibility of his giving up was almost more than she could bear. Softly—as though she were afraid to hear his answer—she asked, "And what are you afraid of, Beauregard?"

"The dowger is afraid of our fears."

Slowly, ever so slowly, Mary gifted the dog with one of her lovely smiles—

almost a smile of appreciation—for Beauregard had just given her the perfect gift. It was something she'd always wanted and yet she hadn't even known how dearly desired until it was received. She lay down, motioning for everyone else to do the same. "You're so right, Beauregard, our dear symbol of Truth. That's why I'm going to tell you all a story, a very wonderful story."

Kit immediately snuggled up to Simon, and Simon laid his head on Beauregard's back. Mr. and Mrs. Beaver, still clinging to each other, sat next to Caleb, and Atticus sprawled out on the other side of Beauregard. Each one listened intently to Mary, and the tinkling music of hope and encouragement highlighted her words.

"Close your eyes," Mary soothingly whispered. "Listen, concentrate, and hear the heart of the story. And know the Father of all Creatures in a way which you may have never known Him before." She took a deep breath and began, "It was the beginning of all time. And His spoken word…*was*. Our words and actions can be two different things entirely, but the Father's word simply *is*. He stretched out His great hand and spoke the world into existence. His breathed words became visible, tangible, living reality. Forests, rivers, the Great Sand, more rivers, mountains sprang into being. And then creatures, all sizes, all shapes, all forms. Then the father created man, and man gave the species their names, such as bird and beaver and dog and raccoon."

"And deer!" Kit added.

"Yes, Kit, the deer too. But there was yet another task to be done, for to the Father of all Creatures, we're not merely various, indistinguishable members of a group or species or kind. Each and every one of us is known individually and personally by Him."

Kit peeked open one eye. "Even baby beavers?"

"Especially baby beavers!" Mary chuckled. "I'm afraid the Father must watch quite diligently to keep His eye upon such squirmy little ones. Now close that peeking eye, Kit."

Kit complied, and soon the comforting, soothing voice of Mary lulled him again, just as it did all the others. Oh, they weren't asleep. Far from it, for each one was fully aware of Mary…of himself or herself…and fully aware of the Father of all Creatures' presence among them.

"The task before the Father was to name each one of His children…each and every child that would be His throughout all time. I call it a task, but this wasn't work as we know work to be. Oh no, it was pure joy for Him to name His own, so he joyfully began this awesome mission of naming. First was…Beauregard. One of His most inspired creations was…" (Beauregard pulled up his great jowls in a mighty smile at Mary's choice of words.) "…this wonderfully simple dog who would delight in the Truth. And that name! Why, have you ever heard anything more glorious? To simply pronounce it— *Beauregard*—is to nearly mimic the voice of angels!" Mary let the melody of her words encircle and fill Beauregard, and she was pleased to see that joining his immense smile was the steady *thump-thump* of his tail—a sign Beauregard was quite content and pleased indeed.

The entire group now became aware of what Mary planned: she would speak of each of them with gifts of love and praise. And oh, each one was most eager for his or her turn. Though they remained relaxed and sprawled about, each listener strained to catch every morsel Mary offered. This "meal" was more delicious than any feast, ever!

"The Father made a rambunctious little beaver, a beaver who'd chase after life with a bounce to his step. No one would ever meet this darling baby without finding him endearing, without desiring to pinch those cheeks. And why would this little one be named Kit? Why, I suppose because he's the very embodiment of cuteness—the "whole Kit 'n' caboodle!" Kit giggled out loud.

"And what of the baby's father? Such dedication! For not only would this papa diligently care for his family, he would also carry out his responsibilities with joy. I say to you all: let it be known that Barton would be willing to give his *very life* for his family." Barton squirmed at the praise, tracing a circle on the ground with his toe, knowing this to be true but, in his humility, feeling uncomfortable with such acclaim. "Because the Father knew Barton's courage would never, ever fail in a time of need, He gave him a name of substance. Of import. A solid name. Barton.

"Then there's the Mama. Oh, what beauty is in that one word! Comfort. Security. Peace. Love. Who provides nourishment in every way? Whom do we cry out to in the night? Whose arms provide the love we long for? *The Mama*." Barton reached out and patted his dear wife, who was so nearly overcome with emotion that she hid her face in her hands. For with all her tender heart, she truly did desire to live up to Mary's description. "Such utter selflessness. By her own choice, this dear beaver would ask for no other name. She would simply be known as *the Mama* for the love of her precious child."

Mary's words moved over them like a loving caress, and her story became a pleasant daydream to replace the frightening nightmares of the night before. They pulled the sweet vision over them like a warm, cuddly blanket, and they snuggled beneath its softness and security with pleasure.

"The Father of all Creatures also created the red-winged blackbird, but when He formed Caleb, the black was so unique and beautiful that it glistened with blue. The scarlet was commanding before all nature because of its glorious color. Why such magnificent coloring?" Mary's voice rose in its intensity, signaling them all to note the gravity of what she was about to say. "Because this blackbird would give magnificent pronouncements for His majesty. No one else could pronounce His decrees as Caleb could. No other could equal his design for the grandness of this task. No one could ever take the place of our own dear Caleb!" The little bird Mary described with such grand words? He hung his noble head, and wept with unabashed joy.

Though Atticus would've vehemently denied it, Mary noted he leaned towards her, eager to hear what she would say about him. It should also be noted that, before she began, Mary smiled to herself—for the love of the creature before her, and the soft heart he attempted (unsuccessfully, it must be noted) to hide from them all. Her voice incredibly soft and tender, she began, "When He made the most lion-hearted raccoon that ever was, the Father decided to call him Atticus, this one who is so valiant, so courageous! And there is yet another distinctive to this particular raccoon, one which cannot be denied. *Heart*. A heart as big as the sky above us, and it is that heart which compels the little raccoon to be so courageous. It is the combination of heart and courage which endears our Atticus to us all!"

Atticus "*a-hemmed!*" a good deal, acting nonchalant, and as though he suddenly had a terribly scratchy cough. But Mary knew Atticus truly was pleased, and once again she smiled in her heart of hearts.

She paused a moment before continuing, "The Father of all Creatures also made more creatures just like the man He had created. One of these we've come to know and love so much: our own Simon-by-the-Way. And though the Father loves him dearly, the young boy struggles to accept that love. For he is afraid of the Father." Simon physically flinched under the directness of the words, and Mary strove to reach out to him even more. "But some day…some day Simon-by-the-Way will fully know how much he is loved. He'll grasp how the Father loves him completely just as he is, for all he is, and that he always will be loved. And he'll also know the Father's touch is good and healing and kind. Then—for the first time—he will reach out for the Father, and allow himself to be enveloped into His embrace." Simon reluctantly opened his eyes to meet Mary's forceful stare. He found only love there, while Mary, sadly, saw only fear in Simon's.

The intense moment of silence was shattered as Kit suddenly sat up. He kept his eyes shut tightly in obedience, and theatrically raised one pudgy little finger to make his point. "Don't forget the deer! Mary, don't forget yourself!"

"Oh, Kit," she nearly sang, as music filled her words. "Yes, in His great mercy He fashioned a deer, an unworthy deer whose only desire was graciously to be used by the Father. A simple name He gave to her…a name for the ages…Mary!

"All of you, turn to me now, and grasp the heart of my story. Each of you was given a glorious name, a name designed and chosen and pronounced by the Father. And though your names describe who you are—each of you, in your wonderful uniqueness—the activity of naming is so much more, ever so much deeper. For the name is a completion, a capturing of the essence of the spirit and soul in each of us just as He is *The Name!*"

The force of *The Name* blew against them, and all were literally pushed to their knees in obeisance to the Glory. They breathed in Mary's words as though there were life inherent in their form—renewing life…energizing life…healing life. They all closed their eyes again, but this time out of reverence and pure awe.

"But still the Father of all Creatures hadn't completed His task, for He also spoke into existence a journey for each of His children, a pathway uniquely designed for each one to follow so he or she might know fully. And become fully known." Mary lifted her majestic head towards the top of the mountain, just as a shadow from a passing cloud shaded her lovely features. "The journey isn't an easy one to follow. There will be grievous dangers and heart-rending pain along the way. Only the most courageous follow it determinedly with stubbornness, won't stray from the pathway, won't ever—*ever!*—give up until the journey is complete.

"What lies at the end of this perilous journey?" she queried, and the strength of her firm belief hovered even in the question. "The Father of all Creatures! He awaits us there—to look into the souls of those He has made, those He has named, those He has known. *Face to face.*"

Mary was quiet for a few moments. Even with their eyes still closed, the little band could feel Mary's searching eyes moving over them. Suddenly she cried out, "Now, look and decide your future, brave little band!" Just in time, they rose to see Mary take a giant, gracefully arching leap from the rocks to a place just beyond them—the beginning to the pathway that would take them up the mountain. "What is your decision? Shall we continue on our journey? Shall we complete it together?"

Barton deliberately stepped forward, a look of great determination upon his whiskered face. "Oh yes, Mary! I'm convinced we should continue." He reached back for Mrs. Beaver's outstretched hand. "But even after your wonderful story, we are still afraid. How do we banish our fears, Mary? Tell us how!"

"Fear will always be with us, Barton, once we have begun our journey. For the dangers have become *real*: they have touched us and become our pain, leaving deep scars. But those who have the strength of character to finish the journey don't focus on the fear. Instead, they ask the Father of all Creatures for the courage to decide to take one step, and then another. And another and another!"

"Like this?" Kit asked, and he bounded forward onto the pathway.

"Oh, yes, Kit!" Mary exclaimed. "Who will take the next courageous step?"

Mr. and Mrs. Beaver exchanged one quick glance and joined Kit, hugging him to them. "You were right, my son," Mr. Barton said to him. "We should finish the journey. With the Father of all Creatures' help, we shall finish together!"

Caleb followed, extending his wings and flying gracefully and purposefully towards the group. Next, Atticus took a dramatic deep breath, and he walked over to them in a most dignified way. (Except for the poodle tail dragging behind him; it would definitely hinder his flair until it had grown out sufficiently.) Atticus's dramatic effect was immediately shattered by Beauregard's uncoordinated plunge into the middle of the group, sending everyone tumbling every which way. Atticus was heard murmuring a few *"horrible, horrendous happenstances!"* and Kit giggled. Mary watched the scene before her with joy. Then she turned to the one who hadn't yet committed to the first step. Simon stood apart from them, with narrowed eyes and a defiant curve about his lips.

He nervously gestured towards the mountain, a flippant motion that hid nothing of his very real fears. "You said I would meet the Father there, that we all would. But you also said I'd meet myself." Simon stuck out his chin and crossed his arms. "What did you mean, Mary? How can I meet *myself?*"

"As we journey, Simon-by-the-Way, we understand better who the Father is. The journey itself becomes our teacher. Slowly we learn about misunderstandings which have caused us to see Him incorrectly. Dearest Simon, all of us somehow distort Who and What He truly is, and because we view Him incorrectly, we can't see ourselves as He sees us, either. So we need to learn the truth about ourselves—see the ugliness dwelling within. That knowledge is painful. It's a hurtful process. But that, my dear friend, is the journey."

Vague memories of Simon's conversation with the pastor flitted across his mind, more assertions about his misunderstanding God's love. Instantly, Simon felt wary, for Mary appeared to be saying the very same thing as the minister had. He narrowed his eyes and scrutinized Mary, searching for the truth. "And you're saying I don't correctly understand this…this Father of all Creatures? God?"

She nodded. "Nor yourself."

"But you're still not explaining how I can supposedly meet myself. That just doesn't make any sense, Mary!"

"None of this will until we complete the journey, Simon-by-the-Way. We three are the image of the Way, the Truth and the Life. All three will be fulfilled as the Father has spoken it to be. I know that—more than any of us— you must gather the greatest amount of courage to take this step. Twice before we've asked you to be brave, to decide to face danger. Now we ask you again. Can you do this, simply knowing and trusting you're safe in the Father's hand? And that we…"—she motioned to all the animals standing before Simon— "your friends, pledge to continue journeying faithfully with you?"

Kit leaned forward, holding out a dimpled hand towards the hesitant boy. The simple gesture was too innocent an offering to deny, and Simon made his decision; he walked forward, grasping the beaver's hand in his own. Kit looked up at him, smiling confidently into Simon's still-wary eyes. "I will help you," Kit announced bravely. "We all will, Simon-by-the-Way."

With nothing more than courageous hearts and a firm decision of will and trust in the Father, the little company began the last part of their journey. They moved forward and resolutely proceeded up the mountain.

They soon discovered the trail wound this way and that a good deal, creating great switchbacks at its steepest points. Beauregard was convinced some curves were so sharp he could literally catch up to his own tail as he climbed. So he'd gallop around each bend, attempting to meet…himself. Mostly, all the determined dog managed to do was plow into someone else, but he certainly added a measure of comic relief for all of them—except Atticus. As usual, Atticus wasn't particularly thrilled with Beauregard's efforts.

They also encountered huge gullies and several downed trees, evidences of the previous night's strong winds and torrential rain. These hindered their progress temporarily, but they always banded together, devising ways to get over or around them. Patches of smooth stones created slippery footing and the constant uphill climb soon caused legs and backs to ache. The journey was still pleasant at this point, however, for there were constant discoveries to hear, smell, and see. The mountain was literally alive and glowing with the fruit of the Father's creation, and they were all charmed by its beauty.

The flowers were especially captivating. No one knew their names, since this was such unfamiliar territory, but that didn't stop them from admiring them. (Atticus grew irritated with Beauregard over correct diction, however. No matter how many times Atticus asked Beauregard to listen carefully and repeat after him, Beauregard's pronunciation of *flowers* still came out sounding like *flouders*.) Delicate, tiny white blossoms were scattered everywhere, peeking out from beneath leaves, mosses, and small plant life. And their fragrance! Kit was constantly wandering off the path to stick his tiny nose into a patch of blossoms. He couldn't resist picking bouquet after bouquet for his mama and Mary, which he shyly produced from behind his back and presented with a sweet grin. Beauregard responded with an exuberant, "Such lovely flouders!" Then Atticus slapped a hand to his forehead again, which caused Beauregard to fret that Atticus's head would soon develop a terrible dent.

A vine—much like honeysuckle, Simon thought—competed with the white flowers' sweet scent, and a yellow daisy bloomed among the rocks. Wild roses, varying in color from white to blushing pink to a deep cherry red, grew in great thorny bushes (Kit avoided picking these after a nasty thorn pierced deep into his hand), and other innumerable varieties of flowers scattered across the mountainside—way beyond Atticus's abilities at counting to ten—were a constant treat to discover.

They encountered other creatures along the way, too—squirrels chattered at them (they spoke so fast that no one could make out a word of what they were saying, though), several birds darted overhead, and Beauregard startled a rabbit with an adorable white cottontail. The poor thing went tearing off in the opposite direction before the truly penitent dog had the chance to apologize for accidentally frightening it so. Several small holes dotted the ground here and there—homes of mice or moles, according to Beauregard, but homes of snakes, according to Atticus. Both Kit and Simon chose to believe Beauregard.

The little group hadn't forgotten the horrible sound from the night before, however, and thus they were constantly keeping watch for any signs of dangerous animals. When all they found along the way were more flowers and small, defenseless creatures—like themselves—they began to think, full of hope, that maybe the frightening howl had merely been an extension of their fears.

The morning passed quite delightfully, and when they were hungry, they all found food to eat and a clear, cool spring to drink from just off the pathway. Simon, Beauregard, and Atticus were bending over the spring, drinking, when Simon mused, "Notice how cold it is? That's because the source is snow—snow that's melting from the very top of the mountain."

Beauregard was pensive for a moment and then said stoically, "Snow's not cold."

Simon chuckled at him and splashed a handful of water onto the dog's nose. "Sure it is! Haven't you ever played in snow? Or built a snowman?" He stopped a moment, adding, "Oops. I guess you'd build a snow*dog*, huh?"

"Yup. The dowger built a snowdog once. Inna snow. What was warm."

"You know there's no sense trying to convince him otherwise," Atticus put in, turning towards Simon and rolling his eyes. "Once Beauregard believes something, it becomes absolute truth in that vast wasteland of his mind. I'm slowly learning it's completely futile to argue with him. He remains in a fog; you grow frustrated. So leave the poor dog blissfully ignorant."

Simon patronizingly patted Beauregard on the head. "Okay, whatever you say, Beauregard. Snow is warm. And snowballs and snowdogs can be made from warm snow. Right?"

He waggled his tail and gave Simon a lick across the cheek. "The dowger says *right*!"

"See?" Atticus whispered into Simon's ear. "He's beyond sarcasm. It's so much easier if you just keep the simple ones happy." He winked at Simon. "Humor them. That's what I advise."

The remainder of the afternoon, as they continued their steady climb upwards, Atticus could be heard mumbling now and then, "Yes sir! Snow is warm. Quite warm! Might even be considered hot to the touch to some. Absolutely scalding, scintillating, seething. Oh yes, indeed," or some such thing. This always caused Beauregard to whirl excitedly in a circle or two, eliciting giggles from Simon and Kit. Atticus was, therefore, characteristically pleased with his constant little jokes at Beauregard's expense. (Not that Beauregard would notice; it was quite impossible to insult him. As a matter of fact, each time Atticus uttered another little ditty, Beauregard took it as unqualified agreement.)

⚮

The next morning, they awoke from a pleasant sleep.

As usual, Kit's eyes popped open first, and immediately he realized something was definitely out of the ordinary, for he was covered with a soft white powder. Tiny, intricate flakes covered him and everything and everyone around him.

He cupped his chubby hands around it, finding that it easily scrunched up into a little ball. Chuckling, Kit sent the ball flying right onto Atticus' sleeping head—oh, of course it had to be this particular head that he accidentally whumped.

"Oomph! What on earth?" Atticus grumbled. He wasn't generally good-humored first thing in the morning anyway, and to be awakened by being bopped in the head…well, that was just too much for any sane creature to endure. Atticus sat up, rubbing the offended spot and spying out the offender. Kit had immediately lain back down next to his mama and papa, but the telltale giggling couldn't be suppressed. His tummy was wobbling and bobbing something fierce.

"Kit! What's the big idea of—?" It wasn't until that exact moment when Atticus, finally prying his sleepy eyes all the way open, noticed the delicate white powder all over them and everything around them. "Hey! What *is* this stuff?"

"It's snow! The dowger *loves* snow!" Beauregard exclaimed happily, and he immediately began to merrily romp around, burying his nose, rolling around on his back with all four legs kicking up in the air, and finally, vaulting about like some giant jackrabbit with enormous springs. Of course, Kit tagged around after the silly dog, laughing hilariously at all his antics and managing to mimic every act rather well, too.

Needless to say, everyone else was awakened (rather abruptly from all the carousing around) and all were surprised and delighted by the snow—a *warm* covering of snow, which Kit proceeded to point out to Atticus.

"Boy! This snow sure feels wonderful!" Kit began. He had a snowball in each fist as he faced Atticus. "It also feels *warm*—just like Beauregard said it would. It's not—let's see, what were some of the words you used?—scalding, sin-till-ting, or seeing." (Kit had a difficult time with words of multiple syllables.) But it sure enough is warm!" What Kit did next has been repeated down through the centuries by children ever since there have been children and snow. He threw both snowballs at Atticus's nose. One missed. The other was right smack on target.

Anyone can imagine what happened next. War had been declared, and the battle was on. Kit and Atticus were already in the thick of it, and now Caleb, Mr. and Mrs. Beaver, and Mary joined in. (One might wonder how animals with hooves or paws or claws could form snowballs, but they all managed rather well.) Snowballs flew through the air, some pelting their intended targets, more landing accidentally on heads or backs or bottoms that just happened to get in the way. Those misfires produced even more snowballs to "get even," the natural course every snowball fight takes, as everyone well knows.

Poor Beauregard was truly at a loss, however. The only purpose he understood balls to have was for *chasing*. Every time one went flying through the air, Beauregard attempted to retrieve it. Of course, the snowballs broke into bits as soon as they hit their targets—whether the ground or an animal— and that left the simple dog absolutely bewildered. Thus for the entire snowball fight, Beauregard ran frantically from one target to another after burying his head in the snow (which stuck to his muzzle, making him look as though he had a white beard) while searching for the non-existent balls. Only Beauregard could be smack in the middle of a grand snowball fight and miss the entire battle.

Eventually they grew tired of this sport, however, and turned their attention to making snow angels and other various snow creatures: a snowdog (of course), snowbeavers (one for each member of the family), snowbirds, snowdeer and one snowman. They took turns flopping over into some fresh snow and pumping legs up and down, cheering on everyone's efforts. Atticus insisted such childish activities were beneath him, but when it was discovered he was secretly using that time to sneak about and make more snowballs, the battle was on again. Except this time around, Atticus had a definite advantage due to his ready-made pile of weapons.

They were all in the midst of another mad frenzy of running about through a mass of airborne snowballs when a sharp cry from Mrs. Beaver brought all activity to a sudden halt. She had ventured a ways out from the group (searching for fresh ammunition), and everyone came running, assuming she'd been injured by an errant missile.

"What is it, my dear?" Mr. Beaver asked, his voice full of concern.

Kit came scampering up to latch onto her too, crying out, "Mama! Are you all right?"

Mrs. Beaver's wide eyes and opened mouth reflected no pain—only stark terror—and she held them back while pointing a shaking finger to the ground just beyond them. "Look there," she whispered huskily, panic clipping her words. "Look at the tracks in the snow!"

They recognized immediately that no one in their group had made the tracks, for they were huge. A large pad was clearly visible, with an accompanying imprint of four shockingly long, sharp claws.

"Oh my. Oh my," Atticus mumbled. "What creature is that, Caleb? I don't suppose they could be your prints, Beauregard? Were you wandering around over here?"

Beauregard shook his head. "The dowger was playing in the warm snow with Kit. The dowger wasn't over here."

"Besides," Mary added, "these are much bigger than yours would be, Beauregard." She glanced around at them, quickly measuring the extent of their fear. "Put your foot next to one paw print, Beauregard, and let's compare."

Beauregard lumbered over to the frightening tracks and stood still for just a moment before backing away. And then seven noses and one beak studied the Beauregard print, contrasting it to the unknown one beside it.

It was twice as big, and the nails were more than twice as long.

They were all so terrified that no one uttered a sound for a few moments. Atticus whispered, "No wonder the creature's howl sounded so ghastly, so evil. It's a wolf, Mary. A *giant* wolf. How can eight defenseless creatures survive against something like that?"

"Come away from here," Mary encouraged them. "Let's gather under the willow where we slept, and we'll discuss this."

It was a somber group that returned to the snow creatures and remaining snowballs—acute reminders of such carefree happiness only moments ago— and plopped down onto the snow-covered ground. Their eyes constantly darted beyond their little group, seeking out any movements among the trees surrounding them, any strange shadows, or any sounds of breaking twigs and rustling branches. Instead of sitting in a semi-circle, facing Mary, the animals all pointed their sensitive noses outwards, towards the forest.

"This will never do," Caleb immediately announced. "We must designate guards from now on. Take turns at watches. That way only the assigned sentry will need to be constantly alert while the remainder rests. I volunteer to take the first watch so the rest of you can turn your attention to Mary." Caleb flew up into the graceful, swaying branches of the willow. "I'm going to follow the tracks," he told them, "and see where they came from, where they're going. That should give us some knowledge of what this animal is about. Any words for me before I leave?"

"Be careful," Kit said, as he snuggled up against his mama and stuck a thumb into his mouth.

Caleb smiled, nodding his head, and flew off in the direction of the dreadful prints.

They waited for his return, fidgeting a good bit in their anxiousness. Though they all watched diligently for Caleb, when he returned and his shadow passed over Atticus and Mary, they jumped. Atticus immediately scrambled up to the top of Simon's head again, frantically clutching tufts of hair.

"*Atticus.* Get down! Why on earth must you insist on perching on my head every time you're scared?" Simon grumbled. "And please, bald may look good on you, but I'd like to keep my hair, if you don't mind!"

Atticus looked a bit chagrined at his over-reaction. He recovered his dignity in no time, nimbly jumping off Simon's head and making his way across his shoulder—even seeming to swagger a bit as he did so. He eased down Simon's arm to the ground, where he proceeded to gracefully sit and give them all a very supercilious look, insisting, "Actually, I only climbed up there to take a quick look around. For everyone's protection." He cleared his throat. "A-hem."

"Is the view better atop Simon-by-the-Way's head? The dowger could look, too," Beauregard asked, leaning forward on his haunches as if he were ready to pounce onto Simon's head.

"Absolutely not!" Simon fumed, and he gingerly patted his head, searching for any bald spots. "The top of my head is not a lookout post!"

"Of course it isn't," Caleb said calmly. "I'll always have the best vantage point from the air. Let's all compose ourselves a bit now. Take deep breaths. Be reasonable." He winked at Simon, and turned to meet everyone's eyes with a reassuring look. "The trail indicated the creature came down from way up the mountain and then retraced its tracks. It's nowhere near us anymore."

In a matter-of-fact tone, Simon stated, "But it came to seek us out. To check on our progress."

"We can't know that for certain, Simon-by-the-Way."

"Oh, can't we? Mary thinks so." Simon turned to face her, searching for the truth in her eyes.

"I'm not the one to ask. Beauregard is," Mary replied, and they all looked expectantly towards the great dog, who wearily laid his head on Simon's sneakers.

Beauregard slowly rolled his sorrowful eyes up to meet Simon's. "He is the one. Blue eyes mirror the rage and pain." Sighing, Beauregard said no more.

CHAPTER 13

"Beware the Jabberwock, my son!
The jaw that bite, the claws that catch!
Beware the Jubjub bird, and shun
The frumious Bandersnatch!

He took his vorpal sword in hand:
Long time the manxome foe he sought—
So rested he by the Tumtum tree,
And stook awhile in thought.

And, as in uffish thought he stood,
The Jabberwock, with eyes of flame,
Came Whifflling through the tulgey wood,
And burbled as it came!"

They were all mystified by Beauregard's response, for the simple dog never used such things as riddles or symbols or pronouns, even. Atticus poked a bony finger into Beauregard's ribs. "Speak plainly. What on earth does that bit of nonsense mean, Beauregard?"

He shrugged his shoulders. "The dowger doesn't know."

"You don't know? Well, of course, that makes perfect sense!" Atticus put a hand on each hip and stood frowning at the poor dog, whose only response was to thump his tail against the ground. "You haven't understood one minuscule part of this entire journey, and still we've followed your great words of wisdom to the Great Sand, across a violent river, and now you ask us to believe in a response which even you admit to not having the slightest understanding of its meaning!"

Beauregard grinned at him. "Yup. That's what the dowger says."

"This is all part of the journey, don't you see?" Mary asked.

"But what does it mean—'blue eyes mirror the rage and pain'?" Simon anxiously looked to Mary for an answer, subconsciously chewing his bottom lip and rubbing his hands together. He avoided looking into Mary's eyes because a glaring truth convicted him: Simon was the only one in their little group with blue eyes.

Mary shook her head. "I'm sorry, Simon-by-the-Way. I have no answers for you. But even though I don't understand this prophecy now, I assume we all will, eventually. One truth I do know, however: the Father of all Creatures sent this snow as a merciful protection for us, to help us discover the animal's tracks. Because of His gentle care, we've been warned of the animal's presence and we can plan to be on guard. Just think of the miracle! Snow—amazingly warm, to keep us from being cold. Recording paw prints, to warn us of the animal's proximity. And glowing white, to illuminate any creature skulking about at night. What a gift!"

Beauregard thumped his tail again. "The dowger knowed the snow would be warm." He turned to Atticus, giving him a wide grin. "And Atticus agreed with the dowger. Atticus knowed the snow would be warm too, huh, Atticus?"

Marveling at the extent of the dog's simpleness, Atticus could just barely be heard to mutter, "Even agreeing with the dog is dangerous. Is there no limit to his muddleheadedness? Unbelievable."

"But how do we proceed?" Barton interjected, ever concerned for the safety of his family. "How can we protect ourselves from this horrible creature?"

"We'll always be on guard—all of us," Caleb stated, assuming an authoritative voice to reassure them. "I'll fly about our little company as we travel, sometimes scouting out a good ways, watching for any movement. Whenever we stop—to eat, drink, rest or sleep at night—we'll take turns at the watch. We'll know if it comes anywhere near us again."

Simon looked skeptical. "But those plans only tell us if it's here. What will we do if we see it?" He glanced about the little group, suddenly realizing how utterly defenseless they were. "What could we possibly do if…if it decides to attack us?"

There was complete silence for a moment. Not even breathing could be heard, for they all held their breaths as they contemplated the horror Simon had placed before them.

"We'll be cared for in the same manner we have been since we took the very first step on this long journey," Mary whispered into the quiet, "by the Father of all Creatures' strong and yet gentle hand. Alone, we are totally defenseless and at the beast's mercy. But we are *not* alone. Nor have we ever been. We cannot see him. But He is with us!"

Empowered and emboldened with the vision of the Father's protective great hand around them, the little company continued bravely up the mountain. The snow eventually disappeared, although Simon was terribly confused about how and where it went. (This was one time when he wished he could be like Beauregard, easily and simply accepting things at face value, unanswered questions not pestering at him.) It seemed to melt away just like the snow he had always known, but because this unique snow wasn't cold—it had existed for some time in the warm sun of the morning—it didn't really *thaw*. It appeared to just slip away into the crevices and tiny holes of the rich soil covering the mountain.

No one veered off the pathway, and everyone kept a close eye upon the wiggly, rambunctious Kit, who was prone to ambitious wandering about. Kit was terribly disappointed that he was no longer allowed to pick flowers—the best ones, the most tempting blooms, were always just off the trail. Mrs. Beaver was quite insistent that it was entirely too dangerous. Caleb and Mary agreed, giving everyone the strictest of instructions to stay extremely close to the group. If anyone was hungry or thirsty, they were to venture out only as a group.

Caleb constantly flew above them, widening his circle of patrol now and then so he could reassure everyone no danger was near. His vigilance was a great comfort to them all. Surprisingly, they slept peacefully throughout the long night as Caleb, Barton, Simon, and then Beauregard each took a turn at keeping watch. The gentle snowfall returned, illuminating the mountainside in the soft moonlight just as Mary had said it would. Each sentry could clearly discern any unusual movements, any shifting of shadows not a normal part of the mountain's nightly rhythm and pattern. Yet, as they continued their climb up the pathway the next morning, they came upon the tracks once again.

Simon was instantly filled with terror. "It came down again. To see how far we've come. To see how far *I've* come!"

"No! You mustn't think that way," Mary insisted, and she nudged at Simon until he would turn towards her instead of staring at the frightening prints in the snow. "You know our foremost rule is that we'll always stay together, always face whatever is ahead of us as one, for in this unity comes our strength. Simon-by-the-Way, you mustn't think you will face this creature, whatever it is, by yourself. If it confronts us, then we shall fight it together. And the Father of all Creatures will be our protector!"

Simon nodded his head, but there was a hint of something in what Mary said, in the way she said it. Fear still pounded in his heart, and along with it, suspicion.

Caleb flew ahead once again and determined the beast had traveled down from above and then retraced its steps. As they climbed higher and higher, they were all aware that the distance between them and their adversary diminished with each passing hour. No longer was there a safe span to separate them from whatever it was that watched them, or from what they feared hunted them. There would be no singing this day, no light-hearted bantering or teasing. They were tense, and all eyes constantly darted this way and that, searching the forest for any strange movements or sounds. When they lay down to sleep on the third night of their journey up the mountain, they found only a fitful sleep awaited them. Just as the creature stealthily pursued them in the moonlit night, it also lurked about in the corners of their minds, pursuing them in the hazy images of frightening dreams.

It was with heavy and fearful hearts they began the fourth day's journey. They knew they were not far from the top of the mountain—and whatever it was that awaited them there.

The haggard little group set out at a near crawl, dragging and shuffling feet through the snow at a slow, pitiful pace. The difficulty was that no one wanted to be the first to come upon the dreaded tracks. Everyone was most certain the tracks were out there somewhere…waiting to be discovered. So they purposefully dawdled, climbing at such a sluggish pace that Kit could stand it no longer.

"Come on, everybody!" he fussed at them. "We've already gone a good distance—even as slow as we're going—and we haven't seen anything. Maybe the nasty beast has decided to leave us alone after all!"

"Kit's right," Caleb said. "Maybe the creature has given up. I'm going to fly up the mountain a ways and see if there's any sight of it. I'll be back soon."

They watched Caleb fly off, and then they scoured the immediate vicinity for any signs of the tracks. They were so intent that they were surprised by Caleb's quick return. He was obviously elated and anxious to share good news as he happily fluttered above them, winging excitedly from one tree branch to another with a bad case of the fidgets.

"Caleb, would you kindly settle on a suitable perch and bless us with your news," Atticus instructed. "It's quite apparent you have something good to share and we are in dire need of a bit of a 'picker-upper.' Now stop flustering and deliver your verdict if you please!"

"Oh, my. Oh, yes," Caleb puffed. He was out of breath—partly from the air at higher elevation and partly because of sheer excitement—and could barely speak. "Wonderful news: I saw (*pant, pant*) absolutely no sign of the creature (*let me catch my breath!*) whatsoever. No tracks. No prints. Nothing!"

"Mama, will it leave us alone now? Is it gone away for good?" Kit asked.

"I pray so, little one," his mama answered, giving Kit a quick hug. "Oh, how I pray so."

Simon looked over at Mary, searching her eyes for some clue of what she thought the news meant for them…for him. But she was closed to him, closed to them all as she stared intently towards the top of the mountain. And Mary said not one word as she simply began climbing, silently, up the pathway.

"Is Mary excited to get to the very top? The dowger is," Beauregard playfully asked, as he ran boisterous circles around her.

But Mary appeared to not even hear or see him. She merely stared ahead, climbing steadfastly towards the goal that was now so close.

Too close, Simon thought to himself.

Their trek soon turned much more difficult, however. They encountered huge boulders, one after another, pressing up against each other in such a way that they couldn't simply hike around them. Instead, they were forced to climb over the great stones. No sooner would they manage to scale one, pausing a moment to catch their breaths (all of them were experiencing shortness of breath due to the altitude), when they would discover yet another they needed to scale. The boulder trail seemed endless and they were dispirited and nearly exhausted, when finally the terrain changed once more.

They emerged above the tree line, and there they stood in amazement, gaping at the view before them. The starkness of the landscape was a profound change: from forest to sparse undergrowth; from shade to being laid bare before the elements; from a focus on the ground which made them feel like an insignificant part of the mountain, to a focus out and beyond and up which compelled them to survey the very world, it seemed. The view was majestic and frightening at the same time. They were nearly to the top, and suddenly they felt exposed and incredibly vulnerable. For the first time, they were cold, as the piercing winds beat against them, penetrating even thick fur until their bodies shivered violently from its effects.

"Mama," Kit shouted, for his little voice was nearly carried off by the wind, "my teeth are shaking!"

She smiled down at him, wrapping her arms about him in an attempt to provide a mother's nurturing warmth. "I think you mean they're chattering, dearest."

"That, too!" Kit exclaimed, and he snuggled even tighter up against her.

But the moment of tenderness was shattered by a scream, a cry of absolute terror that was sucked into the vast expanse below them by the relentless wind. Simon crumpled and dropped to his knees, instantly weak and cowering. He didn't move a muscle, but sat rigid in his terror, never taking his eyes from the specter that stood on a crag of the mountain just above them. It was all their greatest fears: the wolf.

Silhouetted against a suddenly overcast sky, the massive animal's ears were raised and alert as it sought to catch their slightest intake of breath. Its great mouth hung open and panting, as if it eagerly awaited them. Dark grey with uneven blotches of black, the beast glared down upon them, evil radiating from luminous, malevolent eyes. What shocked them most was the color; the wolf's eyes were a startling blue. They stared intently at only one target, piercing into the mirror-image eyes of Simon.

Beauregard darted to plant himself firmly in front of the entire company, and he hung his head low to the ground, ears held tensely back and jowls raised, baring threatening teeth. A fierce growl rumbled deep in his throat and he hunched even lower. He took one slow step forward in warning to the wolf that he, Beauregard, intended to give no ground, that he would defend his friends—*to the death*.

"No, Beauregard!" Mary cried out to him in a panic-stricken voice. "This isn't your battle!" But Mary didn't move—not towards Beauregard and not towards the wolf still crouched above them. In that moment, Simon knew without doubt exactly what Mary meant, what she intended. *You will meet yourself*, she'd told him, and Simon had felt taunted by the words. Mary had constantly alluded to the journey being the most dangerous for Simon, how he would struggle to *know himself*, that this *face-to-face* meeting would be excruciatingly painful. Simon nearly laughed out loud in his delirious terror. *All along Mary planned for this to be* my *battle*, Simon thought. *She expects me— Simon-by-the-Way as they all call me—to lead the way, to solely fight the great wolf, to save the rest of them so they can complete the journey up the mountain. Well, I won't do it!*

Tearing his eyes from the beast before him, Simon looked at Mary with raging hate. "You always meant for this to happen!" he spat out at her. "Why do you hate me so much? Why does everybody hate me? My father, now you—" Simon glared at them all in righteous judgment "—every one of you! And your Father of all Creatures, your God…if He planned this journey as you say, then he hates me the most. Well, I won't give my life for you. I won't!"

Simon jumped up and bolted back down the mountain, escaping the horror behind him, leaving the creatures who had betrayed him. Stumbling, falling as he flung himself blindly down the pathway, Simon watched the dirt trail change to pavement right before his eyes. No longer was he racing down a mountain; instead, he was tearing across his own familiar street. He could hear Abbey calling to him in a plaintive wail, "Simon, hurry! Come help me. I need you. *Simon!*"

CHAPTER 14

"But I don't want to go among mad people,"
Alice remarked.
"Oh, you can't help that," said the Cat:
"we're all mad here. I'm mad. You're mad."
"How do you know I'm mad?" said Alice.
"You must be," said the Cat, "or you wouldn't
have come here."

Simon instantly realized where Abbey was and why she needed him. Instinct directed him to the source of Abbey's distress—Mr. McCauley, the mean neighbor who had threatened Simon many times. For some reason, Abbey must have ventured into Mr. McCauley's yard, and the grumpy old man intended to make her pay dearly for trespassing on his precious manicured lawn. *I won't let him put a finger on her,* Simon fumed to himself. *I'll show him—I will!* The anger he'd felt towards Mary was seething and boiling nearly uncontrollably by now, and Simon was ready to give vent to it. He would gladly give Mr. McCauley the privilege of feeling the effects of the explosion of that pent-up rage.

Simon ran with all his might, furiously pumping arms and legs as he jumped over uneven cement and assorted neighborhood toys scattered about. "I'm coming, Abbey," he mumbled, pushing himself even faster. Over and over in his mind he promised this: *For once, just this once, I will protect her. I will protect her!*

As he approached Mr. McCauley's yard, he slowed his pace slightly in order to search for any sign of Abbey or the hated old man. Simon's eyes traveled to Mr. McCauley's garden, planted in perfectly measured rows; to the cement porch stretching along the entire front—complete with *No Trespassing!* and *No Soliciting!* signs all along the porch railing; to the wide strip of grass along the right side of the house.

That strip was the route Simon had biked across before, the shortcut kids in the neighborhood used consistently. It was the object of dares proposed and accepted, the starting point for initiation rites, the place where the challenge was such a temptation that every child in the neighborhood had scooted across that short stretch of grass at some point in his or her childhood journey just for the privilege of boasting, *"Hey! I crossed old McCauley's property. And survived!"* Simon immediately chose to head there, not hesitating for even a moment. He crossed the line from sidewalk to Mr. McCauley's property and found Abbey, frantically darting back and forth in the far back corner of the lot.

Simon had once witnessed a neighbor's dog cornering a stray cat. The poor tabby had rushed wildly back and forth like a crazed creature until it was trapped with no place to go, finally screaming in terror—a scream Simon could still plainly hear in his memory. Now Abbey was caught and entrapped in much the same manner, being pursued by Mr. McCauley, complete with an upraised cane, ready to strike. Simon covered the remaining ground in a heartbeat, screaming out *No!* at the top of his lungs. He lunged forward, pitching his entire body at Mr. McCauley's knees in an attempt to knock him down.

The cane flew from the outstretched hand, dropping a safe distance away. Both Mr. McCauley and Simon went sprawling onto the grass—Mr. McCauley falling with a great *"oomph!"* onto his side while Simon tumbled and rolled several times before finally coming to a stop up against the fence behind Abbey. She rushed over to Simon and huddled down next to him, clutching at his arm and sobbing hysterically, "Oh, Simon. You came just in time! I was only chasing after my ball and he was going to hit me. I didn't do anything bad—honest, Simon, I didn't!"

"You hoodlums!" Mr. McCauley spit out from between clenched teeth as he readjusted the thick-lensed glasses, ran a hand through thinning hair and slowly raised himself up onto one elbow to glare at them. "If you've thrown out my back I'll sue you for every penny you've got! Just wait 'til your mother hears about this. I'd tell that good-for-nothing father of yours too if he were still alive, but—"

"You just shut up about him!" Simon hissed back at the old man. "And he wasn't a good-for-nothing, either!"

Mr. McCauley sat up easily—Simon was convinced the old grouch was too hardened and mean to sustain any type of injury—and groped about for his cane. "Juvenile delinquents. Spoiled brats. Incorrigible little heathens. That's what the entire pack of you neighborhood kids are!" Locating the cane and clutching it between knotted fingers, he used it as a crutch and pulled himself up. Simon and Abbey clung to each other, staring up at Mr. McCauley with wide eyes, paralyzed in fear. "I'm going to call the cops on you, that's what I'll do. But first I'm going to give you something that evidently your father never did. And he *was* a good-for-nothing, 'cause it's plain the drunk never did discipline either of you two brats worth a hoot. Well, somebody certainly needs to. And that's why I'm going to give you both a good, old-fashioned beating right now!"

"Run, Abbey!" Simon yelled as he pushed her up and away from him all at once. Abbey nearly fell as she was propelled forward, caught her balance at the last moment and ran frantically towards home, never pausing to look back until she reached the safety of the street. Only then did she turn around to see how Simon was faring.

Abbey saw Mr. McCauley—and it was as if he moved in eerie slow motion—raise his cane into the air over his head. His silhouette was bent and gnarled from his aged form, but as he rose above Simon, he looked to be a giant compared to the slight form huddled beneath him. Simon reacted instinctively, repeating what he had done countless times in the past. He put both hands out before him in one simple, pitiful act of submission. Cowering prostrate before the old man, Simon waited, flinching, for the blows to come.

He felt them fall, as he always had when his dad threw his raging fists or belt; but at the same time...he didn't. Oh, he felt the pain on his fragile skin. Simon would carry the evidences of this beating—black-and-blue marks that joined faded ones given earlier by his father. The memories, however, would be pushed into a hidden recess of his mind that Simon wouldn't allow himself to even admit existed. As always, Simon would create a new reality; in his mind, it would be another child who received the sting of that wicked cane.

Ever so slowly, though, sounds of other voices reached him—voices screaming hysterically until Simon finally looked up to see Abbey standing on the sidewalk, sobbing and pointing towards him. Then his mother was there, grabbing the cane from Mr. McCauley and heaving it out and away so violently it soared across the street before landing on the pavement and splintering into a dozen pieces. Gathering Simon into her arms and standing up in one swift motion, she cradled him like a baby, rocking back and forth and kissing his head. "Oh, Simon, my darling, my darling!" she mumbled over and over. She turned and gave Mr. McCauley a venomous stare, warning, "I want you to know I intend to call the police about this, Mr. McCauley. I've put up with your threats too long and now my children have paid the price for my negligence. Just like I tolerated my husband's drinking and bad temper until now, so that Simon just, he simply just…" She stopped suddenly, a sob catching in her throat. Turning her back to the old man, Laura carried Simon home.

Abbey tagged after her mom and Simon, weeping softly and feeling alarmed that Simon was being carried in their mother's arms—as if he were nothing more than a helpless baby. "Mommy," Abbey asked anxiously, "is Simon all right?"

"I don't know, Abbey," Laura replied, her words still catching in her throat. "Let's get him home and then we'll see, okay?"

Abbey opened the screen door and Laura crossed the threshold, gently laying Simon on the worn couch. She knelt on the floor next to him, pushing sweaty curls from his forehead and kissing him tenderly once again. "Simon, are you all right? Do I need to call an ambulance? Or should I take you to the doctor?"

Simon shook his head. "I'm all right, Mom, really I am. The old man is kind of frail, you know." He shrugged his shoulders. "I'm not even sure if he really hit me or just missed and—"

"Simon, I saw him hit you!" Laura's voice raised in intensity and volume with each word, and then she shook her head. Taking a deep breath and shutting her eyes a moment, Laura added in a softer voice, "You can't deny it this time, Simon. I saw him. *I saw what he did to you.*"

"I don't know what you *think* you saw, but I'm okay. Really I am." Simon's voice was calm, too unnervingly composed.

Laura stared at the raised, red welts on his arms, and without taking her eyes from the glaring marks, she asked, "Abbey, did Mr. McCauley hurt you at all?"

"No, Mommy. He tried, but Simon tackled him. Just like a really big football player! And then I ran quick to get you."

"Can you go up to your room and read for a while? I need to talk with Simon. Alone. Is that okay? Can you do that?" She turned to face Abbey, to gauge from Abbey's response if she was still too upset to be alone.

Abbey glanced from her mother to Simon and then nodded her head 'yes.' "Sure, Mommy. I have a book I'm supposed to read for school."

Laura pulled Abbey to her, giving her a quick, intense hug. "You're absolutely positive Mr. McCauley didn't hurt you?" She lightly ran her fingers along Abbey's arms, quickly scanned her legs and face. "He didn't touch you? You're sure you're perfectly all right?"

"I'm fine, Mommy. Simon came just in time." She smiled down at him, thanking him with her eyes. "I'll go upstairs now." She'd skipped up several steps before she stopped and asked, "Mommy, will the policemen arrest Mr. McCauley? Will he go to jail?"

Laura sighed. "I don't know, Abbey. But I certainly hope so."

"He said he was going to send me and Simon to jail. And we'd rot away there forever."

"Abbey, I promise you," Laura stated firmly and calmly, "neither you nor Simon is going to jail. If anyone is, it will be Mr. McCauley. Okay?"

Abbey nodded. "Okay."

She waited until Abbey's footsteps could be heard upstairs, and then Laura turned back to Simon. Easing into a more comfortable position on the floor, Laura leaned towards Simon while softly rubbing his cheek with one hand. "Simon, it's time we had an honest talk about your dad. About everything that's happened."

Simon avoided looking into her eyes. Lying on the couch, scrutinizing the cracked, peeling ceiling, he answered nonchalantly, "Okay. So what do you want to talk about?"

"First, I want you to know your dad wasn't always so...so angry. Or violent. When we first started dating, he could be incredibly gentle and tender." Tears filled her eyes, and she wiped at her nose. "Those times are hard to remember, but it's true. He once was a very kind man. But later, especially after you were born, he started changing, drastically."

"It was because of me," Simon stated emphatically, flatly. "I always knew it was my fault."

"No, Simon, that's where you're very wrong. You see, your dad's father beat him when he was young, so that was all your father knew. It was the only way he knew to work out his pain. And in his sick, twisted reasoning, the only way he could show you he cared. By doing the same thing to you his father had done to him."

"I've told you before, he hurt Abbey. Not me."

Laura was silent for a few moments, and then whispered softly, "Simon, look at me. Please."

He sighed as if irritated, but obeyed.

"I want you to sit up, okay?"

Simon sat up and faced his mom. She rose to a kneeling position before him and reached for his arms, gently turning them slightly so the wicked-looking welts were visible. Simon glanced down and winced.

"How did you get these, Simon?" She stared deeply into his bright blue eyes. When Simon attempted to look away, she gently pulled his chin back so he had to face her. "Look at these welts, son. How did you get them?"

"I, uh, I don't remember. Must've fallen off my bike again. Accidents happen, you know."

"You didn't fall off your bike just now. You got these welts another way, and you need to remember, Simon." She reached up to softly put a hand to each of his cheeks. Her eyes flooded with tears. "It's time, Simon. I'm here with you. I'll help you. It's time to remember the truth. Please?"

A few moments passed as he hesitated, deciding, and then his own indigo eyes filled with tears, too. The drops fell from his eyes, one after another, running down the pathways of his freckled cheeks, collecting in the cupped palms that his mother held to his face. "I always pretended it was either Abbey or another boy," Simon whispered, so softly she could barely hear him. "I'd hold out my hands, trying to stop him, but then…then I'd just kind of slip away in my mind." The tears continued to flow, heavier now, and his mother's tears flowed with his. "See, if it was someone else, well, then dad could still love *me*, Simon. 'Cause he couldn't ever love someone he'd beat like that. He couldn't possibly."

She was quiet for a moment, overwhelmed by his pain, *her* pain for him. "Oh, Simon, I know this must be almost impossible to grasp and believe, but he *did* love you. Somehow you just have to understand and accept what I'm saying. He was terribly sick, hurting too much inside. And I'm…I'm also to blame!" She stopped, choking on a sob but still not taking her eyes from Simon's, not reaching to wipe away the tears streaming down her face. "I didn't know, or else I chose not to know because of my own cowardice. Oh, my darling boy, can you ever forgive me?"

Simon fell into his mother's arms, and they sat on the floor while his mother tenderly rocked him back and forth. With one hand still on his wet cheek, she held him firmly against her chest, and the tears of mother and son mingled and became one as they sobbed out their hurt together.

Finally, the tears were spent, and the gentle rocking became the rhythm for a lullaby, one Simon's mother had used to soothe away many a hurt over the years. The sweet melody brought a quick dart of pain to Simon, however, for it was too reminiscent of Mary. "Mom," Simon asked, sniffing, "have you ever had a dream that was so real you thought you were really living the dream?"

She was pensive a moment before answering, "I guess so. Maybe when it was something I wanted so much…to be real. Hopeful dreams like that get so mixed up with truth that sometimes you can't tell the difference. Or else you don't *want* to tell the difference."

Simon took a deep breath and went on, "I've been dreaming about another place, Mom. A wonderful place with the first real friends I've ever had—a red-winged blackbird who's so beautiful. A beaver family with the cutest baby you've ever seen and this raccoon…well, you just have to meet him to believe what he's like. And there's this dog—oh, Mom, you know I've always wanted a dog and Dad would never let us get one. But this one is absolutely everything I've ever wanted a dog to be. You'd just laugh yourself silly to see him chase after his ball! And there's also a deer who, well, I don't know what she wants from me and I'm frightened and so confused." He nervously glanced up at Laura to see her reaction. "Do you think I'm going crazy?"

"No, my darling. I do not." She kissed his forehead. "Sometimes when we have such deep needs and we don't know how to even begin to understand them, we search for answers through different means. Through different ways, maybe, to attempt getting those needs met."

"Needs? What needs do I have?"

The emotion caught and lodged in Laura's throat, and she swallowed, struggling to answer, "You needed a father's love, Simon. You desperately wanted *God's* love."

Simon hesitated, reflecting on what she'd implied, and asked, "And you still think Dad loved me?"

"I know he did, Simon. You should have seen the glow in his eyes the first time he held you. Such a tiny bundle in his arms! And he cradled you to him as if you were the most precious thing on earth."

"Are you sure that wasn't Abbey? 'Cause Mom, it's *me* he hated. Only me." Simon swallowed, collecting his courage, speaking barely above a whisper. "He never beat Abbey. He only hit me. Honest, Mom, it's not that I wanted Abbey to…you know. I wasn't jealous of her. It's just that then I knew it was only me he hated."

She pulled his chin up so he had to look into her eyes. "No, Simon, believe me—he did love you, and he did once hold you with loving hands. But it all got lost and mixed up in his sick mind. His father abused him, and so he passed that onto you, his *son*. As you grew, I saw the subtle changes in him, the warning signs of his past abuse. But I never actually saw him beat you, and you wouldn't tell me, and down deep…well, I just didn't want to believe it could really happen to us." Laura paused a moment. "I was afraid and in denial, Simon, but I still should've sought help. And that's exactly what we need to do now. Our pastor has recommended a counselor, and I want us all to go. Will you do that?"

Simon sighed. "I suppose, if you want me to."

"He talked to me about how you'd naturally confuse your dad's love— and apparent lack of it—with God's. Oh, Simon, you must know—this one thing is more important than anything else I've told you today—you absolutely *must* know and believe that God loves you. He loves you dearly and completely, accepting you just as you are. He is *not* cruel and He doesn't seek to hurt his children."

"But I've been hurting. For as long as I can remember." The pain in his voice was tangible, weary in the way of an old man. Laura sought to hug him to her so fiercely that the hurt could somehow leave her son…and become her own instead.

"Pain is a part of living in this world, Simon. No one has all happiness— and no pain. I know you've had more to bear than any child should ever know. But God didn't do that to you, Simon. He doesn't want His children to suffer." She struggled for the right words, the explanations that would drive him *towards* God, not away. "Our pastor was just talking to me about Jesus's pain, how He'd never done anything wrong, not a single thing! Yet He suffered tremendously—to the point of dying for me, for my sin. And for you, Simon, and your sin."

"I tried to be good so Dad would love me. It never helped any."

"You don't have to earn God's love, Simon. And as a matter of fact, you can't. He simply gives it freely. You just accept the gift."

Simon was silent for a few moments before he huskily whispered, "I can't just yet. There's too much…still too much unsettled."

"In what way? What do you mean?"

He pulled away from her in his obvious embarrassment. "The dream. I know this sounds weird, but there's so many things I don't understand yet. And somehow I just know that…that the answers I need still are there. In the dream."

Laura's eyes widened and she sucked in her breath. "Simon, remember what we said. A hopeful dream seems real only because we want it to be real. Because, for a time, we need it to be. But we have to go beyond that at some point. We've got to let go and try to understand what drove us there—"

"I know why I went there, Mom. But I don't understand the purpose of it all—why the journey was necessary and what 'the Way, the Truth, and the Life' means."

She drew her brows together, puzzled. "Jesus said *He* was the Way, the Truth, and the Life, Simon. It means He alone is our salvation, that He would be the sacrifice for our sins. You must've heard that verse in Sunday school."

"But me, the dog, and the deer…oh, never mind. I can't even begin to explain it all, Mom, it's so confusing. I just know I have to go back. I have to see it to the end."

Something in Simon's explanation was alarming to her, and she grabbed up his hands. "Simon, I'm worried. In the morgue, I remember…you said something like, 'I killed them.' And I've always wondered about that. Were you confusing reality with this dream somehow?" To his answering nod, she continued, "I don't know why—this makes absolutely no sense at all—but for some reason I sense this is dangerous. You're just too vulnerable." She blurted out, "Let's go see the counselor this afternoon. I'll call him right now and we can—"

"Look at the time, Mom," Simon said, pointing towards the tired old cuckoo hanging next to the front door. "It's nearly six o'clock." He deliberately worked to keep his voice calm, keeping the very real terror he felt coursing through him from being heard in his words—and from showing on his face.

"We'll go tomorrow. Promise. Okay?" He smiled up at her innocently.

Laura hesitated for just a moment, but finally assessed that coupling the tremendous strain of today with seeing a counselor for the first time would be too much for Simon to handle. She'd pushed him incredibly far already, and she sensed Simon could take no more. "Okay. But only because you promised to go tomorrow. And as early as we can get an appointment, agreed?" She lightly ran her fingers across his still-red welts, holding him at arm's length, and said, "We've just barely scratched the surface of all this, Simon. But it's a good start, a wonderful beginning. You've been awfully brave and I'm so proud of you." Once again Laura gave him a hug and added, "Now, how about if you help me get supper started—stick the leftover meat loaf in the microwave—while I call the police. I'm going to press charges against Mr. McCauley and I want them to see these welts and bruises."

The police came later that evening, taking down Simon and Laura's statements. They made no promises, but assured them they would do their best to see that Mr. McCauley suffered the consequences for his actions. Laura, Abbey, and Simon peered through the cracks in the front curtains as the policemen proceeded to Mr. McCauley's house. In all the excitement and unsettling questions and unusual attention, Simon still felt uneasy and distracted, distanced somehow from all that was happening. It was as if his heart and mind were really somewhere else…in another world, in a dream world inhabited by a deer, a dog…and a terribly confused boy.

When his mother came to kiss him good-night and tuck him into bed, she nervously fidgeted with Simon's covers. Positioning the sheet one way and then yanking the bedspread another, continually looking for excuses to stay a while longer in his room, she lingered, nagging at Simon about leaving "dirty clothes lying all over the floor." She pointed out his dresser drawers, which were "so messy he'd never be able to find anything in here," and fretted about his plants from his science project, which he "hadn't watered regularly and so certainly would never grow adequately now."

Responding to her anxiousness, Simon remarked casually, "Mom, I'm really worn out. I just want to go to sleep, okay?"

Laura moved over to Simon and eased down on his bed, reaching out to tenderly brush hair from his forehead. "You must be awfully tired. I hope you sleep well, darling." She leaned down and kissed his cheek but still sat there, hesitating, nervously twisting the wedding band she still wore. Then she asked, nonchalantly, "Do you suppose you'll have the same dream you were talking about before?" Her matter-of-fact voice was betrayed by her eyes, however, for they were alight with concerns for her son.

"Um, I doubt it. I think I'm so tired I'll sleep like a dog."

She grinned at him. "I think the expression is to sleep like a *log*."

"Oh, well, whatever. I bet I'm so exhausted I don't dream at all, Mom." He abruptly sat up and gave her a quick peck on the cheek. "See you in the morning." And then Simon snuggled down into the covers, closing his eyes as if he were already drifting off to sleep.

Laura sat there for a few moments and couldn't help but reach out to touch him. She pulled the covers up again and adjusted the sheet once more, smoothing out a wrinkle in the bedspread and patting Simon's arm. Finally, she leaned down to give him one last kiss on the top of his head. Standing up slowly, taking a deep, uneasy breath, she whispered, "I love you, Simon. So very much. Sweet dreams, my darling." Finally, she reached to turn out the light.

Simon yawned and mumbled, "I love you too, Mom." And then he was quiet and perfectly still, purposefully making his breathing audible and regular.

He listened to her footsteps pad across the hallway to check on Abbey and go down the stairs before he finally dared to open his eyes. When he could hear her in the kitchen washing the supper dishes, Simon reached down to search for the flashlight he kept beneath his bed.

He tested it under the covers first, flicking the tiny switch and feeling instant relief that the batteries were still good and the light was plenty bright. Then, cautiously, he eased out of bed and crept towards his dresser. He'd planned ahead, putting clothes out and leaving them lying purposefully on the floor, ready to slip on. Unfortunately, those were the very ones his mother had nagged him about, and she'd gathered them up to throw in the wash. Now he had to cautiously ease open drawers—avoiding the groan the dresser normally made—and pick out clothes without alerting his mother.

Once he was fully dressed and had tied on his sneakers, he tip-toed over to the mirror. This time, when he held up the flashlight and aimed the light onto its surface, he sucked in his breath in surprise. The light didn't reflect off the surface anywhere, and as Simon moved the light from one corner to another and up and down the entire length of it, the light moved through the mirror and was absorbed into the other world. The strange irregularity now covered every inch of the mirror.

He flicked off the light and sat back down on his bed, for suddenly his breathing was labored and he could feel his heart beating—pounding!—against his chest. *If I don't go through again,* Simon thought to himself, *I'll never know what it all means. I'll never be able to face myself in a mirror again. And I know that I'll never find God—The Father of all Creatures. Or Whoever He is.* He took a deep breath and put a trembling hand to his breast. *And if I do go through*—he put his hands over his eyes, almost as though he were seeing the horrendous scene unfold right before him—*I'll die!*

Tears came unbidden again, and they ran down already chapped cheeks from earlier weeping. "Like I told Mom before," he whispered to no one in the darkness, "my life has been full of nothing but pain for as long as I can remember. I guess I'd rather die anyway."

He wiped roughly at any remaining tears with the edge of his t-shirt. "Good-bye, Mom. Good-bye, Abbey. I love you both." Then Simon leaned forward into the portal for the last time and easily slipped through.

CHAPTER 15

"I can't believe that!" said Alice.
"Ca'n't you?" the Queen said in a pitying
tone. "Try again: draw a long breath,
and shut your eyes."
Alice laughed. "There's no use trying,"
she said: "one ca'n't believe
impossible things."
"I daresay you haven't had much practice,"
said the Queen. "When I was your age, I
always did it for half-an-hour a day. Why,
sometimes I've believed as many as six
impossible things before breakfast."

Simon tumbled into the other world, and all he could do was hope something would stop his wild, out-of-control descent as he somersaulted down the mountain pathway. He tucked his head as he rolled, banging elbows, knees, and shins against rocks and logs before he finally, mercifully, came to a halt when he wedged up against a tree. Attempting to catch his breath—and gather his courage—Simon sat there for a moment before he stood up on shaking legs. Then he ran back up the mountain towards the evil awaiting him there—towards his own death.

When he cleared the tree line Simon stopped, attempting to take in the entire scene unfolding before him. Beauregard still crouched tensely at the front of the group, growling, ready to pounce when needed. Something above attracted Simon's attention, and he glanced up to see Caleb erratically darting about while hysterically screaming out high-pitched, frantic *chack! chack!*s. Slightly off to one side, Atticus stood with both arms outstretched as he held back and protected the entire beaver family huddled behind him. Simon noted Mary, just apart from the rest of the group, visibly shivering in her fear

Summoning all the courage he could, Simon looked up to the rocks where the wolf had been standing over them. It hadn't yet moved from its position, but when it saw Simon, the terrifying creature lifted its jowls in an angry sneer, revealing the most wicked teeth Simon had ever seen. Yellow, long, and razor sharp, the teeth were highlighted by the cavernous mouth. With revulsion, Simon watched saliva drip from the huge jaws to the rocks below. The beast stretched out one huge paw as it jumped with powerful agility to the next lower rock. It was slowly, methodically making its way towards them.

Simon gasped, uncertain where to go and what to do, paralyzed by fear. One fact was horribly obvious as they all watched the wolf deliberately pick its way down the stony cliff: the wolf's eyes never left its prey. Those malevolent blue eyes still bored into Simon's—and Simon's alone.

"Simon," a voice soothingly whispered. Just a hint of a melody wrapped itself around the words. "It is for you, for your hate…for your pain…that I do this."

Simon heard the words, but he didn't note who spoke them, for all his attention was pulled towards the wolf—who suddenly reared up and lunged downward, effortlessly clearing the last pile of rocks. Picking up its pace, the great beast strode fiercely towards the little band. Each step forward was accentuated by massive front paws which dug into the ground, sending gouged clumps of dirt flying up into the air.

Beauregard leaned forward, slowly inching towards the beast before it could reach his friends. With the wolf still approaching at an incredible speed, however, Simon watched in utter amazement as Mary dashed towards Beauregard. Taking a giant leap with her powerful limbs, she lowered her head and rammed Beauregard's side, throwing her weight against the unsuspecting dog's ribs. Because of the tremendous force of the blow and because he was caught completely off-guard, Beauregard was thrown off balance and pushed away.

Seemingly oblivious to the tumbling dog and the deer, the wolf continued to bear down on its target; evil eyes stared into the terrorized, mirror-image eyes of Simon. It opened its massive mouth, revealing the sword-like teeth. Simon—as he had always done before—sucked in his breath, held out shaking hands and stood trembling, waiting for the inevitable pain to come. Nearly upon its prey and sensing the immediacy of the kill, the beast tensed to pounce forward on the helpless victim. Suddenly, Mary rushed forward again—and this time she moved directly into the path of the savage wolf.

Several voices screamed out—Kit's, Atticus's, Mrs. Beaver's—and Caleb swooped down at the wolf's massive head in a brave effort to capture its attention. But there was nothing to be done. The wolf shrugged off the small bird's insignificant attempt, and then the battle was over as quickly as it had begun. Simon watched, frozen in complete horror, as the beast vented its wrath upon the defenseless, fragile deer who had so courageously stepped into the danger. The wolf grabbed Mary by her throat—her beautiful, gracefully arching neck—and violently shook her, effortlessly tossing her body back and forth, instantly tearing at tender flesh and sending blood splaying across the ground at Simon's feet—Mary's blood, precious blood spilled so Simon might yet live.

When the monstrous creature finally dropped her broken body onto the ground, it raised its giant, grotesque head to the skies and howled out the victory of its kill. The sound echoed against the rocks and ripped at Simon's soul. The evil beast was no victor, no triumphant conqueror, however—for when the wolf turned to stare into Simon's eyes, it suddenly slipped away into nothingness. In a matter of seconds, it had vanished.

Caleb, Beauregard, Atticus, and the beavers all rushed to Mary's side, where they discovered she was still alive, though just barely. Only the slightest rise and fall of her side could be seen, her once lively limbs paralyzed. She stared ahead with unfocused, sightless eyes.

Poor, dearest Beauregard was absolutely beside himself, alternately howling, crying disconsolately, and pacing towards Mary and then away from her. "Oh, Mary! Dearest Mary!" he wailed over and over. "Why wouldn't Mary let the dowger fight the beast? Why did Mary push the dowger out of the way? Oh, Mary, *why*?"

Atticus, stunned silent and without even one word to utter in his grief, merely sat beside Mary, stroking her, petting her, attempting to ease her pain with a loving touch. Kit sobbed hysterically and clutched at Mary's fur with pudgy hands. He clung to her back in spite of the blood that covered her, that had splashed across the ground where the little company now hovered in their grief. Sitting hunched over with his wings covering his head, Caleb tried to hide his despair. Mr. and Mrs. Beaver clung to each other for comfort, as they had so many times before on the long journey. They huddled next to Mary's nose, waiting for any sign, any indication she might be able to speak to them. Only Simon, hesitant to approach Mary because of his overwhelming guilt in how he had so mistakenly misjudged her, slumped down a few feet away from them. Then Mr. Beaver leaned forward, as if he'd just heard something. He motioned for Simon to come near.

"Hurry!" Barton called out to him, beckoning anxiously. "There isn't much time!"

Simon couldn't take his eyes from Mary's eerily still form, and merely shook his head.

Beauregard stopped his nervous pacing, and, turning to face Simon, stated firmly, "The dowger says it's time, Simon-by-the-Way. Come to the Truth." In a much softer voice, he encouraged him, "The dowger loves you. The dowger will help you."

The remembrance of his mother's words moved and pushed against his mind…along with her touch, her tears, her love. After Beauregard nudged him gently with his nose—and Simon gave the loving dog a quick, impulsive hug for reassurance and courage—he rushed forward and fell to the ground by Mary. Clutching her by the neck, he buried his face in her blood-soaked fur.

"Oh, Mary!" he cried, choking out muffled words in between his uncontrollable weeping. "Can you ever forgive me for doubting you? For hating you? And why…oh, Mary, why did you do this for me? *Why* would you do this for me?"

She struggled to speak, to breathe deeply enough through the pain to say what she needed to. With a raspy voice filled with love, she whispered,

"Your hate will die with me, Simon-by-the-Way. And then you...you shall truly know the Father of all Creature's love for the first time. It's such a wondrous thing!"

His tears mingled with Mary's blood, and Simon could taste the sweetness of it as he continued to bury his guilty face in her coat. "But I'm not worthy of it! I wasn't worthy of my father's love. I'm not worthy of yours. And I could never be worthy of God's! How can I accept what I can't—what I'll never be able to earn?"

"Simon-by-the-Way," she struggled to say, for her labored breathing was becoming even more shallow. "Look into my eyes."

"I can't! Don't ask me to, Mary, *please*."

"Simon-by-the-Way, look into my eyes!"

Weak from his sobbing, Simon wearily lifted his head from the beloved fur, and turned to peer into the once-lovely eyes of the deer. They were clouded now, completely sightless, physically beautiful no longer. The realization pierced Simon's heart, but what was no longer lovely still contained Love. She spoke so softly that Simon needed to lean in right next to Mary; he could feel her fragile breath upon his cheek. Only then did Simon hear Mary whisper, "Say good-bye to my dear friends for me. Tell them I love them so much! And I have loved you, Simon-by-the-Way, more than—." Her eyes suddenly flew open wider and she gasped in pain. "Oh my dearest. Now know the Father's love!" Then Mary breathed no more.

"No, *please*. Don't leave me, Mary!" Simon cried, but her spirit was already gone.

As Simon continued to lie there, sobbing unashamedly with his face buried in Mary's fur, he felt a strange movement beneath him. The mountain itself began rumbling, almost rhythmically, as if a heart had just begun beating deep in the earth. The rest of the little band—who had been lying prostrate, weeping before their beloved friend—lifted curious faces to the sound, sniffing the air in their confusion. Suddenly, a great roaring rushed at them, a cacophony of sound that set everything in motion, blurring the lines and edges of rocks and trees and sky. Clouds and sun, caught up in the mass

of noise, swirled into the mighty *whoosh!* until they coalesced into something...
something entirely new. Out of chaos, disorder was taking form again with
lines and edges, but Simon couldn't yet make out what. Every member of
the company had inched backwards in fearsome awe, so that now they all
huddled together, wide-eyed, gaping at what slowly evolved before them: a
giant mirror. And just below the enormous mirror, abandoned, motionless,
and with eyes closed, lay Mary.

Simon and each one of the creatures in the little company gasped in
amazement and fear, for the mirror pulsated with a life of its own, and it was a
terrible thing. Reflecting each one's faults and weaknesses and sins in minute
detail, the mirror revealed all, and they were overcome with shame. They
bowed their heads, hiding themselves, cowering before the evidence proving
what Simon had just pointed out: No, Simon was not worthy. But neither
was anyone else. *Not one.* They had finished the journey; they had done as the
Father of all Creatures had asked. Mary had even given her very life. But it was
not enough. So as they lay prostrate before the mirror, they cowered in shame
and fear. For they only saw and knew their sin.

Is this what Mary meant by being fully known? Simon wondered, shivering
at the frightening sight before him—the blatant wickedness of his own heart.
But this is awful! How could she have wanted to see this?

And then they heard the Voice.

"My children," He said, and in those two words alone they recognized
many things—all they had ever longed for; completion; wholeness; healing, in
a way they could not even begin to describe. Each heard his or her own name
somehow, as though He were speaking to all, and yet to each one individually,
at once. *Caleb. Mr. Barton and the Mama. Kit. Atticus. Beauregard. Simon,* the
Voice said...and yet did not say. He indeed was Lord of All and yet each one's
Father at the very same moment. "I know you feel despair, for the mirror
only reflects back all your sin, condemning you. But there is hope, my dear
ones! Look up and view beyond the looking glass. See the One who alone can
transform darkness to light, death to life. Look through the mirror to see the
One who *is* worthy!"

Kit peeked up first, for he held the simple faith of a child. Drawing in a great breath of awe and wonder, Kit encouraged them, "Look up, Mama! Papa! Everyone! *Oh my.* He's just ever so…so *bee-utiful!*"

Meekly they raised their eyes to seek the One, and instantly all were held captive and spellbound by Him—a Man surrounded by an aura of blazing light—who stood beyond the mirror. At first they thought the light came from behind him, making him glow with a radiance which nearly blinded their eyes in its perfect purity, enabling them to view the Man even through the looking glass. They realized, however, that He *was* the Light, that the splendor emanated *from Him.*

The Man gazed down at the broken deer before him, holding out his hands, palms up. "Mary, my servant." Even though they knew Mary could no longer respond, it was as if he were beckoning her to him. "You have journeyed so faithfully. I forgive you all and now you shall have what you so desired. You shall see face to face!"

Suddenly the mirror moved and shifted within itself, metamorphosing until it was no longer a mirror. The reflecting silver shimmered and swirled up and out into the sky until there was nothing left but a perfectly clear sheet of glass, a giant pane devoid of imperfections, any flaws whatsoever. Simon and the creatures were astounded for the shaming reflections were gone—replaced and filled entirely with the Man's presence before them. When before Mary's image had simply been reflected back to them—with all of her flaws and the crimson blood evident upon her—now the perception completely changed. They no longer saw a mere reflected image of Mary, for her appearance was miraculously transformed to become like the splendorous One who stood before them. At the same time, she was still Mary, more beautiful and perfectly whole than they'd ever known her to be. She was fully like the Man— glorious in his image—and fully Mary, all in the same moment.

Clearly the glass was no ordinary pane, for the Man stretched out his arms right through it to them, and this time they noticed revealing pierce marks on his wrists. "I know my own children," he said, "and my own know me. Sweet Mary. Come to me now." He bent down, and, reaching through the glass again, tenderly picked up the beautiful deer and pulled her back through the pane where he gently cradled her in His arms. The watching creatures felt an all-consuming longing to be caressed by those same loving hands, an intense ache to be held in those protective arms. They knew with every ounce of their beings that in His arms was the place of eternal and total joy. This was *home*.

"Mary," the Man said softly, looking fully into her face.

She stirred and opened her eyes, gazing up into the eyes of Love Himself. "It's you!" she cried.

The music of the Resurrection caught and flamed in her voice.

Awed by the scene before them and drinking in its beauty, the members of the little company didn't move at all until Caleb, physically needing a means to release and express his adulation, flew to the very rock where the wolf had stood earlier. Lifting his wings, he joyfully proclaimed triumphant, victorious tidings: "All the Father's Creatures, listen to this Word. Rejoice, for Mary is *alive*! The journey of the Three who image the Way, the Truth, and Life has been completed! The Father and the Father alone has graciously guided the Three, protecting them as they completed the task set before them. Mary has gazed into the Mirror which changed to Glass—the Glass illuminated by the One Who Is Worthy—becoming fully known. Lift up your voices in exaltation! Give all glory and honor and praise to the Father of all Creatures! Sing of his worth before all time and now and forever, shouting Amen and Amen and Amen!"

The responding chorus of contagious worship arose from everywhere and everything, for even the rocks and trees could not keep from crying out, joining the mountain itself, the plants below their feet, the clouds and sky and sun above, joining Beauregard, Atticus, Mr. and Mrs. Beaver, Kit and, most importantly, Simon. They sang as one great, universal congregation, lifting a song of praise that filled the earth and everything in it, creating a symphony that would exist for all time for the One who was the object of their adoration!

As suddenly as the worship had exploded into being, a hush fell over them all. The Man lifted his eyes from Mary and concentrated fully on Simon.

"*Simon.*" Had the young boy ever heard his name spoken with such tenderness? "You also are my child."

The radiant eyes of the One who stood before him bore into Simon's. For a moment, Simon nearly panicked and glanced away, for looking into those eyes was like staring into the sun. The intensity of the brightness didn't bring about physical pain, but it was emotionally clear and sharp and revealing. Reflected in the Man's eyes, Simon saw his hatred for his dad and the resulting rage he'd directed toward God. He realized how he'd defiantly blamed everyone—his mother, the pastor, Mary, mostly God. Every nuance of his sin was right there before him, all the memory, all the shame of it. But the miracle was this: in that same instant, Simon knew without doubt that the Man was actually offering his love, his total and complete love. The thought moved swiftly through his mind, *Could he really love me* that *much? To forgive all? God, is it true?*

The Man nodded to Simon as though his every thought had been heard out loud. "I know what you have endured." The Man's eyes filled with tears. "You thought you bore it alone, but I was always with you. I felt each blow with you, my child. When you go back to your world—for you must go back, Simon, to finish your story there—you will experience pain again. That is a part of living in a sinful world. But know now that you can always turn to me for inner healing and love. I will never abandon you, my child. Feel my touch now, and know my love."

He turned and gently placed Mary next to him (she was fully healed and able to stand now) and stretched his arms out to the boy, inviting him to come of his own free will. Simon hesitated only a moment, looking towards his friends for reassurance. All were gesturing and nodding vigorously; Beauregard even gave him a slight push with his great cold nose. That was all it took. Simon ran and nearly leaped into an embrace which enfolded him tightly within loving arms, a hug pulling him fiercely against his breast.

The Man pulled Simon to arm's length so he could look into the boy's face again. "The Journey of the Three is complete. Mary has obeyed by giving her life. Beauregard obeyed by proclaiming the truth. And you, Simon, have you found the Way?"

"I think so," he whispered.

"You must *know*, Simon. You must know that *I am* the Way, the Truth and the Life. I am the Light of the World who guided you across the intense heat of the Great Sand. I am the Living Water who carried you over the raging river. I am the Rock who is mightier than any evil upon the crag of the mountain, any sin you may try to hide within your heart. *I am the I am!*"

The words themselves embodied power, for no sooner were they spoken than Simon and the animals felt the earth beneath them tremble again. It was as though the rumbling was a mighty hand that shifted the colors of the magnificent vision before them: the edges of the glass began to change, dissipating as their lines became hazy and began blending with the sky behind it. The Man hugged Simon to him again and placed him next to Beauregard. Gradually, the Man and Mary became fainter, more difficult to see. Simon squinted in an attempt to keep everything in focus, and reached out to grab at the pane.

"Simon, rejoin your friends, for Mary and I must leave you now." He reached towards Mary and she eagerly and gracefully leaped into his arms. "But some day you all will join us, and I will welcome you here. You will be *home*."

He then gave them one last gift. While he still tenderly cradled Mary in the crook of his arm, he reached through the fading pane of glass and scratched behind a satiny Beauregard ear (which made him sigh with pleasure), traced the intricacy of a tiny Atticus paw. He tickled a Kit whisker (eliciting a delighted giggle from the beaver), stroked a Mr. Beaver tail, patted a Mama Beaver tummy and rubbed the smooth and glorious red on Caleb's wing. Lastly, his hand rested on the breast of Simon, and the boy felt the warmth of his caress as though he were branded with love. These were the very places where he had touched them earlier when they had slept so peacefully by the stream. He'd put his mark upon his creatures before; he marked them again now. They all bowed once more before the Man, wondering at the tenderness of his touch, pleasuring in the tingle that remained upon them. "Faithful servants, you have earned your rest. Return to your homes in peace. And know that I am *always* with you!"

"What about Mary? Can't she come with us?" Simon asked, clutching at the glass but feeling it continue to dissolve even as he struggled desperately to hold onto it.

"Mary has moved to the other side now." The voice grew fainter with each word. "But there is one last gift she would give to each of you, a legacy she would have you possess." Simon and all the creatures anxiously leaned forward to catch the parting words, for they were vanishing as quickly as the image before them.

Mary turned to face the little company. Radiance spilled from the Man's face to hers, to those who watched them. "I love you all, my dearest friends!" Mary declared, although it was barely audible. "Continue to love each other, Mr. and Mrs. Beaver. Caleb, don't ever stop proclaiming his glorious pronouncements, calling for praise from all creation. How I shall miss your delightful ways, Atticus, and Beauregard, continue to seek and share the simple truth you are blessed with." Her melodious voice became more and more difficult to hear, and everyone strained to catch every last, precious word Mary uttered. "Darling Kit, you must never stop your joyous, youthful bouncing. And Simon-by-the-Way, this gift I—"

They could hear no more then, for Mary's voice was a mere *shhh!* in the now-familiar, deafening wind that surged against the glass, sending it swirling, until the entire pane was absorbed into the skies above them. But just before the Man and Mary disappeared, Mary's music visibly lifted from her in a great swelling crescendo, darting above them all to dance across the clouds. Beauregard jumped up and waggled his tail, Simon laughed out loud, and Kit clapped his little hands in pure delight as the playful notes merrily explored the glorious world around them, skipping above the sun, hopping along its rays and sending sparkles of glistening light scampering in all directions—almost like fireworks, but so much more glorious, ever so much more brilliant and dazzling. The beautiful melody converged into a single line (although a frenetic one, zinging this way and that), seeking a new home, journeying across the sky until it would find its ultimate destination. The notes swelled in one last jubilant song—pure laughter, in musical form. They paused before the waiting boy and Simon reached out with eager palms upraised, gathering the notes in, pulling the lilting melody joyfully to his breast. Mary's gift to Simon—her music—entered his heart and became Simon's song!

The little company looked up, hoping for one last sight of Mary. All they glimpsed, however, was one final burst of light, one shooting star flaming across the now empty sky. They turned to each other, realizing they were now alone. After such celebration, their hearts were suddenly heavy as they realized that the only part of their journey remaining was to say good-bye.

They gathered together as they had done so many times before, although the absence of Mary—so often the center of their attention and the very heart of their little band—left an obvious, painful vacancy. No one spoke her name aloud, but Kit sniffed and each one stared at the empty space in their little circle.

Simon felt a lump rise in his throat and he slumped forward, putting his chin into his hands. "The journey was the hardest thing I've ever done, but still, I don't want to say good-bye. I don't want to go home." He gave Beauregard a forlorn, pleading look. "I want to stay here with you. Why can't I?"

Beauregard leaned towards his friend, presenting his head for some petting. Simon obliged, but he found no comfort even in this familiar endearment.

"The beautiful Man said we were all to go home, didn't he?" Kit asked, looking at each one in turn and nodding his tiny chin. "I miss my home and the dam and our creek and the riverbank and the yummy bark we haven't seen anywhere else since we left. What's it called, Mama?" But Kit wasn't really interested in an answer, so he rambled on, "And I miss my friend Tudburry—he's a turtle, Simon-by-the-Way—and well, I just can't hardly wait to see it all again." He climbed up into Simon's lap, huffing and puffing in his obvious excitement. When he leaned against Simon's tummy as he'd done countless times before, Kit searched his face for answers. "Don't you miss your home, Simon-by-the-Way?"

Simon sighed. "I guess so. I really love my mom. And Abbey too, of course. But I...well, I'll just miss you all so much." His eyes filled with tears and he hugged the irresistible little beaver. "Mr. and Mrs. Beaver, Kit, you all were so brave to build the dam for us. And then you were even more courageous to go searching for Atticus. I said some hateful things then. Can you ever forgive me?"

Beauregard moved to the other side of the little circle so Barton and Mrs. Beaver could stand next to Simon, and Kit joined them by squishing in between the two. They looked up at Simon with sincerity glowing in their tiny, beady eyes and Simon stroked their soft fur. "You were forgiven long before the words were uttered," Barton said earnestly.

Mrs. Beaver wiped at a tear and sniffed, "We cherish you most dearly, Simon-by-the-Way. You have become…like another son to us. It will be terribly lonely without you!" She beckoned to Simon, and when he leaned over, she placed one tender, motherly kiss on his cheek. And then all three of them clung to each other while Mrs. Beaver wept softly against Barton's shoulder.

Caleb had been perched on Beauregard's back, but he flew up onto Simon's shoulder. Fidgeting about as he shifted his weight from one foot to the other, Caleb cleared his throat—suddenly wiping at a glistening eye with one wing—and huskily began, "You have grown to be nearly a man, for you have faced grave danger. And you have done so with courage." Caleb stopped to clear his voice again. "I am proud of you—proud you were a part of our company—and I shall also miss you greatly."

"Oh, Caleb," Simon whispered, for he, too, could barely talk, "I failed miserably so many times. I don't think I was brave at all."

"Didn't you valiantly commit to continue at each point of decision?" Caleb asked. "Didn't you complete the journey? Didn't you see the prophecy fulfilled?"

Simon nodded.

"Then you have journeyed well. And the songs of praise from our children and our children's children,"—Caleb glanced around at all of them when he said this—"will include the mighty name of Simon-by-the-Way."

Simon wiped away a tear and reached up to stroke the brilliant feathers. They still filled him with wonder, and he loved caressing them. "You have taught me so much, Caleb. I want to be just like you some day."

Caleb, completely overcome by the compliment, merely hung his beak down onto Simon's neck, unabashedly allowing tears to trickle onto Simon's shirt.

Simon swallowed hard then, for Atticus suddenly appeared before him. With a final dramatic touch, Atticus crossed his arms over his chest and held a defiant chin up high, insisting, "I won't be maudlin. I refuse to be sad. My memories are too lovely, too bountiful, too blessedly...too blessedly... too blessedly—"

"Be...*hic!*...eau...*hic!*...tiful?" Kit offered, hiccuping through his tears.

"Dear Kit, that was rather impressive. And there are all together four syllables in beautiful—why, that's as high as Beauregard can count!" Atticus winked at Kit and Simon, and Simon was able to give him a hint of a smile in return. "Besides, Kit, you have expressed my sentiments exactly. And still I say, I won't cry, I simply will not." A telltale tear formed in one of the roguish, masked eyes, however. Another "impostor" followed in the other eye. Atticus blinked several times as he rolled his eyes skyward, "a-hemming" repeatedly and acting as though he were simply clearing his eyes of some irritating foreign matter. "There's no need for crying, truly there's not. It wastes one's resources, actually, and I've always been quite cautious about that sort of thing. Raccoons and water don't mix well anyway. My poor, dear tail certainly discovered that to be entirely true. Neither too little water nor too much is..." He held up the pitiful tail, rubbing the bare skin anxiously between his miniature hands. "Of course, every once in a while, sometimes I—"

"Atticus." That was all Simon needed to say. The dear raccoon with the courageous heart ran into Simon's extended arms and cried softly against his chest.

Eventually, Simon gently placed Atticus down and stood. Kit snuggled even more tightly up against his mama and papa, finding just the tiniest bit of solace in the thumb that had found its way into his mouth. Caleb and Atticus consoled one another as they all turned to watch the simple dog say his final good-bye.

Beauregard hunched way down, inching forward so low to the ground that his belly rubbed against the mountain's tender plant life. His great snout swayed back and forth and he shook his head pathetically, murmuring over and over, "The dowger is sad. Oh, yes, the dowger is so sad." When he'd crawled to Simon's feet, he sighed a great sigh, resting his head on the dirty sneakers one last time. And when he rolled his large brown eyes up to Simon, tears flowed freely from their depths. "The dowger misses Mary already. The dowger will miss Simon-by-the-Way, too. Will Simon-by-the-Way miss the dowger?"

"Oh, Beauregard!" Simon flung himself down on top of the great, loving dog. He wrapped his arms around his neck and once again buried his weeping face in the fur of one he loved so passionately.

"The dowger wants to give Simon-by-the-Way a gift like Mary did. The gift's not as good, though. Mary's gift was wunnerful. Mary's gift was gooder." Beauregard pushed his pathetic ball forward with his nose, nudging it until it rolled right next to Simon's feet. The ragged thing had been so loved—so chewed—that it was rather a mess. The poor dog sighed. "But it's the only gift the dowger has to give. So the dowger's ball is Simon-by-the-Way's ball now. Then Simon-by-the-Way will never forget the dowger."

The sweet, simple offering was almost more than Simon could bear and he cried out, "I could never forget you, Beauregard. Not ever! I could never forget *any* of you." He reached out, grabbing the precious, priceless ball with one hand and touching each of his friends with the other. His gaze moved around the group, taking in and committing to memory every little detail of each one's appearance and personality. "You are the first real friends I've ever had, and I could never tell you how thankful I am for your friendship. Or how much I love you. How much I will *always* love you."

Suddenly, the animals before him began to fade in color just slightly. Atticus's mask wasn't quite as black. The scarlet on Caleb—always so wondrously brilliant—slowly began to fade to a dull, washed-out red. The fur along the edges of their thick, beautiful coats was suddenly hazy, indistinct in the separation of animal and background. "*Oh, no.* Not yet!" Simon cried out hysterically, and he frantically clutched at Beauregard, attempting to stop the process. "I'm not ready yet, and I haven't finished saying good-bye!" But even as he clung to the beloved dog beneath him, as Atticus reached out to him with one tiny hand and Kit bounced towards him, Simon could feel the sucking motion draw him up and out and away from them all. For one moment he was clutching nothing but air. And then he was hugging a pillow between otherwise empty arms, a pillow that was quickly being soaked with a grieving boy's tears.

CHAPTER 16

"So I wasn't dreaming, after all,"
she said to herself, "unless—unless
we're all part of the same dream."

Simon would never have believed that he'd sleep that night, but he did—soundly, out of complete exhaustion, with no dreams that he could recall. When he woke up, it was with a heavy, aching heart.

He scanned the boundaries of his room, seeking some measure of comfort in their familiarity. With a depressed sigh, Simon noted the sunshine streaming in through his window and recognized it was going to be a pretty day, even if he wouldn't enjoy it. His eyes flitted to the nightstand where his alarm clock, a deck of cards, a favorite baseball cap, and an old baseball sat, collecting dust. His eye moved to his dresser and the mirror attached above. Scrambling out from his covers, he approached it eagerly at first and then with apprehension.

Simon stood before it for a few moments, inspecting the entire pane of glass. When he finally summoned the courage to examine it with his hands—every single inch, several times—he discovered there wasn't one fraction of the portal remaining. The mirror had closed. The other world was no longer accessible to him.

Plopping wearily back onto his bed, Simon sat there, staring at his reflection. "Was it real?" he whispered to his image. "Or did I just make up every bit of it in some fantastic, ridiculous dream?" But the mirror had no answer for him, and so Simon let himself fall backwards onto his bed. He jerked up instantly, for there was something foreign under his covers—something hard and round, something that obviously didn't belong there. Cautiously, Simon lifted the sheet—and discovered Beauregard's beloved ball.

Tears instantly filled his eyes and he clutched it tightly to his breast. "Oh, Beauregard, you *are* real. But how can I live without you now that I've known you?" He closed his eyes, trying to imagine himself back inside the mirror. "God," Simon prayed, "I know you love me, but it was so hard to leave my friends, and—"

"Simon!" his mother yelled, calling from downstairs. "Are you awake yet?" Come here, please!"

Simon hurriedly dabbed at his tears and, stuffing the treasured ball into the pocket of his pajamas, he shuffled slowly to the top of the stairs where he saw his mother smiling up at him.

"Did you sleep okay?" she asked. "I hope I didn't bother you last night."

"What do you mean?"

"I was so worried I kept tip-toeing into your room every hour or so to see if you were all right. Did you...um...did you have the dream again?"

Simon nodded. "It's okay, Mom. I saw it to the end."

She was obviously still concerned for him because the worried creases remained around her eyes and mouth. Quickly checking him over, Laura's gaze moved from Simon's red-rimmed eyes to his slumping shoulders to the curious bulge in his pocket. "Are you sure you're all right? You don't look as if everything's okay."

"It is. I mean, I am. Honest. It's just that...well, I promise I'll tell you all about it later. But not just now 'cause—"

"No, not now," she agreed, grinning up at him. The weariness instantly fell from her face. "Now you need to come down here and see what our pastor dropped off this morning. It's quite a surprise. Abbey's absolutely delighted!"

Simon's interest was certainly piqued now. He couldn't imagine their pastor bringing anything that either of them would be the slightest bit interested in. He walked down the stairs grudgingly, knowing only wariness. "So what is this surprise?"

"I'm not going to tell you what it is," his mom teased, a sparkle in her eyes now, making her suddenly appear years younger. "You'll just have to come see for yourself."

She led him to the kitchen where Abbey sat on the floor next to a plain cardboard box. When Abbey finally pulled her gaze from the box—whatever was in there was clearly fascinating her—there was a look of pure rapture on her face.

"*Oh Simon,*" she cried. "Come look!"

Simon stood over the box—and instantly fell in love with the most adorable black puppy he'd ever seen. Turning its head to one side as if pondering some grave problem, the pup pulled up floppy ears and blinked huge brown eyes, gazing up at Simon for only a moment before issuing a demanding, "*Yap! Yap!*" It stood up, wiggling every inch of its pudgy little body (its tummy was especially big for one so small), raising its front paws—which were amazingly large in proportion to the rest of him too—and playfully pouncing at Simon. He'd had enough of being confined to the box and was demanding to be picked up. Immediately.

"Oh, Mom," Simon could barely choke out. "I can't believe it!" Gathering up the soft, squishy little body into his outstretched arms, Simon was covered with slobbery kisses across his entire face.

"Isn't he something?" Laura asked, joining Abbey as they both stroked the sleek coat. "It's a Labrador retriever. They're excellent with children, I'm told."

"Oh they are, Mom. They are!"

Abbey and Laura exchanged a questioning look with raised brows. "How do *you* know?" Abbey asked.

"Well, I just do, that's all. And I also know that…that…" The puppy snuffled his face, playfully nipping at an ear now and then amongst the continuing licks. Simon giggled. "I know God is so wonderful. And he loves *me*. Simon." Tears welled up in his eyes. "Oh Mom, he really, really does love me!"

Laura put a hand to his cheek, receiving a spontaneous lick from the pup, too. "Well, what shall we name this mass of wiggles and kisses?" she asked, smiling through her own tears as she watched her son.

"He already has a name, Mom," Simon stated emphatically.

"Already has one?"

"Yup." Simon suddenly remembered the ball and pulled it out of his pocket. The pup took it into his mouth instantly, though it was way too big for his pint-sized bite. He looked so comical that Simon and Abbey burst into laughter.

"I can see he's going to keep us chuckling. *And* busy," his mom mused. "So what is his name, Simon? You're full of surprises this morning."

"God gave him his name. And it's Beauregard!"

There was just a hint of melody in his words.

POST SCRIPT

The Seed of an Idea

The themes for my novels generally emerge from my devotional life, and *Simon's Song* is no exception. Back in 1992, I was reading through I Corinthians, and in my journal I jotted these notes concerning chapter 13, verse 12: "This lovely analogy needs to be a poem or a song. Could it be that sin coats the back of a glass, forming a mirror, where I see only *me*? As I grow spiritually, the sin (the coat of silver) gradually is stripped away, leaving pure, clear glass—until I'm 'fully known,' when I finally see my reflection as Christ." I even drew a picture, trying to put my symbolic analogy into physical form in that way. Needless to say, it was a bit rough at that point. But it was a beginning, and my imagination took off from there.

Ever since I read Walter Wangerin's *The Book of the Dun Cow*, I've aspired to write an allegory of my own. I say *aspired to* because Wangerin's writing is so incredible that I expressed my desire while feeling too intimidated and inferior to actually attempt that lofty goal. Wangerin's characters are unforgettable, his story life changing, and his themes so moving that I read most of it through a film of tears. But at some point, I finally did sit down to begin my story—a story I tell people that, in many ways, wrote itself. For it was as if this tale had a life of its own, and my fingers merely typed out what already existed, somewhere, somehow. It clearly wasn't a money maker, a best seller or marketable, according to publisher after publisher. But it was alive in my imagination, and it pretty much demanded to live on paper too!

Characters with Character

Atticus—I just love that name. It will forever be revered by me because of the father/lawyer in *To Kill a Mockingbird*. Therefore, I chose it because of the associations *Atticus* immediately brought to my mind and heart: warmth, caring, passion, wisdom, courage. This is someone you want to know, and be next to. Clearly my raccoon isn't quite up to that standard—with his bent towards drama thrown in—but Atticus proves his true character in the trials of the journey, and he's as real in my mind as you are, dear reader. I see him drumming his fingers on the tree branch, and throwing his arms up into the air, expressing "Why me?" Atticus makes me smile.

Beauregard is an amalgamation of our two black Labrador retrievers named Bojangles and Wendy. Bojangles was a male, way too smart for his own good (he figured out how to open the neighbor's garage door with his nose, and then proceeded to pilfer dog food and ladies' underwear; needless to say, our neighbors didn't much appreciate that); he was also the fierce protector of our then two young boys, Robby and J.J. Therefore, it was from Bo that Beauregard inherited his courage and protective instincts. Wendy, however, was a sweet female who wasn't quite as bright. From her, Beauregard took on the more gentle nature and a simple innocence. Both dogs were great retrievers, but it was Bojangles who dearly loved a tennis ball (and pretty much only a tennis ball; he turned up his nose at more expensive and better made rubber ones) and would run up and down the hills of Tennessee until he literally dropped from exhaustion. He also had the ball totally drenched with slobber by that time, too—making it feel disgusting to the touch, soaking anything with which it came into contact. Someone once quipped that you mark the stages in your lives by the dogs that you owned. Bo and Wendy were both full-fledged family members, making indelible imprints upon all four of us. In a word, they are both unforgettable.

I've been a dedicated bird watcher for years, and should you peruse my backyard right now, you'd find several feeders (two flat ones for birds like mourning doves, another with a weighted opener designed to out-smart squirrels, a suet feeder for woodpeckers, and a tall cylinder containing thistle seed for finches) plus a bluebird house. A disappointingly *vacant* house (rejected again!). Though redbirds and hummingbirds are my favorites, I wanted a more dramatic-looking bird for this important role of proclaimer: therefore, the red-winged blackbird. The path where I walk and pray is marshy, and blackbirds rule there. I know their throaty call, and I enjoy watching them fly from tall cattails to oak tree, flashing that scarlet color. They truly do fit the bill for majestic, and besides, every time I walk and spy a blackbird—and that happens nearly every time I walk—I can pretend I spot my friend Caleb.

I can't remember why I decided to add the beaver family. The bike path named Ten Mile Canyon from Frisco, Colorado, to Copper Mountain used to be populated with beavers. However, my guess is that the local conservationists didn't appreciate their regularly blocking up Ten Mile Creek, creating havoc, and must surmise that their disappearance is due to a "work related re-location"! However, this beaver family certainly came in handy when the little band needed a dam to cross the river with its dangerous rapids, and

I had fun with the constant interaction of the exuberant Kit with Beauregard. Those two were often my version of Tom and Jerry, while Atticus and Beauregard's banter was more on the order of the straight man and comic duo of George Burns and Gracie Allen.

Just minutes ago I saw a mama deer and her fawn in the open space behind our home. The fawn was quite young, as its spots were still very distinct. I stood mesmerized at my window, observing mother and baby, simply enjoying their graceful movements. And then I smiled with delight as I watched the fawn kick up its heels and scamper around its mother. In my mind, deer seem to define the word *elegant* in the animal kingdom—appearing strong and yet graceful; determined and yet wide-eyed in their defenselessness; non-aggressive and yet resourceful (as in eating my tulips and geraniums, right down to the ground).

As for Simon…he originally was named *Peter*. Advised that my story was too close to another famous tale, set in Narnia, I changed his name (still stubbornly keeping an association to the biblical Peter, however). I have a love and appreciation for coming-of-age fiction, and since I'm familiar with the family dynamics and effects of the disease of alcoholism—I greatly admire my father-in-law (a former alcoholic who hasn't had *one drink* for nearly forty years now; I'm proud of you, Dad!)—I incorporated that struggle into Simon's family to add the tension that story needs.

Why Talking Animals?
Whenever I hear someone say he or she doesn't relate to allegories (too strange, too different, too far from reality), and especially to animals who speak like people, I give this rationale for their viability and vitality: authors are about creating *personalities*. If that's done well, it doesn't matter if the character is an Ent (one of Tolkien's famous talking trees—although we mustn't let the Ents hear us label them that as they'll react quite prickly) or the chicken Pertelote (I can't imagine anyone who wouldn't fall in love with this endearing hen) or Lewis Carroll's famous disappearing Cheshire cat (his unforgettable smile is the last part to disappear, you recall). If the writing is truly skillful, you forget the character's form and zero in on the personal traits that you relate to. Who cares if Kit's a baby beaver? Isn't his bubbly, rambunctious personality one you've witnessed and chuckled about as you were captivated by youngsters at a playground or church nursery?

Truthfully, all of my characters are so very real in my mind: They are living, breathing personalities I was sorry to say good-bye to when I finished that last chapter. I feel a punch to my heart every time I watch Mary sacrifice herself, and I get teary-eyed right along with Simon when the animals begin to disappear. In a way, isn't an allegory with animals a symbolic picture of unconditional love in action? Forgetting the form—not allowing it to detract, and possibly even finding that a "different" form adds value—we love the personality *behind* the physical body. And how many times and in different ways does God repeat the same values: He cares about the heart, my motivations, the desires of my soul, the core of who and what I am. *God looks on the heart*, we're reminded. Mundo Cani (a dog from *The Book of the Dun Cow*), Reepicheep (a mouse in *Prince Caspian*) and Atticus all have huge hearts, and given a chance, they make their way very easily into ours.

My Prayer

Simon's struggle—to accept the generous offer of God's unconditional love and forgiveness when he feels so very unworthy of that gift—is my struggle, too. Just when I think I've finally grasped the meaning of the gospel in all its glorious simplicity and yet at the same time, its complexity, I find that I'm trying to feel deserving of his love by doing something impressive for him. It's a subtle manipulation, but I recognize its existence with shame for the arrogance of the attempt. Sometimes I'm not fully accepting his total forgiveness for a motive or thought that I struggle to forgive myself for. Did I really just try to attempt a *quid pro quo*? Am I placing my forgiveness above God's? Maybe I'm tempted to take credit for an accomplishment, and I'm reminded: *What do you have that you have not been given?* What I'm attempting to demonstrate is that I relate to Simon all too often, for I view the world through his eyes when I'm hurting and weak and needy. And I become like Simon when I view the world through his perspective, judging myself too unworthy to accept his love, his forgiveness, his acceptance of me right now. Exactly as I am—because of Christ's sacrifice in my place.

So this is my prayer for you, that you will risk being more vulnerable before God than you have ever been before, opening the "eyes of your heart" to explore and see where you are like Simon, too. Sadly, the struggle to accept God's love doesn't end in this world. The reality is that our sin gets in the way, blocking our ability to see through that mirror; it's the stubborn grey paint on the back of the window. But when we truly see and are able to grasp God's love and forgiveness to an even greater depth, the paint changes form, becoming notes of joy in our souls.

Then…we too can sing Simon's Song!

A PREVIEW OF CAROLYN'S NEXT BOOK

Coming soon... Satisfying readers' cravings for romance novels with a suspenseful, supernatural touch, this is a faith-filled story of a woman with a mysterious past, an even more unexplainable power, and the need to discover the truth.

Their hit-and-run accidents happen at the same time ... in two separate cars. Julia Johnson survives but her father is killed. His death sparks a search into the mystery of who she is, where she came from, and why someone wants her dead. A fifteenth-century diary may hold the keys to the puzzle. But when she and her Uncle Oliver journey to the Cumberland area of Tennessee to uncover her past and follow the clues, knowing who to trust with her life—and her heart—becomes a deadly game. Guided by a secret, unknown friend (who goes by the name Guy) with whom she shares unexplainable telepathic powers and a connection of the soul, she must seek the faith, courage, and wisdom to stay ahead of her enemies, and live.

THE MELUNGEON DIARY

The night before my break-of-dawn escape, I settled in to have chats with Uncle Ollie and Guy. I figured my cool and calm demeanor would totally fool both of them.

My uncle picked up before the first ring was completed.

"Hey! Are you clairvoyant or what?"

"Julia. How good to hear your voice." I could hear the crackle of a bag of snacks—chips, maybe? "Actually, I was just sitting here having a bite to eat and watching 'Jeopardy,' not feeling particularly bright this evening."

"Tough topics, huh?"

"Very. Either that or I'm just rather dense today. Could also be because I'm feeling a bit under the weather." A significantly loud honking followed.

"You getting a cold?"

"Evidently. Bit of a runny nose. Got a dull headache and I'm cranky. Definitely cranky."

I pictured him sitting in his recliner, alone, and suddenly felt overwhelmingly guilty. A good niece would visit tomorrow to deliver homemade chicken soup. I'd also add to his grief once he discovered my deception. "Um, want me to come over and heat up some soup for you? Sorry I don't have the ingredients on hand to make homemade."

"Julia, darling. Absolutely not. I wouldn't want to expose you to this." He blew his nose again, loud enough to make me flinch. "Besides, could be all I need is a good night's sleep. I'm sure I'll feel much better in the morning. Don't give it another thought. I'll be fine, absolutely fine."

"Well, okay. If you're sure." My options for giving a truthful promise ran quickly through my mind. "I'll call and check on you tomorrow."

"That would be lovely. Night, Julia."

"Oh. One more thing."

"What's that?" He sounded wary, his voice going up a decibel.

"Nothing serious. But remember you told me it would help my memory to put things in the positive?"

"Oh that. Is it working for you?"

"Actually, I can't remember to put things in the positive."

He chuckled. "Clever girl."

"I hope you sleep well and do feel better in the morning, Uncle Ollie. Good night."

I sat there, fretting. My guilt growing like a monster feeding on its own caretaker. *He'll be perfectly fine, it's only a cold*, one voice inside my head whispered. The other sneered back, *What will you tell yourself when it turns more serious and you're not here to care for him, you ungrateful niece?*

–Jules?

Calm yourself, girl. He's so intuitive. You absolutely cannot give yourself away.

–Hey. I've missed you.

–Me too. And I've been thinkin' about our…our impasse, I suppose you could call it.

–Guy, I just can't—

–I know, I know. And you're right. You can't *not* do this, and it wasn't fair of me to ask that of you.

–You mean, you agree with me now?

–To a point, yes.

–What point would that be?

He chuckled, a touch of cynicism mixed in too, but it was mostly pure.

–Jules, oh Jules. I guess the point would be where you put yourself in danger, love.

–But how can I possibly know where that is unless I push this as far as I can? Isn't that the irony of it? If there truly is any danger out there, Guy, I won't meet it until I get to the point where I'm at the heart of this.

–And you're absolutely, one hundred percent fixated on that goal?

Sigh. How to explain what I'm feeling?

–Guy, it's like the outlines of my world have been fuzzy for as long as I can remember. Going back to when no one understood our mind talking, so they turned it into something…something bad, in their eyes. And then when Mom died, it got worse. Know what I've come to realize?

–What, love?

–When Dad told me I was adopted and I got so angry? It really wasn't about me being mad at him. Actually, I think it was because down deep, I knew. I'd always known that sense of not belonging, the fuzzy feeling thing. And so when Dad told me….well, I was more angry at God. And mostly, myself.

–I can understand being mad at God. Anyone in your shoes would've responded that way, I think. I know I would, for sure. But why yourself, Jules? Why would you blame yourself?

Tears filled my eyes again. Would I finally cry for Dad? For me? I reached for the answer that was just beyond my understanding, but it evaded me. Dodged my grasping mind…what was just there…and then, then it was gone. As were the tears.

–I don't know, Guy. I just am.

–Still?

–Oh, definitely still.

–Know what? I'll love you happy, mad, grumpy, joy-filled, depressed, whimsical, whatever.

I smiled.

–Guess you've done that many times over with me already, huh?

And just as sure as if I were looking right at him, I knew Guy nodded. Smiled back at me.

–Good night, Jules. Sleep well, love.

–Night, Guy.

After I'd crawled into bed, I realized I'd talked with everyone who mattered to me that day: Uncle Ollie, Melissa, Guy. Except one.

God, truth is, I've been avoiding you, haven't I?

Because I don't know if I'm doing the right thing. But it's the thing I have to do. Does that make any sense at all? No? Maybe a little? I guess this adventure is like begging forgiveness afterwards rather than asking permission first, huh? But somehow I do sense you being okay with this road trip of mine. That it's destined to be, and I'll find my future somewhere out there in Collinsville, Tennessee.

That future may turn out to be good. Or it may be dangerous. I accept that risk. But whatever it is, Lord, I know I have to find out. I have to meet it.

Please go with me. 'Cause I know I need you too. Whether I find good—or bad.

☙

My plan was off without a hitch.

I slept fairly well, woke at the three-thirty alarm, and stared at the clock as the nearly overwhelming ache hit me again—the reality of Dad's death. *How many mornings would this unwelcome harbinger greet me like this?* I wondered. After showering, getting dressed and packing last-minute items, I piled everything by the back door: Suitcases, purse, pillow, satchel of snacks for me and dog food for Moppit, and a cooler with canned pop. All was accounted for and ready except Moppit, who obviously wouldn't stay put—or worse, would snitch food from my stash. I fed her (she clearly didn't mind the early morning wake-up as long as she received food) and encouraged her to do her business outside.

We were good to go.

The taxi showed up promptly at four-thirty. It was still pitch dark, and so when Moppit and I slipped out the door, I was sure we weren't seen by anyone. Not even nosy Mrs. Fitzsimmons was up at this hour.

The driver and I chatted a bit as he drove us to the mechanic's, and fortunately, we didn't see one black SUV the entire way.

I paid him, and I even waved as he drove off.

Dad's Lexus—realizing it will always be Dad's in my heart and mind, I might as well stick to calling it that—was parked right where it was supposed to be, waiting. After a quick inspection, I noted it truly was as good as new.

I pushed the button to unlock the car, piled my suitcases into the trunk, and opened the door to plop Moppit, my purse, a pillow and a cooler with some drinks and snacks onto the passenger seat. I was just turning to climb in behind the wheel when a slight movement in the back seat caught my eye. Causing me to shriek out loud when the car's soft overhead light illuminated what I'd glimpsed.

A man lay sprawled across the back seat.

8479592R00125

Made in the USA
San Bernardino, CA
12 February 2014